Praise for Chuck Palahniuk and

DAMNED

"Thoroughly original . . . satiric and horrifying, enough so you'll want to repent after you read."   —CNN

"Chuck Palahniuk is William S. Burroughs and David Foster Wallace rolled into one."
> —*The San Diego Union-Tribune*

"*Damned* is typical of Palahniuk's work: a scathing satire that is unfiltered, caustic and smart. . . . [His] descriptions of hell are priceless."
> —*Pittsburgh Tribune-Review*

"Reading a Palahniuk novel is like getting zipped inside a boxer's heavy bag while the author goes to work on you, pounding you until there is nothing left but a big bag of bones and blood and pain."
> —*The Miami Herald*

CHUCK PALAHNIUK

DAMNED

·

Chuck Palahniuk's eleven previous novels are the bestselling *Fight Club*, which was made into a film by David Fincher; *Survivor*; *Invisible Monsters*; *Choke*, which was made into a film by director Clark Gregg; *Lullaby*; *Diary*; *Haunted*; *Rant*; *Snuff*; *Pygmy*; and *Tell-All*. He is also the author of *Fugitives and Refugees*, a nonfiction profile of Portland, Oregon, published as part of the Crown Journeys series, and the nonfiction collection *Stranger Than Fiction*. He lives in the Pacific Northwest.

www.chuckpalahniuk.net

Also by Chuck Palahniuk

Fight Club

Survivor

Invisible Monsters

Choke

Lullaby

Fugitives and Refugees

Diary

Stranger Than Fiction

Haunted

Rant

Snuff

Pygmy

Tell-All

CHUCK PALAHNIUK

DAMNED

·

LIFE IS SHORT.

DEATH IS FOREVER.

ANCHOR BOOKS
A DIVISION OF RANDOM HOUSE, INC.
NEW YORK

FIRST ANCHOR BOOKS EDITION, OCTOBER 2012

The Library of Congress has cataloged the Doubleday edition as follows:
Palahniuk, Chuck.
Damned / Chuck Palahniuk.—1st ed.
p. cm.
1. Hell—Fiction.
2. Future life—Fiction. 3. Dead—Fiction. I. Title.
PZ7.P1754Dam 2011
[E]—dc22   2010044841

Anchor ISBN: 978-0-307-47653-1

Book design by Michael Collica

www.anchorbooks.com

Printed in the United States of America
10   9   8   7   6

DAMNED

.

I.

Are you there, Satan? It's me, Madison. I'm just now arrived here, in Hell, but it's not my fault except for maybe dying from an overdose of marijuana. Maybe I'm in Hell because I'm fat—a Real Porker. If you can go to Hell for having low self-esteem, that's why I'm here. I wish I could lie and tell you I'm bone-thin with blond hair and big ta-tas. But, trust me, I'm fat for a really good reason.

To start with, please let me introduce myself.

ow to best convey the exact sensation of being dead . . .

Yes, I know the word *convey*. I'm dead, not a mental defective.

Trust me, the being-dead part is much easier than the dying part. If you can watch much television, then being dead will be a cinch. Actually, watching television and surfing the Internet are really excellent practice for being dead.

The closest way I can describe death is to compare it to when my mom boots up her notebook computer and hacks into the surveillance system of our house in Mazatlán or Banff. "Look," she'd say, turning the screen sideways for me to see, "it's snowing." Glowing softly on the computer would be the interior of our Milan house, the sitting room, with snow falling outside the big windows, and by long distance, holding down her Control, Alt and W keys, my mom would draw open the sitting room drapes all the way. Pressing the Control and D keys, she'd dim the lights by remote control and we'd both sit, on a train or in a rented town car or aboard a leased jet, watching the pretty winter view through the windows of that empty house displayed on her computer screen. With the Control and F keys, she'd light a fire in the gas fireplace, and we'd listen to the hush of the Italian snow falling, the crackle of the flames via the audio monitors of the security system. After that, my mom would keyboard into the system for our house in Cape Town. Then log on to view our house in Brentwood. She could simultaneously be all places but no place, mooning over sunsets and foliage everywhere except where she actually was. At best, a sentry. At worst, a voyeur.

My mom will kill half a day on her notebook computer just looking at empty rooms full of our furniture. Tweaking the thermostat by remote control. Turning down the lights and choosing the right level of soft music to play in each room. "Just to keep the cat burglars guessing," she'd tell me. She'd toggle from camera to camera, watching the Somali maid clean our house in Paris. Hunched over her computer screen, she'd sigh and say, "My crocus are blooming in London. . . ."

From behind his open business section of the *Times*, my dad would say, "The plural is *crocuses*."

Probably my mom would cackle then, hitting her Control and L keys to lock a maid inside a bathroom from three continents away because the tile didn't look adequately polished. To her this passed for way-wicked, good fun. It's affecting the environment without being physically present. Consumption in absentia. Like having a hit song you recorded decades ago still occupy the mind of a Chinese sweatshop worker you'll never meet. It's power, but a kind of pointless, impotent power.

On the computer screen a maid would place a vase filled with fresh-cut peonies on the windowsill of our house in Dubai, and my mom would spy by satellite, turning down the air-conditioning, colder and colder, with a tapping keystroke via her wireless connection, chilling that house, that one room, meat-locker cold, ski-slope cold, spending a king's ransom on Freon and electric power, trying to make some doomed ten bucks' worth of pretty pink flowers last one more day.

That's what it's like to be dead. Yes, I know the word *absentia*. I'm thirteen years old, not stupid—and being dead, ye gods, do I comprehend the idea of absentia.

Being dead is the very essence of traveling light.

Being *dead*-dead means nonstop, twenty-four/seven, three hundred sixty-five days a year . . . forever.

How it feels when they pump out all of your blood, you don't want me to describe. Probably I shouldn't even tell you I'm dead, because no doubt now you feel awfully superior. Even other fat people feel superior to Dead People. Nevertheless, here it is: my Hideous Admission. I'll fess up and come clean. I'm out of the closet. I'm dead. Now don't hold it against me.

Yes, we all look a little mysterious and absurd to each other, but no one looks as foreign as a dead person does. We can forgive some stranger her choice to practice Catholicism or engage in homosexual acts, but not her submission to death. We hate a backslider. Worse than alcoholism or heroin addiction, dying seems like the greatest weakness, and in a world where people say you're lazy for not shaving your legs, then being dead seems like the ultimate character flaw.

It's as if you've shirked life—simply not made enough serious effort to live up to your full potential. *You quitter!* Being fat and dead—let me tell you—that's the double whammy.

No, it's not fair, but even if you feel sorry for me, you're probably also feeling pretty darn smug that you're alive and no doubt chewing on a mouthful of some poor animal that had the misfortune to live below you on the food chain. I'm not telling you all of this to gain your sympathy. I'm thirteen years old, and a girl, and I'm dead. My name is Madison, and the last thing I need is your stupid condescending pity. No, it's not fair, but it's how people do. The first time we meet another person an insidious little voice in our head says, "I might wear eyeglasses or be chunky around the hips or a girl, but at least I'm not Gay or Black or a Jew." Meaning: I may be me—but at least I have the good sense not to be YOU. So I hesitate to even mention that I'm dead because everyone already feels so darned superior to dead people, even Mexicans and AIDS people. It's like when learning about Alexander the Great in our seventh-grade Influences of Western History class, what keeps running through your head is: "If Alexander was so brave and smart and . . . Great . . . why'd he die?"

Yes, I know the word *insidious*.

Death is the One Big Mistake that none of us EVER plans to make. That's why the bran muffins and the colonoscopies. It's how come you take vitamins and get Pap smears. No, not you—*you're never going to die*—so now you feel all superior to me. Well, go ahead and think that. Keep smearing your skin with sunblock and feeling yourself for lumps. Don't let me spoil the Big Surprise.

But, to be honest, when you're dead probably not even homeless people and retarded people will want to trade you places. I mean, worms get to eat you. It's like a complete violation of all your civil rights. Death ought to be illegal but you don't see Amnesty International starting any letter-writing campaigns. You don't see any rock stars banding together to release hit singles with all the proceeds going to solve MY getting my face chewed off by worms.

My mom would tell you I'm too flip and glib about everything. My mom would say, "Madison, please don't be such a smart aleck." She'd say, "You're *dead*; now just *calm down.*"

Probably me being dead is a gigantic relief to my dad; this way, at least, he won't have to worry about me embarrassing him by getting pregnant. My dad used to say, "Madison, whatever man ends up with you, he's going to have his hands full. . . ." If my dad only knew.

When my goldfish, Mister Wiggles, died we flushed him down the toilet. When my kitten, Tiger Stripe, died I tried the same deal, and we had to call a plumber to snake the pipes. What a big mess. Poor Tiger Stripe. When I died, I won't go into the details, but let's say some Mr. Pervy McPervert mortician got to see me naked and pump out all my blood and commit God only knows what deranged carnal high jinks with my virginal thirteen-year-old body. You can call me glib, but death is about the biggest joke around. After all the permanent waves and ballet lessons my mom paid for, here I am getting a hot-spit tongue bath from some paunchy, depraved mortuary guy.

I can tell you, when you're dead, you pretty much have to give up your demands about boundaries and personal space. Just understand, I didn't die because I was too lazy to live. I didn't die because I wanted to punish my family. And no matter how much I slag my parents, don't get the idea that I hate them. Yes, for a while I hung around, watching my mom hunched over her notebook computer, tapping the keys Control, Alt, and L to lock the door of my bedroom in Rome, my room in Athens, all my rooms around the world. She keyboarded to close all my drapes after that, and turn down the air-conditioning and activate the electrostatic air filtration so not even dust would settle on my dolls and clothes and stuffed animals. It simply makes sense that I should miss my parents more than they miss me, especially when you consider that they only loved me for thirteen years while I loved them for my entire life. Forgive me for not sticking around longer, but I don't want to be dead and just watching everybody while I chill rooms, flicker the lights, and pull the drapes open and shut. I don't want to be simply a voyeur.

No, it's not fair, but what makes earth feel like Hell is our expectation that it should feel like Heaven. Earth is earth. Dead is dead. You'll find out for yourself soon enough. It won't help the situation for you to get all upset.

II.

Are you there, Satan? It's me, Madison. Please don't get the impression that I dislike Hell. No, really, it's way swell. Tons better than I expected. Honestly, it's obvious you've worked very hard for a very long time on the roiling, surging oceans of scalding-hot barf, and the stinking sulfur smell, and the clouds of buzzing black flies.

f my version of Hell fails to impress you, please consider that to be my own shortcoming. I mean, what do I know? Probably any grown-up would pee herself silly, seeing the flying vampire bats and majestic, cascading waterfalls of smelly poop. No doubt the fault is entirely my own, because if I'd ever imagined Hell it was as a fiery version of that classic Hollywood masterpiece *The Breakfast Club*, populated, let's remember, by a hypersocial, pretty cheerleader, a rebel stoner type, a dumb football jock, a brainy geek, and a misanthropic psycho, all locked together in their high school library doing detention on an otherwise ordinary Saturday except with every book and chair being blazing on fire.

Yes, you might be alive and Gay or Old or a Mexican, lording *that* over me, but consider that I've had the actual experience of waking up on my first day in Hell, and you'll just have to take my word for what all this is like. No, it's not fair, but you can forget about the fabled tunnel of bright, spectral-white light and being greeted by the open arms of your long-deceased grandma and grandpa; maybe other people have reported that blissful process, but consider that those people are currently alive, or they remained living for sufficient time to report on their encounter. My point is: Those people enjoyed what's clearly labeled a "near-death experience." I, on the other hand, am dead, with my blood long ago pumped out and worms munching on me. In my book that makes me the higher authority. Other people, like famous Italian poet Dante Alighieri, I'm sorry to say, simply hoisted a generous helping of campy make-believe on the reading public.

Thus, disregard my account of Hell at your own peril.

First off, you wake up lying on the stone floor inside a fairly dismal cell composed of iron bars; and take my stern advice—don't touch anything. The prison cell bars are filthy dirty. If by accident you DO touch the bars, which look a tad slimy with mold and someone else's blood, do NOT touch your face—or your clothes—not if you have any aspiration to stay looking nice until Judgment Day.

And do NOT eat the candy you'll see scattered everywhere on the ground.

The exact means by which I arrived in the underworld remain a little unclear. I recall a chauffeur standing curbside somewhere, next to a parked black Lincoln Town Car, holding a white placard with my name written on it, MADISON SPENCER, in all-caps terrible handwriting. The chauffeur—those people never speak English—had on mirrored sunglasses and a visored chauffeur cap, so most of his face was hidden. I remember him opening the rear door so I could step inside; after that was a way-long drive with the windows tinted so dark I couldn't quite see out, but what I've just described could've been any one of ten bazillion rides I've taken between airports and cities. Whether that Town Car delivered me to Hell, I can't swear, but the next thing is I woke up in this filthy cell.

Probably I woke up because someone was screaming; in Hell, someone is always screaming. Anyone who's ever flown London to Sydney, seated next to or anywhere in the proximity of a fussy baby, you'll no doubt fall right into the swing of things in Hell. What with the strangers and crowding and seemingly endless hours of waiting for nothing to happen, for you Hell will feel like one long, nostalgic hit of déjà vu. Especially if your in-flight movie was *The English Patient*. In Hell, whenever the demons announce they're going to treat everyone to a big-name Hollywood movie, don't get too excited because it's always *The English Patient* or, unfortunately, *The Piano*. It's never *The Breakfast Club*.

In regard to the smell, Hell comes nowhere near as bad as Naples in the summertime during a garbage strike.

If you ask me, people in Hell just scream to hear their own voice and to pass the time. Still, complaining about Hell occurs to me as a tad bit obvious and self-indulgent. Like so many experiences you venture into knowing full well that they'll be terrible, in fact the core pleasure resides in their very innate badness, like eating Swanson frozen chicken potpies at boarding school or a Banquet frozen Salisbury steak on the cook's night out. Or eating really *anything* in Scotland. Allow me to venture that the sole reason we enjoy certain pastimes such as watching the film version of *Valley of the Dolls* arises from the comfort and familiarity of its very inherent poor quality.

In contrast, *The English Patient* tries desperately to be profound and only succeeds in being painfully boring.

If you'll forgive the redundancy: What makes the earth feel like Hell is our expectation that it ought to feel like Heaven. Earth is earth. Hell is Hell. Now, stop with the whining and caterwauling.

On that basis, it does seem clichéd and obvious to arrive in Hell and then weep and gnash and rend your garments because you find yourself immersed in raw sewage or plopped down atop a bed of white-hot razor blades. To scream and thrash seems . . . hypocritical, as if you've bought a ticket and seated yourself to watch *Jean de Florette* and then complain loudly, resentful of the fact that all the actors are speaking French. Or like the people who travel to Las Vegas only to harp about how it's so tacky. Of course, even the casinos that take a stab at elegance with crystal chandeliers and stained glass, even those are crowded with the din and cacophony of plastic slot machines flashing strobe lights to seize your attention. In such a situation the people who whine and moan might imagine they're making a contribution but really they're just being another petty annoyance.

The other most important rule worth repeating is: Don't eat the candy. Not that you'll be even remotely tempted, because it's scattered on the dirty ground, AND it's the candy even fat people and heroin junkies won't eat: rock candy, rock-hard Bazooka bubble gum, Sen-Sen, saltwater taffy, black Crows, and popcorn balls.

Given the fact that you, yourself, are still alive and Black or a Jew or whatever—bully for you, you just keep eating those bran muffins—you'll have to take my word for all of these details, so listen up and pay close attention.

Flanking your cell, other cells stretch to the horizon in both directions, most containing a single person, most of those people screaming. Even as my eyes flutter open, I hear a girl's voice say, "Don't touch the bars. . . ." Standing in the next cell, a teenage girl displays both her hands, spreading the fingers wide to show her palms smeared with smut. There really is the most dreadful mildew problem in Hell. It's like an entire underworld with sick building syndrome.

My neighbor I'd wager is a high school junior, because she has the hip development to hold up a straight-line skirt and she has breasts instead of just frills or smocking to fill out the front of her blouse. Even with smoke clouding the air and the occasional vampire bat fluttering through my line of vision I can see her Manolo Blahnik shoes are counterfeit, the kind you might buy sight unseen over the Internet from a pirate operation in Singapore for five dollars. If you can stomach yet another piece of advice: Do NOT die while wearing cheap shoes. Hell is . . . well, hell on shoes; anything plastic melts, and you don't want to walk barefoot over broken glass for the rest of eternity. When it comes your time, when the proverbial bell tolls for thee, seriously consider wearing a basic low-heel Bass Weejun penny loafer in a dark color that won't show dirt.

This teenage girl in the next cell calls over, asking, "What are you damned for?"

Getting to my feet, stretching my arms. and dusting off the legs of my skort, I reply, "Smoking marijuana, I guess."

Out of courtesy rather than genuine interest I ask the girl about her own cardinal sin.

The girl shrugs her shoulders; pointing one stained, smutty finger toward her feet, she says, "White shoes after Labor Day." Her sad shoes—the ersatz leather is white and already scuffed, and you can never actually polish counterfeit Manolo Blahniks.

"Beautiful shoes," I lie, nodding my head toward her feet. "Are those Manolo Blahniks?"

"Yes," she lies in return, "they are. They cost a fortune."

Another detail to remember about Hell . . . whenever you ask why anyone is damned for all eternity, she'll tell you "jaywalking" or "carrying a black purse with brown shoes" or some such petty nonsense. In Hell you'd be foolish to count on people displaying high standards of honesty. The same goes for earth.

The girl in the next cell takes a step closer and, still looking at me, she says, "You know, you're really pretty."

That statement exposes her as a super, all-out, major-league liar, but I don't say anything in response.

"No, I mean it," she says. "All you need is more eyeliner and some mascara." Already she's digging in her shoulder bag—also white, fake Coach, plastic—picking out tubes of mascara and compacts of turquoise Avon eye shadow. With one dirty hand, the girl waves for me to lean my face between the bars.

It's my experience that girls tend to be terrifically smart until they grow breasts. You may dismiss this observation as my personal prejudice, based on my own tender age, but thirteen years seems to be when human beings reach their fullest flower of intelligence, personality, and pluck. Both girls and boys. Not to boast, but I believe a person is her most truly exceptional at the age of thirteen—look at Pippi Longstocking, Pollyanna, Tom Sawyer, and Dennis the Menace—before she finds herself conflicted and steered by hormones and crushing gender expectations. Let girls get their menstruation or boys have their first wet dream, and they instantly forget their own brilliance and talent. Again, here's a reference to my Influences of Western History textbook—for a long time after puberty, it's like the dark ages that fell between the Athenian Enlightenment and the Italian Renaissance. Girls get their boobs and forget they were ever so gutsy and smart. Boys, too, can display their own brand of clever and funny behavior, but let them get that first erection and they go complete *moron* for the next sixty years. For both genders, adolescence occurs as a kind of Ice Age of Dumbness.

And, yes, I know the word *gender*. Ye gods! I may be pudgy and flat-chested and nearsighted and dead, but I am NOT a moron.

Yes, and I know that when a supersexy older girl with hips and breasts and nice hair wants to take off your glasses and to paint you a smoky eye she's merely trying to enroll you in a beauty contest she's already won. It's a kind of slummy, condescending gesture, like when rich people ask poor people where they summer. To me, this smacks of a blatant, insensitive "let them eat cake" type of chauvinism.

Either that, or the attractive older girl is a lesbian. Either way, I don't offer my face even as she stands ready, brandishing a gloppy mascara brush like a fairy godmother's magic wand, to turn me into some floozy Cinderella. To be honest, whenever I watch the classic John Hughes film *The*

Breakfast Club, and Molly Ringwald leads poor Ally Sheedy into the girl's bathroom, then brings her out with those hideous 1980s smears of rouge under each cheekbone and Ally's hair tied back with that preppy ribbon and her lips painted that dated *red*-red like a cheap China doll version of Ringwald's own sellout Whorey Vanderwhore *Vogue* magazine conformity, poor Ally reduced to a kind of living, breathing Nagel print, I always yell at the television, "Run, Ally!" Really, I scream, "Wash your face, Ally, and *just run!*"

Instead of submitting my face, I say, "I'd better not, not until my eczema clears up some."

At this, the magic mascara wand jerks back. The Avon eye shadows and lipsticks all clatter back into the fake Coach bag even as her eyes squint, searching my face for signs of inflamed, red, flaky skin and open sores.

It's like my mom will tell you: "Every new maid wants to fold your underwear a different way." Meaning: You have to stay smart and not let yourself be pushed around.

Other cells cluster around our two, some cells empty, others occupied by lone people. No doubt the football jock, the rebel stoner, the brainy geek, the psycho, all serving detention here, forever.

No, it's not fair, but chances are good that I'll be in this cell for centuries to come, pretending to suffer psoriasis even while hypocrite people scream and complain about the humidity and the smell, and my Whorey Vanderwhore neighbor squats down to try to spit-shine her cheapo, white plastic shoes with a crumpled wad of Kleenex. Even against the stink of poop and smoke and sulfur, you can smell her dime-store perfume like a mixed-fruit flavor of chewing gum or instant grape drink. To be honest, I'd rather smell poop, but who can hold their breath for a million-plus years? So, simply out of courtesy I say, "Thanks anyway, about offering the makeover, I mean." Out of sheer politeness, I force myself to smile and say, "I'm Madison."

At this, the teenage girl almost lunges toward the bars which separate us. All breasts and hips and high-heeled shoes, now obviously, pathetically grateful for my companionship, she grins to show me her every mass-produced, porcelain-veneered incisor. In her pierced earlobes, she's even wearing diamond earrings—so very Claire Standish of her—only vulgar, dime-size, dazzle-cut cubic zirconium. Saying, "I'm Babette," dropping the wad of tissue, she thrusts a smutty, stained hand between the bars for me to shake.

III.

Are you there, Satan? It's me, Madison. Please don't feel hurt, Satan, but my parents raised me to believe you didn't exist. My mom and dad said you and God were invented in the superstitious, backward pea brains of hillbilly preachers and Republican hypocrites.

ccording to my parents, there's no such place as Hell. If you asked them, they'd probably tell you I'm already reincarnated as a butterfly or a stem cell or a dove. I mean, my parents both said how important it was for me to see them walking around naked all the time or I'd grow up to be totally a Miss Pervy McPervert. They told me that nothing was a sin, just a poor life choice. Poor impulse control. That nothing is evil. Any concept of right versus wrong, according to them, is merely a cultural construct relative to one specific time and place. They said that if anything should force us to modify our personal behavior it should be our allegiance to a social contract, not some vague, externally imposed threat of flaming punishment. Nothing is wicked, they insisted, and even serial killers deserve cable television and counseling, because multiple murderers have suffered, too.

In the spirit of the classic John Hughes film *The Breakfast Club*, I've begun to write an essay in the same manner the student detainees at Shermer High School were required to write one thousand words on the theme of "Who Do You Think You Are?"

Yeah, I know the word *construct*. Put yourself in my penny loafers: I'm locked in a barred cell in Hell, thirteen years old and doomed to be thirteen forever, but I'm not totally self-unaware.

What's worse is how my mom even said all her Gaia Earth Mother baloney in *Vanity Fair* magazine when she was promoting her last movie release. The magazine took her picture arriving at the Oscars red carpet with my dad driving them both in a dinky electric car, but really, when nobody's looking they go everywhere in a leased Gulfstream jet, even if it's just to pick up their dry cleaning, which they send to have cleaned in France. That one film, she got nominated for playing a nun who gets bored and unfulfilled, so she ditches her vows to do prostitution and heroin and have some abortions before she gets her own top-rated daytime talk show and marries Richard Gere. A total of nobody went to the film in theatrical release, but the critics creamed all over it. Critics and movie reviewers really, *really* count on there being no actual Hell.

My guess is I feel about *The Breakfast Club* the same way my mom feels about Virginia Woolf. I mean, she had to take Xanax just to read *The Hours* and still cried for almost a year.

In *Vanity Fair* my mom said the only true evil was how big oil companies were using global warming to push innocent baby polar bears closer to extinction. Even worse was she said, "My daughter, Madison, and I have struggled for years over her tragic childhood obesity." So, yes, I comprehend the term *passive-aggressive*.

Other kids went to Sunday school. I went to Ecology Camp. In Fiji. Other girls learned to recite the Ten Commandments. I learned to reduce my carbon footprint. In our Aboriginal Skills workshop, *in Fiji*, we used certified organically grown, sustainably harvested fair-trade palm fronds to weave these crappy wallets that everybody threw away. Ecology Camp cost about a million dollars, but we still all had to share the same filthy bamboo toilet stick to wipe our butts. Instead of Christmas, we had Earth Day. If there was a Hell, my mom said you'd go there for wearing fur coats or buying a cream rinse tested on baby rabbits by escaped Nazi scientists in France. My dad said that if there was a devil it was Ann Coulter. If there's a mortal sin, my mom says it's Styrofoam. Most times they'd spout this environmental dogma while walking around naked with the curtains open so that I wouldn't grow up to become a little Miss Whorey Vanderwhore.

Sometimes the devil was Big Tobacco. Sometimes, Japanese drift nets.

Even worse, it's not as if we traveled to Ecology Camp aboard sampans, gently pushed along by the Pacific currents. No, every single kid got there on a separate private jet, burning through about a gazillion fossil-fuel gallons of dinosaur juice the likes of which this planet will never see again. Each child was borne aloft; provisioned with his or her body weight in organic fig bars and free-trade yogurt snacks sealed within single-use Mylar packaging designed not to biodegrade before the future date of NEVER, all of this burden of homesick children and between-meal calories and video gaming systems would rocket toward Fiji at faster than the speed of SOUND.

What a fat load of good that did . . . now look at me: dead from a marijuana overdose and damned to Hell, scratching my cheeks raw in an attempt to convince my next-door-cell neighbor I suffer from communicable psoriasis. Surrounded by a million-million stale popcorn balls. On the plus side, in Hell you're no longer slave to a corporeal self, and this can be a blessing to the truly fastidious. Not to put too fine a point on it, but you've no more of the tedious, endless stoking and scrubbing and evacuation of the various holes required to keep a physical body functional. Should you find yourself in Hell your cell will feature no toilet nor water nor bed, nor will you miss them. No one sleeps in Hell except as a possible defensive posture in retaliation during yet another punitive presentation of *The English Patient*.

No doubt my mom and dad meant well, but it's really hard to argue with the fact that I'm trapped within a corroded iron cage boasting a scenic view of a raging excrement waterfall—actual poop, I mean, not just *The English Patient*—NOT that I'm complaining. Trust me, the last thing Hell seems to need, in a coals-to-Newcastle way, is one more complainer.

Yes, I know the word *excrement*. I'm trapped and bored, not brain damaged.

And it was my parents who told me to act out, a little, and experiment with recreational drugs.

No, it's not fair, but I guess the worst thing they taught me was to hope. If you just planted trees and collected litter, they said, then life would turn out okay. All you had to do was compost your wet garbage and cover your house roof with solar cells and you'd have nothing to worry about. Renewable wind energy. Biodiesel. Whales. That's what my parents considered our spiritual salvation. We'd see approximately a quatrillion Catholics throwing incense at some plaster statue, or a billion-zillion Muslims all lined up on their knees and facing New York City, and my dad would say, "Those poor ignorant bastards . . ."

It's one thing for my parents to behave all secular human-ist and gamble with their own eternal souls; however, it's altogether *not* all right that they also gambled with mine: They placed their bets with such self-righteous bravado, but I'm the one who lost.

We'd see Baptist people on television waving baby dolls impaled on wooden sticks and dripping with fake ketchup blood in front of some doctor's clinic, and I really could believe that all religions were way-bat-shit loony. In con-trast, my dad always preached that if I ate enough dietary fiber and recycled any plastic bottles that had a neck, I'd be fine. If I asked about Heaven or Hell, my mom gave me a Xanax.

Now—go figure—I'm waiting to get my tongue yanked out and fried in bacon grease and garlic. Probably demons plan to stub out their cigars in my armpits.

Don't get me wrong. Hell isn't so dreadful, not com-pared to Ecology Camp, and especially not compared to junior high school. Call me jaded, but not much compares to having your legs waxed or getting your navel piercing done at a mall kiosk. Or bulimia. Not that I'm a totally eating-disordered Miss Slutty von Slutski.

My biggest gripe is still hope. In Hell, hope is a really, really bad habit, like smoking cigarettes or fingernail biting.

Hope is something really tough and tenacious you have to give up. It's an addiction to break.

Yes, I know the word *tenacious*. I'm thirteen and disillusioned and a little lonely, but I'm not simpleminded.

No matter how hard I try to resist the impulse, I keep hoping I'll still have my first menstruation. I keep hoping I'll grow really big boobs, like Babette in the adjacent cell. Or reach a hand into my skort pocket and find a Xanax. I cross my fingers that if a demon dunks me in a vat of boiling lava I'll get thrown together naked with River Phoenix, and that he'll say I'm cute and try to kiss me.

The problem is, in Hell there is no hope.

Who Do I Think I Am? In a thousand words . . . I don't have a clue, but I'll start by abandoning hope. Please help me, Satan. That would make me so happy. Help me give up my addiction to hope. Thank you.

IV.

*Are you there, Satan? It's me, Madison. I thought I saw
you, today, and waved madly like some fevered groupie
to get your attention. Hell continues to unfold as an
interesting, exciting place, and I've begun to learn some
rudimentary demonology so I won't feel like an idiot
forever. Really, there's almost no time to feel homesick.*

*Today I even made friends with a boy who has dreamy
brown eyes.*

 o be completely technical about the mat-
ter, time in Hell doesn't consist of days
and nights, only a constant low-light con-
dition accented by the flickering orange
glow of flames, billowing white clouds of steam, and black
clouds of smoke. These elements combine to create a per-
petual rustic après-ski atmosphere.

Recognizing that, thank God I wore a self-winding calen-
dar wristwatch. Sorry, Satan, my mistake, I said the G-word.

To all of you alive people walking around, taking your
multivitamins and busy being Lutheran or getting colonoscopies, you need to invest in a good-quality, long-lasting
wristwatch with day and date functions. Don't count on
getting any cell phone reception in Hell, and don't think
for a second you'll have the forethought to die with your
charger cord in hand or even find yourself locked inside
a rusted jail cell with a compatible electrical outlet. That
doesn't mean go buy a Swatch. Swatches equal plastic, and .

plastic melts in Hell. Do yourself a big favor and invest in a high-quality leather wristband or the springy expandable metal kind.

In the event you neglect to equip yourself with an adequate wristwatch, do NOT scope out some bright, proactive thirteen-year-old chubby girl wearing low-heeled Bass Weejuns and horn-rimmed eyeglasses and then keep asking her, "What day is it?" and "What time is it?" The aforementioned intelligent-albeit-beefy girl will simply feign looking at her watch, then tell you, "It's five thousand years since the LAST time you asked me that. . . ."

Yes, I know the word *feign*. I may be a tad annoyed and defensive, but—no matter how nicely you ask with that wheedling tone in your voice—I am NOT your little time-keeping servant bitch slave.

And before you make the effort to give up smoking, take note that smoking cigarettes and cigars is excellent practice for being in Hell.

AND before you make some snide remark, based on my general temperament, that I must be "riding the cotton pony" or suffering from a "red-letter day," need I remind you that I am dead, deceased, and rendered eternally prepubescent and therefore immune to the mindless reproductive biological imperatives that, no doubt, shape every living, breathing moment of your crummy living, breathing life.

Even now I can hear my mom saying, "Madison, you're dead, so just *calm down*."

Increasingly, I'm not sure to which I was more addicted: hope or Xanax.

In the cell next to mine, Babette exhausts her time by

examining her cuticles and buffing her fingernails against the strap of her white shoulder bag. Anytime she glances in my direction, I make a big show of scratching my neck and around my eyes. It never seems to occur to Babette that we're dead, so conditions like psoriasis would be fairly unlikely to continue into the afterlife; however, when you consider her choice of frosted-white nail varnish, it's clear that Babette is no one's idea of a scholarship girl. A Cover Girl, maybe.

Catching my eye, Babette calls over, "What day is this?"

Scratching myself, I call back, "Thursday." Actually, I don't allow my fingernails to make contact with my skin; what I execute is an air-guitar equivalent of scratching; otherwise, my face would be raw as hamburger. The last problem I need is an infection in such dirty, filthy surroundings.

Squinting her eyes, peering at her fingernail beds, Babette says, "I love Thursdays. . . ." She fishes a bottle of white nail varnish out of her fake Coach bag and says, "Thursday feels like Friday, but without the pressure to get out and have fun. It's like Christmas Eve Eve, you know, December twenty-third. . . ." Shaking the little bottle of nail varnish, Babette says, "Thursday is like a really, really good second date, when you still think that the sex might be okay. . . ."

From another cell, fairly close by, someone begins to scream. Alone in their cells, other people slump in the classic postures of catatonic stupor, wearing the soiled costumes of Venetian doges, Napoleonic vivandiers, Maori headhunters. They've clearly been able to abandon all hope and clutch their filthy cage bars. They've flailed and thrashed in complete resignation, and now lie stained, staring, and motionless. The lucky bastards.

Painting her fingernails, Babette asks, "Now . . . what day is it?"

My wristwatch says Thursday. "It's Friday," I lie.

"Your skin looks better today," Babette lies in return.

I counterlie, "Your perfume smells so good."

Babette parries my counterlie with, "I think your breasts grew a little."

That's when I think I see you, Satan. A towering figure steps out of the darkness, striding down alongside a distant row of cages. At least three times as tall as any human being cowering within the bars, the figure drags a forked tail which grows from the base of his spine. His skin sparkles with fish scales. Great black-leather wings sprout from between his shoulder blades—real leather, not like Babette's shabby, fake Manolo Blahniks—and thick horns of bone burst through the scaly surface of his bald pate.

Forgive me my possible breach of hellish protocol, but I can't resist the opportunity. Lifting one hand, waving it above my head as if to flag a passing taxi, I shout, "Hello? Mister Satan?" I shout, "It's me, Madison!"

The horned figure stops beside a cage wherein a mortal man cowers and screams wearing the frayed, sullied uniform of some football team. With jagged eagle talons instead of hands, the horned figure flips the lock on the man's cage, reaches in, and snatches about in the small space while the screaming football man dodges and evades being caught.

Still waving, I call, "Over here!" I shout, "Look over here!" I just want to say hello, to introduce myself. This seems like the polite thing to do.

Finally, one talon clutches the panting, breathless

football man and withdraws him from the iron cage. The captives in all the surrounding cells scream, pulling themselves as far away from the action as possible; each huddles and shivers in some far corner, bug-eyed and hyperventilating. Their combined wails sound hoarse and broken from effort. In the same manner you'd dismember a steamed crab, the horned figure grasps one of the football man's legs and twists it around and around, the hip socket popping and tendons snapping, until the leg pulls free from the torso. Repeating the process, the figure removes each of the man's limbs, lifting each to his own mouth of jagged shark's teeth and biting the meaty, hypertrophied flesh from the man's bones.

All the while, I continue to call, "Hello? When you have a moment, Mister Satan . . . ," uncertain about the etiquette of interrupting such a meal.

After consuming each limb, the horned figure throws the remaining bones back into the football man's original cage. Even the screams are drowned out by the wet sounds of sucking and lip smacking and chewing. Then a thunderous belch. When finally the football man is reduced to a bony thorax, much like the picked-over carcass of a Thanksgiving turkey, all white rib cage and hanging shreds of leftover skin, only then does the horned figure toss the final remains into the cage and once more lock the door.

At this lull I'm spastically leaping in place, waving both arms above my head and shouting. Ever mindful to not come in contact with my own dirty, filthy iron bars, I shout, "Hello?! Madison, here!" I pick up a soiled popcorn ball and lob it, shouting, "I've been dying to meet you!"

Already the loose, bloodied bones of the football man are assembling themselves, pulling back together to form a human being, once more sheathing themselves with muscle and skin, coming back to re-create the man himself, restored in order to be tortured again, indefinitely, forever.

His hunger seemingly satiated, the horned figure turns and begins walking into the distance.

In desperation, I scream. No, it's not fair; I did tell you that to scream in Hell was to exhibit very bad form. I consider screaming to be a complete impropriety, but I scream, "Mister Satan!"

The towering, tailed figure is gone.

From next door, Babette's voice says, "What day is it now?"

If anything, life in Hell is like a vintage Warner Bros. cartoon where characters are forever getting decapitated by guillotines and dismembered by dynamite explosions, then being completely restored in time for the next assault. It's a system not without both its comfort and its monotony.

A voice says, "That's not Satan." From a nearby cell, a teenage boy calls, "That was Ahriman, just a demon of the Iranian desert." The teenage boy wears a short-sleeved, button-down shirt tucked into chinos. He wears a thick submariner's wristwatch with deep-water diver chronograph functions and a built-in calculator. On his feet, he wears crepe-soled Hush Puppies, and his chinos are hemmed so short you can see his white sweat socks. Rolling his eyes, shaking his head, the boy says, "Geez, don't you know *anything* about basic ancient cross-cultural theological anthropology?"

Babette squats down and starts spit-shining her own bad shoes with another wad of Kleenex. "Shut up, nerd," she mutters.

"My mistake," I tell the boy. I point a finger at myself, such a lame gesture—even in the sweltering heat of Hell I can feel myself blushing—and I say, "I'm Madison."

"I know," the boy says. "I've got ears."

Just seeing the boy's brown eyes . . . the terrible, horrible threat of hope swells inside my tubby self.

Ahriman, he explains, is nothing more than a deposed deity native to ancient Persian culture. He was the twin of Ohrmazd, born of the god Zurvan the Creator. Ahriman is responsible for poison, drought, famine, scorpions, mostly stereotypical desert stuff. His own son is named Zohak and has venomous snakes which grow from the skin of his shoulders. According to this teenage boy, the only food these snakes will eat is human brains. All this . . . it's so much the gruesome trivia an adolescent boy would bother to know. So way-totally D&D.

Babette buffs her fingernails against the strap of her bag, ignoring us.

The teenage boy jerks his head in the direction where the horned figure disappeared, saying, "Usually he hangs out on the far side of the Vomit Pond, just west from the River of Hot Saliva, over on the opposite shore of Shit Lake. . . ." The boy shrugs and says, "For a ghoul, he's pretty rad."

Babette's voice pipes up; interrupting, she says, "Ahriman ate me, one time. . . ." Seeing the expression on the boy's face, looking at the tented front of his chinos, Babette says, "NOT in that way, you gross, puny little twerp."

Yes, I might be dead and suffering from a world-class

inferiority complex, but I can recognize an erection when I see one. Even as the stinking, poop-scented air around us swarms with fat, black houseflies, I ask the boy, "What's your name?"

"Leonard," he says.

I ask, "What are you condemned to Hell for?"

"Jerking off," Babette says.

Leonard says, "Jaywalking."

I ask, "Do you like *The Breakfast Club*?"

He says, "What's that?"

I ask, "Do you think I'm pretty?"

The boy, Leonard, his dreamy brown eyes flit all over me, alighting like wasps on my stubby legs, my pop-bottle eyeglasses, my crooked nose and flat chest. He glances at Babette. He looks at me, again, his eyebrows jump up toward his hairline, wrinkling his forehead into long accordion folds. He smiles, but shakes his head, No.

"Just testing," I say, and cover my own smile by pretending to scratch the eczema I don't have on my cheek.

V.

*Are you there, Satan? It's me, Madison. After a
somewhat rocky start, I'm having simply the best
time. I continue to meet new people, and I'm sorry
about the mix-up . . . just imagine: me mistaking just
some regular ordinary, nobody-special demon for you.
I'm learning something new and interesting all the
time from Leonard. On top of that, I've concocted a
way-brilliant idea for how to overcome my insidious
addiction to hope.*

ho could imagine that cross-cultural
anthropological theology could be so
absolutely fascinating! According to Leonard, who really does have the loveliest
brown eyes, all the demons of Hell formerly reigned as
gods in previous cultures.

No, it's not fair, but one man's god is another man's devil.
As each subsequent civilization became a dominant power,
among its first acts was to depose and demonize whoever
the previous culture had worshiped. The Jews attacked
Belial, the god of the Babylonians. The Christians banished Pan and Loki and Mars, the respective deities of the
ancient Greeks and Celts and Romans. The Anglican British banned belief in the Australian aboriginal spirits known
as the Mimi. Satan is depicted with cloven hooves because
Pan had them, and he carries a pitchfork based on the tri-
dent carried by Neptune. As each deity was deposed, it was

relegated to Hell. For gods so long accustomed to receiving tribute and loving attention, of course this status shift put them into a foul mood.

And, ye gods, I knew the word *relegated* before it came out of Leonard's mouth. I might be thirteen and a newbie to the underworld, but don't take me for an idiot.

"Our friend Ahriman was originally cast out of the pantheon by the pre-Zoroastrian Iranians," Leonard says, shaking his index finger in my direction and adding, "but don't be tempted to perceive Essenism as a Judaic avatar of Mazdaism."

Shaking his head, Leonard says, "Nothing related to Nebuchadnezzar the Second and Cyaxares is ever that simple."

Babette gazes at the compact she holds open in one hand, retouching her eye shadow with a little brush. Looking up from her reflection in the tiny mirror, Babette calls to Leonard, "Could you possibly BE more boring?"

Among the early Catholics, he says, the Church found that monotheism couldn't replace the long-beloved polytheism now outdated and considered pagan. Celebrants were too used to petitioning individual deities, so the Church created the various saints, each a counterpart to an earlier deity, representing love, success, recovery from illness, etc. As battles raged and kingdoms rose and fell the god Aryaman was replaced by Sraosha. Mithra supplanted Vishnu. Zoroaster made Mithra obsolete, and with each succeeding god, the prior ruling deity was cast into obscurity and contempt.

"Even the word *demon*," Leonard says, "originates with Christian theologians who misinterpreted '*daimon*' in the writings of Socrates. Originally the word meant 'muse' or 'inspiration,' but its most common definition was 'god.'" He adds that if civilization lasts long enough into the future, one day even Jesus will be skulking around Hades, banished and ticked off.

"Bullshit!" a man yells. The yelling erupts from the jail cell of the football man, where his bare bones foam with red corpuscles, the red bubbles running together to form muscles which swell and stretch to attach with their tendons, the white ligaments braiding, a process both compelling and revolting to watch. Even before a layer of skin has fully enveloped the skull, the mandible drops open to shout, "That's *bullshit*, geek!" The flow of new skin breaks like a pink wave to form lips around the teeth, the lips saying, "You just keep talking that way, twerp! That's exactly why you're stuck here."

Without looking up from her own reflection in her compact mirror, Babette asks, "What are you down here for?"

"Offsides," the football man calls back.

Leonard shouts, "Why am I here?"

I ask, "What's 'offsides'?"

Auburn hair sprouts from the football man's scalp. Curly, coppery hair. Gray eyes inflate within each socket. Even his uniform weaves itself whole from the scraps and threads scattered around his cell floor. Printed across the back of his jersey is a big number 54 and the name Patterson. To me, the football man says, "I had a part of my foot over the scrimmage line when the ref blew his whistle to signal the start of play. That's 'offsides.'"

I ask, "And that's in the *Bible*?"

With all his hair and skin replaced, you can tell the football man is only a high schooler. Sixteen, maybe seventeen years old. Even as he talks, little silver wires weave themselves between his teeth, becoming a mouthful of braces. "Two minutes into the second quarter," he says, "I intercepted a pass and got sacked by a defensive tackle—pow! Now, I'm here."

Again, Leonard shouts, "But *why am I here*?"

"Because you don't believe in the one true God," says Patterson, the football player. Now that he's covered in skin again, his new eyes keep glancing over at Babette.

She doesn't look up from her little mirror, but Babette makes faces, pursing her lips and tossing her hair, fluttering her eyelashes, fast. As my mom would tell you, "Nobody stands that straight when she's not on camera." Meaning: Babette loves the attention.

No, it's not fair. From within their respective cages, Patterson and Leonard both stare at Babette locked within hers. No one looks at me. If I wanted to be ignored I'd have stayed on earth as a ghost, watching my mom and dad walk around naked, opening the drapes and chilling rooms as I bully them to put on some clothes. Even that Ahriman demon showing up to tear me apart and devour me would be better than getting no attention whatsoever.

There it is, again—that nagging tendency to hope. My addiction.

While Patterson and Leonard ogle Babette, and Babette ogles herself, I pretend to watch the vampire bats flit around. I watch the surf crest and break in rolling brown waves on Shit Lake. I pretend to scratch the make-believe psoriasis on my face. In the neighboring cages, sinners huddle, weeping out of old habit. A damned soul dressed in the uniform of a Nazi soldier smashes his face, again and again, into the stone floor of his cell, crushing and collapsing his nose and forehead as if he were tapping a hard-boiled egg against a plate in order to shatter the shell. In the pause between each impact on the stone, his crushed nose and features inflate to their normal appearance. In another cell, a teenage kid wears a black leather biker jacket, an over-size safety pin piercing his cheek, his head shaved except for a stripe of hair, dyed blue and gelled to stand in a spiky Mohawk which runs from his forehead to the nape of his neck. As I watch, the leather-jacket punk reaches up to his cheek and flicks open the safety pin. He draws it out from the holes in his skin, then reaches through the bars of his cage and pokes the point of the open pin into the lock of his cell door, working the point around within the keyhole.

Still gazing at herself in her compact mirror, Babette asks of no one in particular, "What day is it?"

Leonard's arm crooks, instantly, and he looks at his diver's chronograph watch, saying, "It's Thursday. Three-oh-nine p.m." A beat later, he says, "No, wait . . . now it's three ten."

In the middle distance, a looming giant with the head of a lion, shaggy with black fur, with cat claws instead of hands, reaches into a cage and plucks out a wailing, flail-ing sinner, dangling him by his hair. In the same manner you might nibble grapes from a bunch, the demon's lips close around the man's leg. The demon's furry lion cheeks sink inward, hollowed, and the man's screams grow louder as the meat is sucked from the living bone. With one leg reduced to hanging bone, the demon begins to suck the meat from the second leg.

Despite all of this ruckus, Leonard and Patterson continue to watch Babette, who watches herself. The Ice Age of Dumbness.

With a muted clank, the punk wearing the leather jacket twists the tip of his safety pin sideways within the lock on his cell door to trip the mechanism. He pulls the pin free, then wipes it against his blue jeans until the point is clean of rust and slime before thrusting it back into its previous place, piercing his cheek. At that the punk swings the cell door open and steps out of his cage. His Mohawk stands so tall the blue hair brushes the top of the doorframe.

Swaggering down the row of cells, the blue-Mohawk punk peers into each cage. Inside one lies an Egyptian pharaoh or somebody who went to Hell for praying to the wrong god, crumpled on the floor, gibbering and drooling, one arm sprawled so that the hand rests near the cage bars. A fat diamond ring glitters on one finger, the stone in the four-carat range, D-grade, not cubic zirconium like Babette's cheapo earrings. Next to that cage, the punk kid stops and stoops. Reaching through the bars, he slips the ring off the wasted finger. The kid pockets the diamond ring inside his motorcycle jacket. Standing, he catches me watching him and saunters toward my cell.

He wears black motorcycle boots—note: an excellent footwear choice for Hades—the ankle of one boot wrapped with a bicycle chain, his other ankle wrapped with a knotted, soiled red bandanna. Pimples swell into red points dotting his pale chin and forehead, in contrast to his bright green eyes. As the Mohawk punk struts closer, one hand slips into his jacket pocket and scoops out something. From a long toss away, still walking, he says, "Catch," and his hand swings, tossing the object, which flashes in a long, high arc, flying between my cage bars, falling to the point where my hands clap together to catch it.

Acting the part of a complete Miss Slutty Slutovitch, Babette continues to ignore Patterson and Leonard but holds her compact angled to spy on the punk kid, scrutinizing him so closely that when the thrown object flashes, the bright flash bounces off her mirror, reflected into her eyes.

"What's a nice girl like you," the Mohawk kid asks me, "doing in a place like this?" When he talks the safety pin in his cheek jerks around, flashing orange in the firelight. He struts up to the bars of my cell and winks one green eye at me, but looks at Babette without looking directly at her. He's clearly touched the dirty iron bars, then touched his face, his jeans, his boots, smearing the filth all over himself.

No, it's not fair, but dirt does manage to make some people look more sexy.

"My name is Madison," I tell him, "and I'm a hope-aholic."

Yes, I know the word *tool*. I may be dead and jailbait and boy-crazy, but I can still be used to make another girl jealous. Warm from the punk's pocket, lying in the palm of my hand is the stolen diamond ring. My first gift from a boy.

Drawing the oversize safety pin from his cheek, the Mohawk kid pokes the sharp point into my keyhole and begins to pick the lock.

VI.

Are you there, Satan? It's me, Madison. I assume that membership in Hell gives you access to a zillion-million A-list celebrities. . . . About the only person I'm not excited to meet is my dead grandpa. My long-dead Papadaddy Ben. Long Story. Please credit the impulse to my youthful curiosity, but I can't resist the opportunity to get sprung and take a quick look-see ramble to check out the lay of my new neighborhood.

pare me, please, your dime-store psychology, but I really do hope the devil will like me. Note, again, my lingering attachment to the H-word. My being here, locked in a slimy cage, it would seem a forgone conclusion that God isn't my biggest fan, and my parents, it now appears, are largely out of the picture, as are my favorite teachers, nutrition coaches, really all the authority figures I've tried to please for the past thirteen years. Therefore it's not surprising that I've transferred all my immature needs for attention and affection to the only parental adult available: Satan.

There they both are: the H-word and the G-word, proof of my tenacious addiction to all things upbeat and optimistic. To be honest, all my effort thus far to remain spotless, mind my posture, present myself as perky, affect a cheerful smile, is calculated to endear myself to Satan. In my best-case scenario I see myself assuming a kind of sidekick or comic-relief role, becoming a perky, chubby, sassy girl child who tags along with the Prince of Lies, cracking wise-ass jokes and propping up his flagging ego. So ingrained is my spunky nature that I can't even allow the Prince of Darkness to indulge in the doldrums. I truly am a sort of flesh-and-blood form of Zoloft. Perhaps that explains Satan's general absence: He's simply waiting for my verve to exhaust itself before he makes himself known.

Yes, I understand that much about pop psychology. I may be dead and vivacious, but I'm not in denial concerning the manic first impression I can make.

Even my own dad would tell you, "She's a dervish." Meaning: I tend to wear people out.

It's for that reason that when the blue-Mohawk punk unlocks my cell door and swings it open on creaky, rusted hinges I step back deeper into the cage rather than forward to gain my freedom. Despite the diamond ring the punk's just tossed me, which now resides on the middle finger of my right hand, I resist my wanderlust. I ask the kid his name.

"Me?" he says, stabbing the oversize safety pin through his cheek. He says, "Just call me Archer."

Still lingering in my cell, I ask, "What are you in for?"

"Me?" the kid, Archer, says. "I went and got my old man's AK-47 semi. . . ." Dropping to one knee, he shoulders an invisible rifle, saying, "And I blew away my old man and old lady. I slaughtered my kid brother and sister. After them, my granny. Then our collie dog, Lassie . . ." Punctuating each sentence, Archer pulls an invisible trigger, sighting down the barrel of his phantom rifle. With each trigger pull, his shoulder jerks back as if pushed by recoil, his tall blue hair fluttering. Still sighting through an invisible scope, Archer says, "I flushed my Ritalin down the toilet and drove my folks' car to school and took out the varsity football team and three teachers . . . all of them, dead, dead, dead." As he stands, he brings the bore of the imaginary rifle barrel to his mouth, purses his lips, and blows away invisible gun smoke.

"Bullshit," shouts a voice, Patterson, the football player, fully restored to a teenage boy with red hair and gray eyes and the large number 54 on his jersey. In one hand, he carries a helmet. His feet scratch the stone floor, the soles of his shoes tapping and skittering with sharp steel cleats. "That's total bullshit," Patterson says, shaking his head. "I saw your paperwork when you first got here. It said you're nothing but a lousy shoplifter."

Leonard, the geek, laughs.

Archer snatches a rock-hard popcorn ball off the ground and wings it, line-drive fast, against the geek's ear.

Exploded popcorn and the pens from his pocket fly everywhere. Leonard falls silent.

"Get this," Patterson says. "According to his file Mr. Serial Killer, here, was trying to steal a loaf of bread and a batch of disposable diapers."

At this Babette looks up from her mirror and says, "Diapers?"

Archer strides over to the bars of Patterson's cell, thrusting his chin between the bars; snarling through clenched teeth, Archer says, "Shut up, jockstrap!"

Babette says, "You have a baby?"

Turning toward her, Archer shouts, "Shut up!"

"Get back into your cell," Leonard shouts, "before you get us all in trouble."

"What?" Archer shouts. He swaggers over, at the same time extracting the safety pin from his cheek, then begins to pick the lock of Leonard's cage door. "You afraid this will go on your *permanent record*, twerp?" Tripping the lock, Archer says, "You afraid you might not get into an Ivy League college?" On that note he swings the barred door open.

Grabbing the door, yanking it shut, Leonard says, "Don't." Unlocked, the door won't stay shut and swings open. Holding it closed, Leonard says, "Lock it, quick, before some demon comes along. . . ."

Already, Archer's blue head is swaggering over to Babette's cell; pin in hand, he's saying, "Hey, sweet thang, I know a scenic spot overlooking the west edge of the Sea of Insects that will take your breath away," and he begins picking her lock.

Leonard continues to pull on the bars of his cell door, holding it shut.

My door hangs open. I close my hand into a fist around my new diamond ring.

Patterson shouts, "You loser, you couldn't find your way across to the far side of Shit Lake."

As he swings open Babette's door, Archer shouts, "Then join us, jockstrap. Show me."

Dropping her cosmetics back into her fake Coach bag, Babette says, "Yeah . . . if you're brave enough." Pointlessly, she pinches her already short skirt and lifts the hem as if to prevent it from dragging. Being a total Miss Harlotty O'Harlot, her legs showing almost to her panty-hose crotch, Babette steps through her open door, picking her way delicately in her fake Manolo Blahniks.

Leonard stoops to collect his scattered pens. He brushes the bits of sticky popcorn from his hair.

Archer swaggers over to Patterson's cell. Holding the safety pin outside the bars, beyond Patterson's reach, baiting him, Archer says, "You up for a little field trip?"

To get Leonard's attention I tell him my theory about behavior modification therapies versus plain, old-fashioned exorcisms. How nowadays if any of my friends, my alive girlfriends, sat in their bedrooms all day throwing up, the diagnosis would be bulimia. Rather than engage a priest to confront the girl about her behavior, express love and concern, and evict the occupying demon, contemporary families engage a behavioral therapist. It's weird to think that as recently as the 1970s religious leaders were throwing holy water on adolescent girls with eating disorders.

My hope really does spring eternal; but, darn it, Leonard isn't listening.

By now, Archer has sprung Patterson. Babette joins them and the trio is already strolling toward the fiery horizon amid screams and swarms of black houseflies. Patterson offers his hand to steady Babette on her high heels. Archer sneers, but it might just be the pin lanced through his cheek.

Even as I continue to talk, expounding on my theory about Xanax addiction being caused by demonic possession, Leonard of the lovely brown eyes throws open his cell door and bolts after the vanishing hikers. My last only new friend in Hell, Leonard's scrambling over the terrain of aged Gummi Bears and smoldering coal. His head swiveling, on the lookout for possible demons, he's calling, "Wait!

Wait up!" Rushing after the fading blue point of Archer's Mohawk hair.

When all four of them are almost gone, reduced by distance to mere rule-breaking dots in the landscape of bubbling poop and discarded Jujubes, only then do I walk through my own cell door and take my first forbidden Bass Weejun steps in their pursuit.

VII.

Are you there, Satan? It's me, Madison. Like so many tourists, we've embarked on our little walkabout to explore Hell. We take note of the general topography. We view a few interesting landmarks. And I'm prompted to make a small confession.

he group of us skirted around the margin of the flaky, greasy Dandruff Desert, where scorching winds as hot as a billion hair dryers blow the scabs of dead skin into drifts as tall as the Matterhorn. We traipsed past the Great Plains of Broken Glass. After a fair trek, we stood on a bluff of volcanic cinders overlooking a vast pale ocean which stretched to the horizon. No wave or ripple disturbed its opalescent surface: a shade of soiled ivory similar to the scuffed faux leather of Babette's counterfeit Manolo Blahnik shoes.

Even as we watch, the viscous tide composed of this off-white ooze seems to rise and consume a finger's width of the ashy, cindery beach. So thick is the corrupt liquid that it appears more to roll up the shoreline than to wash ashore as this flood tide creeps in. Apparently, on this particular ocean, the tide never ebbs and is always flowing, always a rising flood tide.

"Check it out," Archer says, and waves one leather-jacketed arm in a wide arc to frame the view. "Ladies and gentlemen, may I present the Great Ocean of Wasted Sperm. . . ."

All ejaculate, according to Archer, expelled in masturbatory emissions over the course of human history, at least since Onan—it all trickles down to accumulate here. Likewise, he explains, all blood shed on Earth trickles down and collects in Hell. All tears. Every spit gob spat on the ground ends up hereabouts.

"Since the introduction of VHS tapes and the Internet," Archer says, "this ocean has been rising at record rates."

I think of my Papadaddy Ben and shudder. To repeat, Long Story.

In Hell, porn is creating an effect equivalent to that of global warming on earth.

The group of us take a step backward, away from the rising, shimmering ooze.

"Now that this twerp is dead," Patterson says, as he cuffs Leonard on the back of the head, "maybe the ol' sperm sea won't be filling up so fast."

Leonard rubs his own scalp, wincing, and says, "Don't look now, Patterson, but I think I can see some of your ball juice floating out there."

Looking at Babette, Archer licks his tongue around his lips and says, "One of these days we're going to be up to our eyeballs. . . ."

Babette looks at the diamond ring on my finger.

Archer, still ogling her, says, "Hey, Babs, you ever been up to your foxy eyes in hot sperm?"

And pivoting on one scuffed heel, Babette says, "Back off, Sid Vicious. I'm not your Nancy Spungen." Waving for us to follow her, fluttering her white-painted fingernails, Babette looks at Patterson in his football jersey and says, "It's your turn. Now you show us someplace interesting."

Patterson swallows, shrugs his shoulders, and says, "You guys want to see the Swamp of Partial-birth Abortions?"

We, the rest of us, all shake our heads, No. Slowly. In unison, for a long time, no, no, no. Definitely not.

As Babette strides away from the Ocean of Wasted Sperm, Patterson trots to catch up with her. The pair of them link arms, walking together. The team captain and the head cheerleader. The rest of us, Leonard and Archer and I, follow a few steps behind.

To be honest, I keep wishing we could all talk. Chew the fat. And, yes, I know that wishing is another symptom of hope, but I can't help it. As we amble along, trudging over steaming brimstone beds of sulfur and coal, I want to ask if anyone else feels an intense sense of shame. By dying, do they feel as if they've disappointed everyone who ever bothered to love them? After all the effort that so many people made to raise them, to feed and teach them, do Archer or Leonard or Babette feel a crushing sense of having failed their loved ones? Do they worry that dying constitutes the biggest sin they could possibly commit? Have they considered the possibility that, by dying, each of us has generated pain and sorrow which our survivors must suffer for the remainder of their lives?

In dying—worse than flunking a grade in school, or getting arrested, or knocking up some prom date—perhaps we've majorly, irreversibly fucked up.

But nobody brings up the subject, so I don't either.

If you asked my mom, she'd tell you that I've always been a little coward. As my mom would say, "Madison, you're dead . . . now, stop being so *needy.*"

Probably everyone in the world looks like a coward when compared to my mom and dad. My parents were always leasing a jet to fly round-trip to Zaire and bring home an adopted brother or sister for Christmas—not that we celebrated Christmas—but the same way my friends might find a puppy or kitten under their holiday tree, I'd find a new sibling from some obscure, postcolonial, living-nightmare place. My parents meant well, but the road to Hell is paved with publicity stunts. Any adoption occurred within the media cycle of my mom's film releases or my dad's IPOs, announced with a gale-force flurry of press releases and photo ops. Following the media blitz, my new adopted brother or sister would be warehoused in an appropriate boarding school, no longer starving, now offered an education and a brighter future, but never again present at our dinner table.

Walking along, now backtracking across the Great Plains of Broken Glass, Leonard explains how ancient Greeks conceived of the afterlife as Hades, a place where both the corrupt and the innocent went to forget the sins and egos left over from their lives on earth. Jews believed in Sheol, which translated as "the place of waiting," again, where all souls collected, regardless of their crimes and virtues, to rest and find peace through discarding their past transgressions and attachments on earth. Kind of Hell as going to detox or rehab instead of Hell as burning punishment. For most of human history, Leonard says, people have perceived of Hell as a sort of inpatient clinic where we go to kick our addiction to life.

Without breaking stride, Leonard says, "John Scotus Eriugena wrote during the ninth century that Hell is where your own desires take you, stealing you away from God and the original plans God had for fulfilling your soul's perfection."

I say maybe we should swing by that swamp of terminated pregnancies. There's a good possibility that I might run into a long-lost sibling or two.

Yes, I may be flip and glib, but I know what constitutes a healthy psychological defense mechanism.

Droning on while we walk, Leonard lectures about the power structure of Hades. He describes how midway through the fifteenth century, an Austrian Jew named Alphonsus de Spina converted to Christianity, becoming a Franciscan monk, then a bishop, and finally compiling a list of the demonic entities who populate Hell. His numbers ran into the millions.

"If you see anyone with a goat's horned head, a woman's breasts, and the black wings of a huge raven," Leonard says, "that would be the demon Baphomet." Counting in the air, waving an index finger in the manner of a conductor cueing the sections of an orchestra, Leonard says, "You have the Hebrew Shedim, the Greek demon kings Abaddon and Apollyon. Abigor commands sixty legions of devils. Alocer commands thirty-six legions. Furfur, a royal count of Hell, commands twenty-six legions. . . ."

Just as the earth is ruled by a hierarchy of leaders, Leonard says, so too is Hell. Most theologians, including

Alphonsus de Spina, describe Hell as having ten orders of demons. Among those are 66 princes, each overseeing 6,666 legions, and each legion comprises 6,666 demons. Among them is Valafar, the grand duke of Hell; Rimmon, the chief physician of Hell; Ukobach, the leading engineer of Hell, and reputed to have invented fireworks and presented them as a gift to mankind. Leonard rattles off the names: Zaebos, who boasts the head of a crocodile on his shoulders . . . Kobal, the patron demon of human comedians . . . Succorbenoth, the demon of hate. . . .

Leonard says, "It's like Dungeons and Dragons, only to the tenth power." He says, "Seriously, the biggest brains of the Middle Ages devoted their entire lives to this type of theological bean counting and number crunching."

Shaking my head, I say that I wish my parents had.

Periodically along our journey, Leonard stops to point out a figure in the distance. One, flying across the orange sky, flapping pale wings of melting dripping wax, this is Troian, the night demon of Russian culture. Flying along a different trajectory, peering down with the wide head and luminous eyes of an owl, this is Tlacatecolototl, the Mexican god of evil. Wrapped in cyclone winds of rain and dust, there are Japanese Oni demons, who traditionally live at the center of hurricanes.

What the Human Genome Project would represent for future researchers, Leonard explains, this great inventory represented for previous centuries of world leaders.

According to the bishop de Spina, a third of Heaven's angels were cast into Hell, and this divine downsizing, this celestial housecleaning, took nine full days—two days longer than it took God to create the Earth. In all, a total of 133,306,668 angels—including much-revered former cherubim, potentates, seraphim, and dominations—were forcibly relocated, among them Asbeel and Gaap, Oza and Marut and Urakabarameel.

Ahead of us, where she walks arm in arm with Patterson, Babette cuts loose with a peal of laughter, loud and shrill and as fake as her counterfeit shoes.

Archer glares at their backs, the big safety pin bunched in the muscles of his clenched jaw.

Leonard name-drops about the different demons whom we might stumble across: Baal, Beelzebub, Belial, Liberace, Diabolos, Mara, Pazuzu—an Assyrian with a bat's head and scorpion's tail—Lamashtu—a Sumerian she-devil who suckles a pig with one breast and a dog with the other—or Namtaru—the Mesopotamian version of our modern grim reaper. We look for Satan with the same intensity that my mom and dad looked for God.

In retrospect my parents were always pushing me to expand my consciousness by huffing glue or gasoline or chewing peyote buttons. Simply because they'd done their time, wasted their teen years lolling in the muddy fields of Vermont and the salt flats of Nevada, naked except for rainbow face paints and a thick coating of sweaty filth, their heads festooned with fifty pounds of fetid dreadlocks, teeming with crab lice and pretending to find enlightenment . . . that does NOT mean I have to make that same mistake.

Sorry, Satan, once again I've said the G-word.

Without breaking stride, Leonard nods and points to indicate the former deities of now-defunct cultures, now warehoused in the underworld. Among them: Benoth, a god of the Babylonians; Dagon, an idol of the Philistines; Astarte, goddess of the Sidonians; Tartak, the god of the Hevites.

My suspicion is that my parents treasure their sordid recollections of episodes at Woodstock and Burning Man not because those pastimes led to wisdom, but because such folly was inseparable from a period of their lives when they were young and unburdened by obligation; they had free time, muscle tone, and their futures still looked like a great, grand adventure. Furthermore, both my mother and father had been free of social status and therefore had nothing to lose by cavorting nude, their swollen genitals smeared with muck.

Thus, because they had ingested drugs and flirted with brain damage, they insisted I should do likewise. I was forever opening my boxed lunch at school to discover a cheese sandwich, a carton of apple juice, carrot sticks, and a five-hundred-milligram Percocet. Tucked within my Christmas stocking—not that we celebrated Christmas— would be three oranges, a sugar mouse, a harmonica, and quaaludes. In my Easter basket—not that we called the event Easter—instead of jelly beans, I'd find lumps of hash-ish. Would that I could forget the scene at my twelfth birth-day party where I flailed at a piñata, wielding a broomstick in front of my peers and their respective former-hippie, former-Rasta, former-anarchist throwback parents. The moment the colorful papier-mâché burst, instead of Tootsie Rolls or Hershey's Kisses, everyone present was showered with Vicodins, Darvons, Percodans, amyl nitrate ampoules, LSD stamps, and assorted barbiturates. The now-wealthy, now-middle-aged parents were ecstatic, while my little friends and I couldn't help but feel a tad bit cheated.

That, and it doesn't take a brain surgeon to understand that very few twelve-year-olds would actually enjoy attending a clothing-optional birthday party.

Some of the most gruesome images in Hell seem downright laughable when compared to seeing an entire generation of adults stripped nude and wrestling on the floor, grasping and panting in frantic competition for a scattered handful of codeine spansules.

These were the same people who worried that I might grow up to become a Miss Nymphy Nymphoheimer.

At present, Archer, Leonard, and I trail after Babette and Patterson, navigating a switchback route through hummocks of discarded toe- and fingernail parings, between sloughing gray hillocks heaped with every thin crescent of nail ever trimmed. Some nail fragments are painted pink or red or blue. As we tread along the narrow canyons, thin rivulets of loose fingernails trickle down. Trickling toenails threaten to become full-fledged avalanches which could bury us alive (alive?) in their talus of prickly keratin. Overhead arches the flaming orange sky, and down branching canyons, dwarfed in the distance, we can glimpse communities of cages where our fellow doomed souls sit in permanent soiled desolation.

As we meander, Leonard continues to recite the names of demons we might encounter: Mevet, the Judaic demon of death; Lilith, who steals children; Reshev, the plague demon; Azazel, demon of deserts; Astaroth . . . Robert Mapplethorpe . . . Lucifer . . . Behemoth . . .

Ahead of us, Patterson and Babette stroll up a gentle slope, topping a rise which blocks the view beyond. Reaching the crest, the two of them stop. Even from behind we can see Babette's body stiffen. In reaction to what she now sees in the distance, both her hands come up to cover her face, her fingers cupped over her eyes. Babette bends slightly from the waist, bracing her hands against her thighs, and turns away from the view, stretching her neck as if about to retch. Patterson turns to see us, jerking his head for us to hurry and catch up. To witness some new atrocity just over this next horizon.

Archer and Leonard and I trudge along, mounting the slope of nail parings, soft under each labored step, like snow or loose sand, climbing until we stand alongside Patterson and Babette, at the edge of a steep cliff. Half a step ahead of us, the land drops away, and below us boils a sea of insects which stretches to the horizon . . . beetles, centipedes, fire ants, earwigs, wasps, spiders, grubs, locusts, and what-all churning constantly, a shifting soft quicksand composed of pincers, feelers, segmented legs, stingers, shells, and teeth, darkly iridescent, largely black but speckled with hornet yellows and bright grasshopper greens. Their constant clicking and rustling generates a din not unlike the crashing surf of a briny ocean on earth.

"Cool, huh?" says Patterson, waving his football helmet in one hand as if to direct our attention over this morass of seething, undulating horrors. He says, "Check it out . . . the Sea of Insects."

Gazing down into the surging swells and rolling troughs of clamoring bugs, Leonard sneers in righteous disgust, saying, "Spiders are not insects."

Not to belabor the point, but counterfeit luxury goods truly represent a false economy. To witness, Babette's plastic shoes look to be falling apart, the straps severed and the soles loose and flapping—subjecting her lithe feet to fingernail and busted-glass abrasions—while my own sturdy Bass Weejun loafers barely appear to be broken in by our lengthy underworld trek.

As we gaze out across the vast squirming, humming pudding of insect life, a scream approaches us from behind. There, sprinting between the hills of nail parings, panting and running, comes a bearded figure dressed in the toga of a Roman senator. Craning his neck to glance backward over his shoulder, the man races toward us, screaming the word *Psezpolnica*. Screaming, "Psezpolnica!"

At the cliff's edge, teetering near where we stand, the lunatic toga man points a quaking finger in the direction he's come. Beseeching us with his wide-open eyes, he screams, "Psezpolnica!" and dives, plummeting, flailing, falling to vanish beneath the seething surface of bug life. Once, twice, three times the toga man comes up for air; his mouth is choked with beetles. Crickets and spiders sting and strip the flesh from his twitching arms. Earwigs swarm, eating deep into his eye sockets, and millipedes weave through ragged, bloody holes nibbled between his now-exposed rib bones.

As we watch in horror, wondering what could drive a person to such an extreme course of action . . . Babette, Patterson, Leonard, Archer, and I . . . we turn in unison to see a lumbering, towering figure approach.

VIII.

Are you there, Satan? It's me, Madison. It might amuse you to hear we were beset by a demon of thrilling size. This precipitated the most amazing act of heroism and self-sacrifice—really, from the least likely person among our company. In addition I've included more of my own background, in the event you're interested in learning more about me as a bewitching, fully faceted overweight person.

s our little group stands atop the ridge overlooking the Sea of Insects, a looming figure stomps toward us. Each of its thundering footfalls trembles the surrounding hillocks, bringing down dusty cascades of ancient finger- and toenail clippings, and the figure stands so tall that we can discern only the silhouette of it as outlined against the flaming orange sky. So violently does the giant's weight shake the ground that the cliff on which we stand heaves and shimmers beneath us, the loose nail parings threatening to subside and deposit us into the seething, devouring bugs.

It's Leonard who speaks first, whispering only the single word, "Psezpolnica."

In our immediate distress, Babette appears to be far too self-absorbed, the poor quality of her fashion accessories too blatant a metaphor—impossible to ignore—representing her choice of surface appeal over inner quality. Patterson, the athlete, seems frozen in his conventional, traditional attitudes, a person for whom the rules of the universe were fixed very early and will always remain unchanged. In contrast, the rebellious Archer presents himself as a knee-jerk rejection of . . . everything. Of my newfound companions Leonard shows the most promise of evolving into something more than an acquaintance. And, yes, once more I recognize *promise* as a symptom of my nagging, deeply ingrained tendency to hope.

Prompted by this hope, made manifest by my instinct for self-preservation, when Patterson very slowly fits his football helmet over his head and says, "Run," my stout legs don't hesitate. As Archer and Babette and Patterson each flee on their own tangent, I run beside Leonard.

"Psezpolnica," he pants, legs working against the soft, malleable layers of nails, his bent arms pumping the air for momentum, Leonard says, "The Serbians call her 'the tornado woman of midday.'" Gasping for breath, running beside me, his shirt pocketful of pens bouncing against his skinny chest, Leonard says, "Her specialty is driving people insane, lopping off their heads and ripping them limb from limb. . . ."

In a glance, I look back to see a woman who towers as tall as a tornado, her face so distant it seems tiny against the sky, as straight-up and high above me as the sun at noon. Like a flaring funnel cloud, her long black hair whips and streams out from her head, and she hesitates as if deciding which of us to pursue.

Beyond the giantess, Babette staggers, both of her cheesy, way-shoddy shoes flapping around her feet, hobbling and tripping her. Patterson hunches his shoulders, dodging and weaving, his cleats throwing up a rooster tail of nail filings as if he were running a football through some defensive line, headed for a touchdown. Archer rips off his leather jacket and tosses it aside, sprinting full-tilt, the chains looped around his one boot clanking.

The tornado demon crouches, reaching lower with a hand, the fingers spread as wide as a parachute, steadily lowering toward the stumbling, screaming figure of Babette.

Granted, there exists an element of play in all of this panic; having witnessed the demon Ahriman render and consume Patterson, and Patterson's subsequent regeneration to a redheaded, gray-eyed footballer, on some level I'm aware that my absolute death is no longer possible. All of that said, the process of being plucked apart and devoured still seems like it would sting like all get-out.

As the towering tornado demon reaches to snatch a screaming Babette, Leonard shouts for her to dive. Cupping both his hands to make a megaphone around his mouth, Leonard shouts, "Dive and dig!"

So that you might learn from my ignorance, it's a tried-and-true strategy when escaping danger in Hell to dig into the nearest available terrain. Hell offers scant cover, no flora to speak of—except for the inexplicable accumulations of Beemans gum, Walnettos, Sugar Daddys, and popcorn balls—thus the only consistent, ready manner in which to conceal oneself is to tunnel until completely buried, in this case by the vast accumulation of castoff fingernail shards.

Distasteful as this might sound, for this piece of advice, you owe me.

Not that you're ever actually going to die. Perish the

thought. Not with your hours and hours invested in aerobic exercise.

On the other hand, if you do find yourself dead and in Hell, menaced by Pszpolnica, do as Leonard would recommend: Dive and dig.

My hands burrow into a hillside of loose, cascading parings, and with every inch I dig a steady landslide of the same avalanches down upon me, prickly and itchy, abrasive but not entirely unpleasant, until I'm completely interred, Leonard interred at my side.

About my own death, my *death*-death, I remember very little. My mother was launching a feature film, and my father had gained a controlling interest in something— Brazil, I think—so of course they'd brought home an adopted child from . . . someplace awful. My brother du jour, his name was Goran. He of the brutish, hooded eyes and beetling brow, an orphan sourced from some war-torn, former-socialist hamlet, Goran had been starved of the early physical contact and imprinting required for a human being to develop any sense of empathy. With his reptilian gaze and broad pit-bull jaw, he arrived forever and always as damaged goods, but this only added to his appeal. Unlike any of my previous siblings, now apportioned to various boarding schools and long forgotten, I found myself quite smitten with Goran.

For his part, Goran had merely to cast his churlish, ravenous eyes upon my parents' wealth and lifestyle, and he was determined to curry my acceptance. Add to those factors one overly large baggy of marijuana supplied by my dad, plus my impulse to finally smoke the nasty herb, if only to bond with Goran, and that's the sum total I'm able to recall about the circumstances of my fatal overdose.

Currently, lying fully buried in a grave of fingernails, I listen to my heartbeat. I hear my breath rushing in my nostrils. Yes, without a doubt, it's hope that makes my heart continue to beat, my lungs to breathe. Old habits die hard. Above me, the ground heaves and shifts with every step of the tornado demon. The parings trickle into my ears, stifling any sound of Babette's screams. Stifling the clicking din from the Sea of Insects. I lie buried here, counting my heartbeats, resisting an urge to dig one hand sideways in search of Leonard's hand.

In the next instant my arms are pinned to my sides. The fingernails press in close, tightly around me, and I'm lifted into the stinking sulfurous air, rising into the flaming orange sky.

The fingers of a huge hand are clasped around me as tight as a straitjacket. This giant hand has been thrust into the loose soil and has plucked me the way one might pull a carrot or radish from its buried slumber.

Ye gods, I might be the privileged, wealthy, insulated scion of celebrity parents, but I still know where babies and carrots come from . . . although I was never entirely certain where Goran originated.

Soaring into the air, I can survey it all: the Sea of Insects, the Great Plains of Broken Glass, the Great Ocean of Wasted Sperm, an endless array of cages containing the damned. Below me spreads the whole geography of Hell, including demons wandering hither and yon to gobble hapless victims. At the highest point of my ascent, a canyon of wet teeth await. A wind of rank, wet breath buffets me with a stink worse than the communal toilets at Ecology Camp. There heaves a monstrous tongue carpeted with taste buds the size of red mushrooms. All of this ringed by lips as fat as greased tractor tires.

The hand brings me to the mouth, where my arms stretch to brace against the upper lip. My feet push against the lower lip, and like a fishbone I hold myself too wide and rigid to be swallowed. Under my hands, the lips feel surprisingly plush, leathery like a banquette in a good restaurant, but very warm. Like touching the upholstery of a Jaguar someone's just driven from Paris to Rennes.

So vast is the demon's face that all I can see is the mouth. In my peripheral vision, I'm vaguely aware of eyes above me, broad and glassy as department store windows, except curved outward, bulging. Those eyes, fenced by the black pickets of huge eyelashes. I'm conscious of a nose the size of a mud hut with two open doorways, each door hung with a curtain of fine nostril hairs.

The hand pushes me against the teeth. The tongue thrusts to make wet contact with the buttoned front of my cardigan sweater.

In the moment I am resigned to my immediate fate, to be masticated and swallowed, my bones cast aside like the skeleton of every Cornish game hen I've ever eaten, at that instant the mouth screams. What occurs seems less like a scream than an air-raid siren blasting point-blank into my face. My hair, my cheeks and clothing, these are all blown and rippling, snapping like a flag in a hurricane.

One of my Bass Weejuns slips from my foot, falling, tumbling, dropping to land on the ground beside a tiny figure sporting a bold blue Mohawk. Even at this distance, I can see it's Archer standing beside the giant's sizable bare foot. Having removed the oversize safety pin from his cheek, Archer is plunging the point, repeatedly removing it and plunging it, again and again, into the tip of the demon's big toe.

In the melee which ensues, I feel myself half dropped, half heaved, half lowered until I land in the soft, scratchy fingernails. The same moment as my impact, hands grasp me, human hands, Leonard's hands, and pull me to shelter beneath the slurry of nail parings . . . but not before I see the same parachute hand which caught me now catch Archer and lift him—cursing, kicking his boots, slashing with his pin—to where the teeth snap shut, and in a single bite guillotine off his vivid blue head.

IX.

Are you there, Satan? It's me, Madison. Before I tell you the following you must promise, cross your heart and hope to die, that you won't EVER share this secret with another person. I mean it. You see, I'm well aware that you're the Prince of Lies, but I need you to swear. You'll have to guarantee your confidentiality if we're to have a relationship of any significant depth and honesty.

ast winter, if you must know, I found myself alone at boarding school during the holiday break. It goes without saying that I'm recounting an event from my past life. Christmas occurred to my parents as just another ordinary day, and the rest of my classmates were leaving for ski vacations or Greek islands, so, for my part, there was nothing to do except put on a game face and assure them, girl by girl, that my own family would be along at any moment to collect me. That final day of autumn term, the residence hall emptied out. The dining hall shut down. As did the lecture halls. Even the faculty departed the campus with their packed bags, leaving me in almost complete solitude.

I say "almost" because a night watchman, possibly a team of them, continued to prowl the school grounds, checking locked doors and turning down thermostats, their flashlight beams occasionally sweeping the landscape at night like searchlights in an old prison movie.

A month previous, my parents had adopted Goran, he

of the haunted eyes and heavy Count Dracula accent. Although he was only one year older than me, Goran's forehead was already etched with wrinkles. His cheeks, hollowed. His eyebrows grew as wild and tangled as the forested slopes of the Carpathian Mountains, so matted and bristling that if you looked too closely among the hairs you'd expect to see marauding packs of wolves, ruined castles, and stooped Gypsy women gathering firewood. Even at the age of fourteen, Goran's eyes, his voice pitched deep as a foghorn, it all gave the impression that he'd witnessed his entire extended family tortured to death as slave labor in the salt mines of some remote gulag, bloodhounds baying after them across ice floes, and leather whips cracking at their backs.

Ah . . . Goran. No Heathcliff nor Rhett Butler was ever so swarthy nor rudely fashioned. He seemed to exist in his own permanent isolation, insulated by some terrible history of hardship and deprivation, and I envied him that. I did so, so long to be tortured.

Next to Goran, even adult men sounded silly and chatty and insignificant. Even my father. Especially my father.

Lying in bed, alone in a Swiss residence hall built to house three hundred girls, in temperatures barely warm enough to prevent the pipes from freezing, I pictured Goran, the way blue veins branched under the transparent skin of his temples. How his hair grew so thick it wouldn't comb down, the stand-up kind of hair you'd cultivate while studying Marxist philosophy over tiny cups of bitter espresso in smoke-filled coffeehouses, awaiting your perfect opportunity to lob a burning dynamite stick into the open touring car of some Austrian archduke and ignite a world war.

My mom and dad were doubtless introducing poor Goran to the assembled media outlets represented at Park City, Utah; or Cannes; or the Venice Film Festival, while I was hiding out beneath six blankets surviving on hoarded Fig Newtons and Vichy water—*avec gaz.*

No, it's not fair, but I was clearly getting the better part of the arrangement.

My family assumed I was aboard a yacht, among giggling friends. My mom and dad assumed I *had* friends. The school assumed me to be with my parents and Goran. For two glorious weeks all I had to do was read the Brontës, evade the occasional security guards, and wander about— naked.

In all my thirteen years I'd never even slept in the nude. Of course, my parents paraded unclothed constantly, exposing themselves around the house and on the more exclusive beaches of the French Riviera and the Maldives, but I perennially felt too flat in some places, too fat in some, too skinny in others, simultaneously gawky and plump, too old and too young. It was clearly in violation of the school's rules of deportment, but alone one night, I pulled off my nightgown and slipped into bed, naked.

My mother had never hesitated to suggest I attend this or that weekend retreat focusing on genital awareness and mastering control of one's own pleasure centers, the usual assortment of celebrity mothers and daughters idling in a remote grotto, squatting over hand mirrors and marveling at the infinite pink moods of the cervix, but their sort of workshopped . . . empowerment seemed so clinical. It wasn't a frank, honest workshopping of my sexuality that I wanted. It was Goran I wanted, someone ruddy and moody. Pirates and tightly laced bodices. Masked highwaymen and kidnapped wenches.

The second night I slept naked, I awoke needing to pee. The toilets were down the hall, shared by all the girls on each floor, but I was almost certainly alone in the residence building. So, despite the sacrosanct rules, I peered out of my room, naked and barefooted, checking the dark hallway for a patrolling guard. I ran the cold steps to the bathroom and did my business, all in the dim moonlight filtering through the windows, my breath steaming in the cold air. The third night, I visited the bathroom, again naked, but strolled en route, taking a detour on my return trip to visit the first-floor lounge and sit unclothed on the chilly leather sofas which faced the blank dark mirror of the television screen. My nude reflection in the glass, wan as a pudgy ghost.

Ah, those glory days when I still had an earthly reflection . . .

Really, Satan, please. You have to swear that you won't breathe a word of this.

By my fifth night alone I'd ventured naked to the chemistry lab, sat naked in my usual desk in the Romance Languages classroom, and stood naked on the dais at the head of the dining hall, where the senior faculty normally sat for their meals.

And, yes, while I admit to being dead and having a poor body image and a suppressed sense of my own personal value, I am well aware of my risky, late-night exhibitionism and yen for Goran as symptoms of my budding sexuality. The night air against my skin . . . all of my skin and nipples, and the texture of so many ordinary objects: wooden desks, stairway carpets, tiled hallways—without the usual intervening layers of silk or nylon—it all felt glorious. Around any corner seemed to lurk a possible guard, some strange man wearing a uniform, his boots polished. I imagined each guard with a polished badge, wearing a gun strapped to his belt. Most likely, it would be somebody's Swiss father or grandfather with a mustache, but I pictured Goran. Goran, carrying handcuffs. Goran, his brooding eyes behind dark totalitarian sunglasses. At any moment, the beam of a flashlight might reveal me, the parts of myself I had always kept hidden. I'd be reported and expelled. Everyone would find out.

In my nude ramblings I lingered among the leather-smelling stacks in the library, perusing the books as I walked barefoot over the chill marble floors. I swam unclothed in the pool complex. With only the moonlight to see by, I sneaked into the stainless-steel kitchens and sat cross-legged on the concrete floor, eating chocolate ice cream until my body shook with the accumulated cold. As lithe as an animal . . . a sprite . . . a savage . . . I strode into the chapel and presented my fleshy self to the altar. There, the paintings and statues of the Virgin Mary were always so heavily robed and veiled, crowned and burdened with jewelry. Depictions of the Christ seldom wore more than a thorny halo and a way-tiny loincloth. Sitting on the front pew, I felt the gentle suction of my bare thighs against the polished wood.

By my second week alone, I was sleeping through the

days and wandering sans apparel all night. I'd been naked in almost every room, wandered all the hallways and steam tunnels, entered every space with an unlocked door; however, I had yet to venture outside. Beyond the windows, snow fell, layering over everything and bouncing the moonlight inside. Now, the buildings themselves felt like too much clothing. At this point I slept naked. I walked and ate and read naked so often that the thrill had evaporated. Even while reading *Forever Amber* with my tits out . . . I'd lost that special forbidden feeling. The only way to renew it would be to go out-of-doors and stand unclothed under the stars or masked in the falling snowflakes, leaving my bare footprints in the drifts.

Other girls I know, they shoplifted to generate this same prepubescent high. Other girls told lies or cut themselves with razors.

No, it's not fair, but one minute you can be wading through clean snow, your feet sinking ankle-deep into the perfect wastelands of snowdrifts which surround a private girls' school near Locarno, and mere days later you can be slogging through the morass of countless discarded fingernail clippings, cast forever into fiery Hell.

That Christmas break which I spent alone, as I first stepped out of the residence hall, entering the snowy night, my skin felt the touch of every snowflake. The cold air made my hair stand up from the roots the way my nipples stood erect, every follicle on my arms and legs becoming a tiny clitoris, and every cell of me awake and alert at rigid attention. Walking, I held my arms straight out in front of myself, mimicking the way ancient Egyptian mummies walk when rising from their stony tombs in old horror films. My hands turned palms-down, my fingers dangled the way Frankenstein's monster shambles when brought to life in black-and-white Universal movies. This was my fallback excuse: that I was sleepwalking. My parasomniac defense. So I walked, step by step, farther into the falling snow, into the darkness as cold as chocolate ice cream, my arms outstretched in the manner of sleepwalking cartoon characters, only naked. Pelted with ice crystals and pretending to be asleep, but more awake than I had ever felt. Every hair and cell of me alert, aching, afraid. Alive.

All of me felt the thrill of being touched at that same instant. You see, I wanted to be discovered. I wanted to be seen at the very height of my prepubescent power, my tits-out, bare-fanny, legally off-limits kiddie-porn Lolita power.

If a guard found me, I'd merely pretend to be ashamed. By then I had a long history of feeling mortified and embarrassed. Reverting back to such feelings would be like second nature. As a guard approached and grabbed my wrist, or threw a blanket over my shoulders to protect my childhood modesty, I'd simply pretend hysterics and insist I had no idea where I was or how I'd come to be there. I'd reject all responsibility for my own actions . . . play the innocent victim. Over the past two weeks of solitude, something within me had changed, but I could still fake being shocked and fragile and demure.

No, this is not how I came to die. As I've mentioned before, I died from smoking an overdose of marijuana. I did not freeze to death.

Nor did a lustful, groping security guard catch me. Darn it.

Arms extended like a somnambulist, I marched around the school grounds, collecting snowflakes in my hair until my feet felt quite numb. Then, fearing frostbite and permanent disfigurement, I sprinted back to the door of my residence hall. As I grasped the steel handle with my damp hands, my fingers and palms froze to the metal. I pulled, but the door had automatically locked the moment it first swung shut, leaving me naked, my hands fixed—frozen— to the handle of a door which wouldn't open, unable to run for help, unable to return to my safe bed, the deadly night piling up around me, ice crystal by ice crystal.

And, yes, I might be a dreamy, romantic, preadolescent girl, but I can recognize a metaphor when one batters me over the head: a young budding lass perched frozen on the threshold between sheltering girlhood and the frigid wasteland of her impending sexual maturation, only a sacrificial layer of her tender, virginal skin holding her captive, blah, blah, blah . . .

And no, the children of wealthy families, consigned to Swiss boarding schools, are nothing if not wily. It was common knowledge among my peers and myself that a crafty student some years before had stolen a key to the residence hall, a master key, and secreted said key beneath a specific rock near the hall's main door. In the event a wanton little Miss Slutty Slutpants sneaked away for a clandestine tryst or to smoke a cigarette and found herself locked out, rather than face reprimand she had merely to use this key held in common for such sinful emergencies and later return it to the usual hiding place. As convenient as this shared key was, under the rock only a few steps away, with my bare hands frozen to the door handle I had no means to reach it.

My mom would tell you, "This is one of those *Hamlet* moments." Meaning: You need to make a significant effort to determine whether you're to be or not to be.

If I scream and yell until a night watchman arrives, I'll be mortified, humiliated, but alive. And if I freeze to death I'll save my dignity, but be . . . well, dead. Probably I'll be a figure of pathos and mystery for future generations of girls at this school. My legacy will be a stringent new set of rules about accounting for every girl. My legacy will be a ghost story which girls my age will tell to scare each other after lights-out. Maybe I'll linger as a naked spirit they glimpse in mirrors, outside windows, at the far end of moonlit corridors. Those future privileged urchins will summon my ghost by repeating: "Maddy Spencer . . . Maddy Spencer . . . ," three times while gazing into a mirror.

Again, that's a form of power, albeit a fairly impotent form of power.

And, yes, I know the word *disassociation*.

As much as I fancy that spooky gothic immortality, I start screaming for a guard. Shouting, "Help!" Shouting, *"Au secours!"* Shouting, *"Bitte, helfen sie mir!"* The falling rush of snow hushes every sound, dampening the acoustics of the entire midnight world, blocking any echo that might carry my voice very far into the dark.

By this time my hands were the hands of a stranger. I could see my bare, blue feet, but they belonged to someone else. As blue as Goran's veins. In a glass pane of the door, I could see my own face reflected, my image framed by the frost of my breath condensing and freezing on the small window. Yes, we all appear somewhat absurd and mysterious to each other, but that girl I saw was no one to me.

Her pain was not my pain. Here was Catherine Earnshaw's dead face haunting the wintry windows of Wuthering Heights, blah, blah, blah. . . .

That waifish me, reflected in moonlight or streetlight, I watched her pulling her fingers away from the steel handle, her skin peeling away still clinging to the metal, leaving the whorls and palm prints like patterns of frost. Abandoning the wrinkled road map of her lifeline, her love line and heart line, I watched this strange girl, her face grim and resolute, walk on frozen stick legs to retrieve the key and save my life. This girl I didn't know, she pulled open the heavy door, her hands sticking once more, tearing away yet another thin layer of this stranger's fragile skin. Her hands, so frozen they didn't bleed. The metal key froze between her fingers so resolutely she was forced to carry it to bed.

Only in bed, smothered between blankets, drifting to sleep, did her skin thaw and the girl's hands began to bleed quietly into her clean, starched white sheets.

X.

Are you there, Satan? It's me, Madison. Please do NOT
get the idea that I'm some Miss Trollopy Van Trollop.
It's true that I've read the Kama Sutra, but why anyone
would bother to attempt such revolting gymnastics
remains largely a mystery to me. In regard to sex, mine
is a kind of complete intellectual understanding with
no real aesthetic appreciation whatsoever. Forgive
my uneducated distaste. While I know what organ
stimulates what, the bizarre, sordid business of phallus
and orifice interaction, the exchange of chromosomes
required for procreation of the species, I have yet to
grasp the appeal. Meaning: yuck.

 t is no accident that I segue from a scene in
which my group is confronted by a tower-
ing nude giantess to a flashback in which I,
myself, am undressed and exploring both
my interior and exterior environs without the usual protec-
tive layers of clothing or shame. In the enormous, exposed
figure of Psezpolnica, no doubt I feel an affinity, perhaps
an admiration for any female who can present herself with
such apparent lack of self-consciousness, seemingly in complete disregard for how she might be judged and exploited
by her audience. Having masqueraded one Halloween as
Simone de Beauvoir, I guess I'll always be a bit de Beauvoir.

The satire of Jonathan Swift remains a staple of English-
speaking primary education—including my own—but it's

usually limited to the first volume of *Gulliver's Travels*; or, in very daring and progressive classrooms, strictly as an illustrative example of irony, students might also read Swift's classic essay "A Modest Proposal." Few teachers would risk introducing the second volume of Lemuel Gulliver's memoirs, his misadventures in the island nation of Brobdingnag, where looming giants capture and make of him a household pet. No, it's far safer to present children, those powerless, diminutive children, with a narrative in which a giant is taken prisoner and manipulated under the control of tiny beings whose sole reason for not murdering him is their fear that his gargantuan corpse might decompose and threaten the overall public health.

It remains unknown to the majority of children that in the kingdom of Brobdingnag, in the second volume, Swift's picaresque travelogue does get a tad bit tawdry and dicey.

These are the salacious tidbits one learns when bothering to do the supplemental reading for extra credit. Especially while spending Christmas vacation naked, alone in an otherwise empty residence hall. In the second volume of Swift's masterpiece, once the giant residents of Brobdingnag capture Gulliver, he's presented at their royal court and is made a kind of mascot, forced to live in the queen's apartments, in very intimate proximity among the very gigantic ladies-in-waiting. It's these ladies who pleasure themselves by removing their clothing and lying together, sharing a bed while our hero is compelled to journey the peaks and valleys of their way-naked bodies. Writing in the guise of his narrator, Swift describes these women—the most-lovely female aristocrats of their society, who would appear so charming and appealing from a distance—as in fact constituting a swampy, reeking Gehenna in actual up-close physical contact. Our minuscule hero stumbles about their spongy, damp flesh, encountering monstrous pubic thickets of hairs, inflamed blemishes, vast cavernous scars, pits, knee-deep wrinkles, stretches of dead flaking skin, and shallow puddles of fetid perspiration.

And yes, it's duly noted that such a landscape depicted by Swift bears a marked resemblance to the actual terrain of Hell. This spreading landscape of noblewomen reclining in their afternoon languor, expecting, really demanding, that this teeny shrunken man bring them to pleasure. All the while, he stumbles and reels in disbelief and utter disgust of them. Overwhelmed with sickness and horror, exhausted, our enslaved Gulliver is forced to labor until the giant women are satisfied. In all of English literature, few passages can match this one of Swift's for its descriptive bluntness and unwelcome, masculine crudity.

My mother would tell you that men—boys, men, males in general—are too stupid, too easily found out, and too lazy to ever succeed as truly gifted liars.

Yes, I might be dead and rather imperious and steadfastly opinionated, but I know the blunt stink of misogyny when I smell it. And that it's very likely Jonathan Swift found himself the victim of childhood sexual abuse, and was now venting his rage in the passive-aggressive avenue of fantasy fiction.

In his own unhelpful way, my father would tell you, "A woman eats to feed her pussy." Meaning: Anything we do to excess is in compensation for not getting a minimum amount of sexual gratification.

My mother would say that men overimbibe alcohol because their penises are thirsty.

Really, being the offspring of former-hippie, former-Rasta, former-punk, former-anarchist parents means that I'm bombarded by no end of earthy truisms.

And no, I've never enjoyed an orgasm of my own, but I have read *The Bridges of Madison County* and *The Color Purple*, and if I learned nothing else from Alice Walker I learned that if you can help a woman discover the curative power of manipulating her own clitoris she'll serve as your loyal devotee and best friend forever.

That said, I stand before the Serbian demon, the towering nude tornado woman known as Psezpolnica.

First, I shuck off my remaining penny loafer and place it at a safe distance from the giant. I pull off my school cardigan, fold it, and settle it neatly on top of the shoe. Unbuttoning the cuffs of my blouse, I roll the sleeves back to each elbow, all the while gazing up the length of the giant's hairy legs, looking skyward to see her shins, the knees, the muscled naked thighs, craning my neck to see the Brobdingnagian mons pubis beyond.

A shrill whistle splits the air, a whistle as loud as a fire siren. On the ground, resting near my stocking feet, Archer's severed head looks up at me, the lips still pursed. "Hey, little girl," the severed head says, "whatever you're planning, don't do it. . . ."

Reaching down, I grab Archer by the long hairs of his blue Mohawk. Carrying the head as I would a purse, I step up onto the arch of the giant's foot.

Dangling from my hand, Archer says, "Getting eaten hurts like hell." He says, "You don't have to do this. . . ."

Transferring the blue hair to my teeth, I bite down, gripping the Mohawk as a pirate would a knife as said pirate climbs the rigging of a ship. In that manner, I climb the copious leg hairs of the giant demon Psezpolnica, scaling the fleshy ridge of her shin. Like Gulliver, I navigate the wrinkled skin of the demon's knees, then continue grasping the coarse body hair, pulling myself ever higher along the giant's thighs. Glancing at the distant ground, I see Babette and Patterson and Leonard, all of them with their heads tipped back, watching my ascension with their mouths gaping open. Looking around, from this height I can see the distant mother-of-pearl shimmer of the sperm ocean, the steam rising off Hot Saliva Lake, the perennial dark cloud of bats that hover above Blood River.

Swinging from his blue hair, gripped between my clenched teeth, Archer's head says, "You're crazy, little girl, you know that?"

Still climbing, I skirt my way around the wrinkled folds of the labia majora, hauling myself, like Jonathan Swift's worst nightmare, through pungent thickets of curling, dense pubic hair.

Above me hangs the foreboding cornice of two enormous breasts. Between them I can discern a chin, above that a rolling pair of chewing lips, and one blue-jeaned leg of Archer's, still shod with a motorcycle boot, dangling out a corner of the giant's mouth.

Even though my knowledge is largely theoretical, based on years of witnessing naked family friends on French beaches, I do know my way around the adult female genitalia. Clinging to the abundance of lush hair, I locate the clitoral hood and deftly manipulate the sheltering skin, thrusting my arm within to find the retracted organ of such fabled womanly pleasure. On this scale, merely brailled blindly within the warm enclosure of the clitoral hood, it feels to be roughly the size and shape of a Virginia ham.

The severed head of Archer watches my actions. Licking his lips, Archer says, "Little girl, you are *sick*. . . ." Smiling, he says, "The bitch monster ate me so, hey, the least I could do is return the favor."

Retrieving my forearm from the warm depths of the fleshy hood, I take the hank of blue hair from my mouth. Holding the head so that I gaze directly into Archer's green eyes, I say, "Take a deep breath, and make yourself useful," and I stuff the grinning, salivating head deep into the hooded depths.

For a beat, not much occurs. Above me the vast mouth continues to masticate the cud of Archer's body, his blue jeans and boots. From below, the trio of Babette, Patterson, and Leonard stare, slack-jawed. Something stirs, moaning and slurping like a ravenous beast, moving within the skin of the clitoral hood. Then gradually, the giant's lips cease to chew. The giant's breathing deepens and slows. A warm pink glow suffuses the acres and acres of skin, a great landscape of blush covering the giant's face, chest, and thighs. A shudder, tremulous as an earthquake, shakes the towering body, and I'm compelled to grip the pubic hairs more tightly lest I plummet to the fingernail fields far below.

Pirates and masked highwaymen and kidnapped wenches.

The giant's knees begin to tremble, to weaken and

buckle a little. The labia become more pronounced and highly colored, flooded with fresh blood flow.

At this point, I reach into the fleshy hood, where the hardening clitoris threatens to eject Archer's slathering, slurping noggin. Grasping the hidden head, I pull it free.

In the open air, slick with the juices of female passion and drooling wildly, Archer gasps a huge breath. His eyes dilated and crossed with pleasure, he shouts. His lips webbed with the noxious fluids inherent in adult sexual congress, Archer shouts, "I AM THE LIZARD KING . . . !"

At that, I stuff his head back to do hidden oral battle with the stiffening, engorged clitoral tissues.

The giant looks down upon me, her eyes also glazed with orgasmic ecstasy. Her head lolling loosely on her neck. Her nipples jut, the size and hardness of sidewalk fire hydrants, the same bright red color.

In the blue-jeaned leg which remains dangling from between Pszepolnica's lips, the severed leg of Archer, clearly outlined within one denim pant leg appears the sizable bulge of a male erection.

Looking up, I meet the giant's loose, sloppy grin with my own cheerful, competent smile. With one hand gripping the pubic hair to maintain my position, my other hand holds Archer's head within the confines of the slippery clitoral hood. That's the hand I risk waving in a friendly gesture while I shout, "Hello, my name is Madison." I shout, "Now that we've met . . . would you mind very much doing me just the smallest favor?"

It's at that moment the hood retracts, the fully erect clitoris popping free to make its appearance, ejecting Archer's eager advances so quickly that his slimy, delirious head plummets, trailed like a vivid blue comet by a broken stream of spittle or vaginal mucosa, tumbling, falling, rocketing to land with a hushed splash amid the loose fingernails far below.

XI.

Are you there, Satan? It's me, Madison. Don't take the following as a scolding. Please regard what I'm about to say as strictly constructive feedback. On the plus side, you've been running one of the largest, most successful enterprises in the history of . . . well, history. You've managed to grow your market share despite overwhelming competition from a direct, omnipotent competitor. You're synonymous with torment and suffering. Nevertheless, if I may be bluntly honest, your level of customer service skills really sucks.

y mom would always say, "You can trust Madison to tell you anything about herself—except the truth." Meaning: Don't expect me to instantly disassemble and leave you simply awash in revelations concerning my deep, personal self. Go ahead and chalk up this reticence to some deep, secret shame on my part, but that's not the case. I may not have been educated beyond the seventh grade, may be insufferably naive and lack solid workplace experience, but I'm not so desperate for attention that I feel compelled to share my most intimate, inner blah, blah, blah.

All you need to know is that I've seen beyond the veil. I'm dead, and in my own admittedly limited life experience, I'd wager that the best people are. Dead, I mean. Although, I'm not sure if anything since my overdose counts as "life experience."

I'm dead, and I'm riding in the cupped palm of a towering giant female demon as she strides across the hellish landscape, just burning up the miles. Accompanying me are my newfound compatriots: Leonard, Patterson, Archer, and Babette. The brain, the jock, the rebel, and the prom queen. Ergonomically speaking, traveling nested within an enormous hand is infinitely comfortable, combining the contour of a Singapore Air first-class seat with the gently rolling feel of a drawing room berth on the Orient Express. From this height, comparable to the cattle level of the Eiffel Tower or the top of the London Eye, we pass various landmarks. And not a small number of condemned A-list celebrities.

The football jock, Patterson, points out the most important locales: the Steaming Dog Pile Mountains . . . the Swamp of Rancid Perspiration . . . a meadow of what could be heather but is actually a luxuriant growth of unchecked toenail fungus.

Riding along, Leonard explains that Pszpolnica stands exactly three hundred cubits tall. Our hostess-slash-SUV is the offspring of angels who gazed down from Heaven and fell madly in lust with mortal women. All this history, Leonard says, comes down from no less a source than Saint Thomas Aquinas, who wrote in the thirteenth century that these angels appeared on earth as incubi—these revved-up, way-horny divine superbeings. The angels did the Hot Nasty Thing with mortal women, and giants such as Pszpolnica were conceived. The horny angels themselves were cast into Hell to become demons. Before you question the bullshitty way this scenario sounds, Saint Thomas Aquinas is nowhere to be found in Hades, so he must've gotten something correct.

Likewise, when earthly men lusted after angels in the cities of Sodom and Gomorrah, Leonard says, God gave them a good thrashing. The full pillar-of-salt treatment.

No, it's not fair, but it would seem that the only immortal being allowed to indulge in a dalliance with mortals is God Himself.

Sorry about how I keep using the G-word. I guess old habits do die hard.

"Keep it up," Patterson says. He cuffs Leonard on the back of the head, adding, "You fucking heretic!"

"Such language," Babette says. "Why don't you just take a dump in my ears!"

Riding along, Archer waves down at a couple demons. Shouting at a hulking blond man with deer antlers sprouting from his head, Archer says, "Yo! Cernunnos, my man!"

Whispering to me, Leonard explains that this is the dethroned Celtic god of stags. He says our Christian devil is depicted with horns as a snide dig at Cernunnos.

Archer flashes a thumbs-up at another demon, this one in the middle distance, a lion-headed man listlessly eating a dead lawyer. Archer cups one hand around his mouth and shouts, "What's up, Mastema?"

"The prince of spirits," Leonard whispers to me.

This entire time, Babette keeps asking, "What time is it?" She asks, "Is it still Thursday?" Sitting off to one side of the enormous palm, her arms folded across her chest, impatiently tapping the toe of one dirty Manolo Blahnik, Babette says, "I can't believe there's no wifi in Hell. . . ."

Our vessel, our hostess, Pszepolnica strides along, her features still lit with a soft postcoital smile.

Her smile is matched only by Archer's, his entire body

regenerated, from his blue Mohawk down to his black boots, his grin so wide it shoves his safety pin almost to one ear.

Far below, a withered old man shambles along, leaning on a cane, dragging a way-long beard. I ask Archer if he's a demon.

"Him?" says Archer, pointing at the old man. "That's Charles fucking Darwin!" Archer hawks a gob of spit, which falls, falls, falls to land near enough to make the old man look up. When they make eye contact, Archer shouts, "Hey, Chuck! You still doing the Devil's work?"

Darwin lifts one withered, veined hand to flip Archer the bird.

As it turns out, the way-fundamentalist Christian creationists were correct. How I wish I could tell my parents: Everybody in Kansas was right. Yes, the inbred snake handlers and holy rollers had more on the ball than my secular humanist, billionaire mom and dad. The dark forces of evil really *did* plant those dinosaur bones and fake fossil records to mislead mankind. Evolution was hokum, and we fell for it hook, line, and sinker.

On the horizon, outlined against the flaming orange sky, a building takes shape.

Craning his head to look up into the vast, floating, full-moon face of our sated giant, Leonard shouts, *"Glavni stab. Ugoditi. Zatim."*

To me, Leonard says, "Serbian." He says, "I picked up a few words in my advanced-placement courses."

The building in the distance is still partly hidden below the curve of the horizon, but as we draw closer and closer, it rises to reveal a sprawling complex of wings and complicated renovations.

As I started to boast earlier, really the best people are dead. Since I've been in Hell I've sighted just oodles of notables from throughout history. Even now, peering over the edge of the giant's palm, I point out a tiny figure and say, "Everybody, look!"

Patterson shields his eyes with one hand, holding it to his forehead like a salute, to cut down on the ambient orange glare. Looking to where I point, he says, "You mean that old guy?"

That "old guy," I tell him, just happens to be Norman Mailer.

You can't turn around in Hell without elbowing somebody important: Marilyn Monroe or Genghis Khan, Clarence Darrow or Cain. James Dean. Susan Sontag. River Phoenix. Kurt Cobain. Honestly, the resident population reads like the guest list of a party that would make both my parents cream. Rudolf Nureyev. John F. Kennedy. Frank Sinatra and Ava Gardner. John Lennon and Jimi Hendrix and Jim Morrison and Janis Joplin. A permanent Woodstock. Probably, if he knew the networking opportunities hereabouts, my dad would immediately gulp down rat poison and throw himself on a samurai sword.

Just to schmooze with Isadora Duncan, my mom would pop open the emergency-exit door and bail out of our Learjet midflight.

Really, just looking around, you feel a twinge of pity for the poor souls who succeeded in getting past the Pearly Gates. One can't help but picture the lackluster VIP lounge in Heaven, a kind of nonalcoholic ice-cream social starring Harriet Beecher Stowe and Mahatma Gandhi. Hardly anyone's idea of a "with-it" social register.

And, yes, I am thirteen years old, fat, and dead—but I am not overcompensating in the same manner as insecure homosexuals who constantly trot out Michelangelo and Noël Coward and Abraham Lincoln in order to bolster their own fragile self-esteem. True, being dead AND in Hell seems to suggest that one has committed the double whammy of Big Mistakes, but at least I find myself mingling in very, capital-V, Very good company.

Trotting along, still borne aloft in our giant's hand, we draw closer to the complex of buildings which now appear to spread far beyond the horizon, covering acres, even square miles of Hellish real estate. Along the outer edges, the buildings' perimeter consists of postmodern pastiche, a collage of styles borrowing heavily from Michael Graves and I. M. Pei, with an assortment of laborers already excavating and laying the foundations for an ever-spreading series of additions ribbed to suggest the undulating forms of Frank Gehry. Within this outer margin stand concentric circles of older additions, like the rings of a bisected tree, each inner ring identifiable with the fashion of an earlier era. Adjacent to the PoMo sections rise the boxy glass towers of the International style. Within those lie the campy futuristic spires of the Art Deco, then the Period Revival of Victorian times, the Federal, the Georgian, the Tudor, Egyptian, Chinese, Tibetan palace architecture, Babylonian minarets, all of it comprising an ever-widening history of building. Even as the edges expand, covering land almost as rapidly as the Great Ocean of Wasted Sperm, at the same time the complex's ancient core is rotting and collapsing.

As Pszpolnica stands at the buildings' outskirts, from

this height we can see that the oldest, inner portions, pre-dating the Etruscan and Incan and Mesopotamian, those towers and chambers at the center have crumbled to decayed wood and clay dust.

Here, this place is the nerve center, the headquarters of Hell.

Leonard shouts upward, *"Ovdje."*

At this, the giant stops walking.

Snaking away from the outermost walls of the building complex, way-long queues of people stand waiting in line. Literally, no exaggeration, miles of the damned. Each queue leads to a different doorway, and every so often the people in a line step forward as someone enters.

Leonard shouts, *"Prekid."* He shouts, *"Ovdje,* please."

Hearing this strange Slavic babble, I wonder how close it comes to the language of Goran's thoughts. The cryptic, mysterious lingo of my beloved Goran's memories and dreams. Goran's native tongue. To be entirely honest, I'm not certain from which war-torn homeland my Goran even harkened.

And yes, I've sworn off hoping, but a girl can still carry a torch.

As we approach the tail end of one long queue, Leonard says, *"Spustati. Sledeic."*

Babette says, "Is this even the same *year*?"

Only in Hell do you wish a wristwatch included the day, date, and *century* functions.

At this, Pszpolnica sinks to one knee, leaning forward to carefully, gently lower us back to the ground.

XII.

Are you there, Satan? It's me, Madison. If you can
tolerate yet another admission on my part, I've never
been very adept at taking tests. Trust me, I'm not trying
to lay the blame elsewhere, but I loathe the kind of
game-show context in which so much of our lives is
determined: proving my memory and mental skills in a
sedentary situation under the pressure of limited time.
While death has its obvious drawbacks, it is a blessing
that I now have an unassailably valid excuse to not
take the SATs. However, it seems that I've not entirely
dodged that dreaded bullet.

t the present I'm sitting in a small room, seated in a straight-backed chair next to a desk. Picture the archetypal all-white room, featuring no windows, which Jungian analysts say best represents death. A demon with cat's claws and folded leathery wings leans close to adjust a blood-pressure cuff which is wrapped around my upper arm, inflating the cuff until I can feel my pulse throbbing along the inside of my elbow. Sticky pads hold the wires of a heart-rate monitor to the skin of my chest, snaking between the buttons on my blouse. Adhesive tape holds another wire which monitors the pulse at my wrist. Other sensors are wired to the front and back of my neck.

"To monitor the tremors in your speech patterns," Leonard explained. One sensor sticks to the cricothyroid muscle on the front of your neck, he says. Another sensor, the cricoarytenoid muscle on the back of your neck, near your spine. As you speak, a low-voltage current runs between the two sensors, registering any microtremors in the muscles which control your voice box, indicating when you're telling an untruth.

The demon with the leathery wings and cat's claws, his breath smells putrid.

This comes after Babette escorted us into the headquarters building, sidestepping the endless lines of waiting people to usher our little party through a crumbled portion of the building's simultaneously unfinished yet decayed facade. Babette shepherded us into a cavernous waiting hall as large as any stadium, wherein countless souls stood around, constituting a sort of Department of Motor Vehicles mélange: people wearing soiled rags next to people wearing Chanel couture and carrying briefcases. All the plastic scoop-seated chairs were booby-trapped with wads of fresh chewing gum, so, really, only the people who've succeeded in abandoning all hope risk sitting down. An enormous reader board sign mounted at the front of the hall said, NOW SERVING NUMBER 5. The distant stone walls and ceiling looked to be brown. Everything earth-toned, sepia, the color of grime, the color of nose pickings. Almost everyone stood, their heads sagging at a slight angle, dispirited, like the heads of broken necks.

The stone floor teemed, almost carpeted by legions of fat cockroaches feasting on the ever-present popcorn balls and nonpareils. Hell is very much like Florida in that the resident bug life never dies. As a result of the steamy heat and immortality, the roaches achieve fat, meaty proportions more associated with mice or squirrels. Babette watched me hopping, one-legged, always holding the opposite leg aloft, storklike, to avoid treading on roaches, and she said, "We need to steal you some high heels."

Even Patterson, wearing his football shoulder pads and jersey, practically danced, skewering an ever-thickening layer of cockroaches smashed under his steel cleats. World-weary Archer also pranced, the chrome chains clanking around his boots, his feet skidding and skating on the crushed beetles. In contrast, even falling to pieces, Babette's fake high-heeled shoes allowed her to stilt-walk, impervious, above the roachy debris.

Outstriding the rest of us, elbowing aside the aeons of people already waiting, Babette arrived at a counter or long desk that ran the entire length of the far wall. There, a row of demons appeared to work as clerks, standing on the opposite side of the desk. Babette plopped her fake Coach bag on the countertop, addressing the demon who stood closest, saying, "Hey, Astraloth." She produced a Big Hunk candy bar from her bag and slid the candy across the counter, leaning into the demon's face, and said, "Give us an A137-B17. The short form. For an appeal and records search." Babette jerked her head in my direction, adding, "It's for the new kid, here."

It was clear Babette meant business.

The air in the waiting hall was so humid that every exhalation hung like a white cloud in front of my face, fogging my glasses. Cockroaches crunched beneath my every footstep.

No, it's not fair, but my mom and dad were always happy

to tell me the sordid details of every sex act or fetish that existed. Other girls might get a training bra at thirteen, but my mom offered to have me fitted for a training diaphragm. Beyond the birds and the bees—and tea-bagging, rimming, and scissoring—my parents never taught me a single thing about death. At most my dad pestered me to use moisturizer with sunblock and to floss my teeth. If they perceived death at all, it was only on the most superficial level, as the wrinkles and gray hairs of very old people fated soon to expire. Therefore they seemed heavily invested in the belief that if one could constantly maintain one's personal appearance and mitigate the signs of aging, then death would never be a pressing issue. To my parents, death existed as merely the logical, albeit extreme, result of not adequately exfoliating your skin. A slippery slope. If one simply failed to practice meticulous grooming, one's life would grind to an end.

And please, if you're still in denial, eating low-sodium, heart-healthy skinless chicken breasts and feeling all self-righteous as you jog on a treadmill, don't pretend you're any more realistic than my loopy parents.

And do NOT get the impression that I miss being alive. AS IF I really regret not getting to grow up and have blood gush out of my woo-woo every month and learn to drive a fossil-fueled internal-combustion vehicle and watch crappy R-rated movies without a parent or guardian, then drink beer out of a keg, frittering away four years to snag a softball degree in art history before some boy squirts me full of sperm and I have to lug some big baby around inside me for almost a whole year. Bummer—sarcasm fully intended—I am really missing out on the Good Times. And, no, this isn't just Sour Grapes. When I look at all the bullshit I'm skipping, sometimes I thank God I overdosed.

There, I said the G-word again. Ye gods! So kill me.

As it turns out, my damnation records have been lost. Or they have yet to arrive. Or my records were accidentally destroyed. Whatever the case, I'm forced to start from scratch, assigned to take a basic lie-detector test and submit for drug testing.

Babette, it seems, is not quite as useless as I'd first imagined. She's sidestepped no small amount of red tape and bureaucratic redundancy, leading our little team through the maze of corridors and offices, bribing low-level bureaucrats with Hershey bars and SweeTarts. Hell is aeons away from establishing a paperless culture, and most of the floor is layered knee-deep in misplaced records, disemboweled manila folders, the discarded polygraph readouts, Butter Rum Life Savers, and cockroaches.

En route to my testing, Archer told me not to cross my arms, not to look to the right or upward. Both of those: physical gestures that betray a liar.

After we submit the filled-out appeal form and slip the attendant demon a Kit Kat bar, Babette wishes me good luck. She gives me a little hug, no doubt leaving dirty handprints all over the back of my cardigan sweater. Babette, Leonard, Patterson, and Archer wait in an outer hallway while I go through a door into the all-white testing room. The polygraph machine. The demon inflating the blood-pressure cuff around my arm.

You might recall this same demon from the classic Hollywood masterpiece *The Exorcist*, where he possessed a little girl who was the spoiled, precocious child of a middle-aged movie star. Talk about déjà vu. Here he is now, watching my eyes for changes in pupil dilation which might betray dishonesty. The demon's wiring my skin to test whether I sweat. What Leonard calls "skin conductivity."

I say that I loved the scene where he made the little girl, Regan, crab-walk backward down the stairs with gore spilling out of her mouth. More out of nerves, I ask whether the demon has had any personal experience possessing people. Did he make any other movies? Does he get any residuals? Who's his agent?

Without looking away from his scrolling readout, those wavering little needles that squiggle lines on the rolling belt of white paper, the demon says, "Is your name Madison Spencer?"

The control questions. To establish a baseline of honest answers.

I say, "Yes."

Tweaking a knob on his machine, the demon asks, "Are you, in fact, thirteen years old?"

Again, yes.

The demon asks, "Do you reject Satan and all his works?"

Easy enough. I shrug and say, "Sure, why not?"

"Please," the demon says, "it's very important that you answer only either 'yes' or 'no.'"

I say, "Sorry."

The demon says, "Do you accept the Lord God as the one true God?"

Way-easy, no sweat, again, I say, "Yes."

The demon says, "Do you recognize Jesus Christ as your personal savior?"

I don't know, not for certain, but I say, "Yes?"

The needles squiggle on the readout paper, not much but a little. I can't feel for sure, but maybe the irises of my eyes suddenly contract. The dogma seems pretty familiar, but this isn't any sort of catechism my parents trained me to recite. The demon's own eyes never leaving the inky, wavering lines, he says, "Are you now or have you ever been a practicing member of the Buddhist religion?"

I say, "What?"

"Yes or no," the demon says.

"What?" I say, "Buddhists don't get to Heaven?"

While my parents fell far short of being perfect, none of their mistakes were intentionally malicious, so it feels downright traitorous to disavow every ideal they did their best to instill in me. Mine is the age-old conundrum of betraying one's parents versus betraying one's deity. Me, I just want to wear a halo and ride on a cloud. I just want to play a harp.

Without missing a beat, the demon says, "Do you believe the Bible to be the one and only true word of God?"

I say, "Does that include the way-crazy, loony parts of Leviticus?"

Plunging forward, the demon says, "In your honest opinion, does life begin at conception?"

Yes, I know I'm supposed to be dead, with no corporeal body and physical needs or physiology, but I start sweating like a pig. My face feels hot with blushing. My teeth sit on edge, softly grinding together. My fists clenching, tight, the bones and muscles take shape under the whitening skin of my knuckles.

I venture, "Yes?"

"Do you sanction mandatory prayer in public schools?" the demon asks.

Yes, I do want to go to Heaven—who doesn't?—but not if it means I have to be a total asshole.

Whether I answer yes or no, those little needles are going to wiggle like crazy, responding to either my dishonesty or my guilt.

The demon says, "Do you view sexual acts between individuals of the same gender to be an abomination?"

I ask if we can come back to that question later.

The demon says, "I'll take that as a 'no.'"

Throughout the history of theology, Leonard tried to explain, religions have argued over the nature of salvation, whether people are proved holy by their good works or by their deep, inner faith. Do people go to Heaven because they acted good? Or do they go to Heaven because it's predestined . . . because they *are good*? That's ancient history, according to Leonard; now the entire system relies on forensic science. Polygraph tests. Psychophysiological detections of deception. Voice stress analysis. You even have to submit hair and urine samples due to the new zero-tolerance policy for drug and alcohol abuse in Heaven.

In secret, putting my hands into the side pockets of my skort, I cross my fingers.

The demon asks, "Does mankind hold ultimate dominion over all earthly plants and animals?"

Fingers crossed, I say, "Yes?"

"Do you approve," the demon says, "of marriage between individuals of differing racial backgrounds?"

The demon continues without hesitation, asking, "Should the Zionist state of Israel be allowed to exist?"

Question after question, I'm stumped. Even fingers crossed. The paradox: Is God a racist, homophobic, anti-Semitic ass? Or is God testing to see if I am?

The demon asks, "Should women be allowed to hold public office? To own real property? To operate motor vehicles?"

Now and then, he leans over the polygraph machine, using a felt-tipped pen to scribble notes next to the read-outs on the rolling banner of paper.

We've journeyed here to the headquarters of Hell because I asked about filing an appeal. My reasoning is . . . if convicted murderers can linger on death row for decades, demanding access to law libraries and gratis public defenders, while scribbling briefs and arguments with blunt crayons and pencil stubs, it seems only fair that I ought to appeal my own eternal sentence.

In the same tone that a supermarket cashier would ask, "Paper or plastic?" or a fast-food server would ask, "Do you want fries with that?" the demon asks, "Are you, yourself, a virgin?"

Since last Christmas, when I froze my hands to the door of my residence hall and was forced to rip off the outermost layers of skin, my hands have yet to totally heal. The lines crisscrossing my palms, the lifeline and love line, are almost erased. My fingerprints look faint, and the new skin feels tight and sensitive. In my pockets, now, it hurts to keep my fingers crossed, but all I can do is just sit here, betraying my parents, betraying my gender and politics, betraying myself to tell some bored demon what I hope is the perfect mix of blah, blah, blah. If anybody should spend eternity in Hell, it's me.

The demon asks, "Do you support the profoundly evil research which utilizes embryonic stem cells?"

I correct his grammar, telling him, "*That* . . . research *that* utilizes . . ."

The demon asks, "Does physician-assisted suicide fly in the face of God's beautiful will?"

The demon asks, "Do you espouse the obvious truth of intelligent design?"

With the needles scribbling my every heartbeat, my respiration rate, my blood pressure, the demon waits, watching for my body to turn traitor on me when he asks, "Are you familiar with the William Morris Agency?"

Despite myself, my hands relax a little and let my fingers slip and stop lying. I say, "Why . . . yes."

And the demon looks up from his machine, smiles, and says, "That's who represents me. . . ."

XIII.

*Are you there, Satan? It's me, Madison. Don't get the
idea that I'm way homesick; but lately, but I've been
thinking about my family. This is no reflection on you
or the fabulousness of Hell. I've just been feeling a tad
nostalgic.*

or my last birthday, my parents announced
we were headed for Los Angeles in order
for my mom to present some awards-show
trophy. My mom had her personal assis-
tant buy no fewer than a thousand-million gilded envelopes
with blank pieces of card stock tucked inside. For the past
week, all my mom's done is practice tearing open these
envelopes, pulling out the cards, and saying, "The Academy
Award for Best Motion Picture goes to . . ." To train herself
not to laugh, my mom asked me to write movie titles on
the cards like *Smokey and the Bandit II* and *Saw IV* and *The
English Patient III.*

We're sitting in the back of a town car, being driven from
some airport to some hotel in Beverly Hills. I'm sitting in
the jump seat facing my mother so she can't see what I
write. After that, I hand the card to her assistant, who tucks
it into an envelope, affixes a gold-foil seal, and hands the
finished product to my mom to rip open.

We're not going to the Beverly Wilshire because that's
where I tried to flush the dead body of my kitten, poor
Tiger Stripe, and a plumber had to come and unclog half

the toilets in the hotel. We're also not going to the house in Brentwood, because this trip is only for, like, seventy-two hours, and my mom doesn't trust Goran and me not to mess up the whole place.

On one blank card, I'm writing *Porky's Revenge*. On another I write *Every Which Way but Loose*. As I write *Nightmare on Elm Street: Freddy's Dead*, I ask my mom where she put my pink blouse with the smocking on the front.

Tearing open an envelope, my mom says, "Did you check your closet in Palm Springs?"

My dad isn't here in the car. He stayed back to supervise work on our jet. Whether this is a joke, I won't even venture a guess, but my dad is redesigning our Learjet to feature an interior crafted of organic brick and hand-hewn pegged beams, with knotty pine floors. All of it sustainably grown by the Amish. Yeah—installed in a jet. To cover the floors, he hoisted all my mom's last-season Versace and Dolce on some Tibetan rag-rug braiders and he's called this "recycling." We'll have a jet outfitted with faux wood-burning fireplaces and antler chandeliers. Macramé plant hangers. Of course, all the brick and wood is just veneer; but trying to take off, the plane will still consume somewhere around the entire daily output of dinosaur juice pumped by Kuwait.

Welcome to the start of another glorious media cycle. All this muss and fuss is to justify their getting the cover of *Architectural Digest*.

Sitting opposite me, my mom tears open an envelope, saying, "This year's Academy Award for Best Picture goes to . . ." She plucks the card out of the envelope and starts to laugh, saying, "Maddy, shame on you!" My mom shows the card to Emily or Amanda or Ellie or Daphne or WHOEVER her PA is this week. The card reads, *The Piano II: Attack of the Finger*. Emily or Audrey or whoever, she doesn't get the joke.

The good news is the Prius is way too dinky for Goran and me to accompany my folks to the awards ceremony. So while my mom's onstage trying not to get a paper cut or crack up laughing from having to give an Oscar to somebody she hates, Goran is supposed to babysit me at the hotel. Be still, my wildly beating heart. Technically, because Goran doesn't speak enough English to order pay-per-view cable porn, I'll be babysitting him, but we're required to watch the awards on television so we can tell mom whether she ought to bother doing them again next season.

That's how come I need my pink blouse—to look hot for Goran. Booting my mom's notebook computer, I press the Control, Alt, and S keys, using the security cams to scan my bedroom closet in Palm Springs. I toggle to the cameras in Berlin and check my bedroom there.

"Check in Geneva," says my mom. "Tell the Somali maid to FedEx it to you."

I hit Ctrl+Alt+G. I hit Ctrl+Alt+B. Checking Geneva. Checking Berlin. Athens. Singapore.

To be honest, Goran is the most likely reason he and I aren't going to this year's Oscars. It's too big a gamble that, when the cameras zoom in on us in our seats, the Spencer children, Goran would be yawning or picking his nose or snoring, slumped in his red velvet theater seat, asleep, with drool trailing out one corner of his sensuously full lips. This is all water under the bridge, but whatever flunky does the screening to identify potential adoptees, he or she definitely lost his or her job for putting Goran's name forward. My parents fund a charity foundation which primarily employs approximately a billion publicists who issue press releases touting my dad's generosity. Yes, they might donate a thousand dollars to build a cinder-block school in Pakistan, but then they'll pay a half million to film a documentary about the school, hold press conferences and media junkets, and make certain the entire world knows what they've accomplished. From his very first photo op Goran was a letdown. He wouldn't weep tears of happiness for the cameras, nor would he refer to his new guardians as anything more endearing than "the Mister and Missus Spencer."

We're all familiar with those television commercials where a cat or dog dives nose-first into its bowl of dried kibble to demonstrate how delicious, but really because the poor animal has been starved beforehand. Well, the same principle should prompt Goran to beam proudly in his new Ralph Lauren togs, or Calvin Klein or whomever my parents are shilling for. Goran is expected to scarf down whatever cage-free, bean-curd delicacy while gulping from a bottle of whatever sponsoring sports beverage, holding the bottle so the label is prominently displayed. It's a lot of work for one battle-scarred orphan, but I've seen kids my folks adopted, as young as four years, from Nepal and Haiti and Bangladesh, simultaneously model my parents' largesse and babyGap and heat-and-serve figs stuffed with pain-free haggis and cumin-infused aioli—plus continually mention whatever film project my mom had going into theatrical release.

I had this one sister for about five minutes—my folks had rescued her from a brothel in Calcutta—but the moment she sensed a camera in the room, she could hug her new Nike shoes and Barbie dolls, weeping such realistic, photogenic tears of joy that she made Julia Roberts look like a slacker.

In contrast, Goran would sip the requisite corn syrup–flavored, vitamin-enhanced energy drink and grimace as if in pain. Goran just flat-out refuses to play this game. All Goran does is scowl at me, but that's all he does to anyone. When his hateful, brooding gaze bores into me, I swear, I feel exactly like Jane Eyre being stared at by Mr. Rochester. I'm Rebecca de Winter under the cold scrutiny of her new husband, Maxim. After a lifetime of being coddled and courted, by servants, by underlings and media sycophants, I find Goran's hateful distain to be utterly irresistible.

The other reason we're not going to the Academy Awards is because I'm a great, huge, roly-poly pig. My mom would never fess up to that, except maybe to *Vanity Fair*.

Even as our driver bears my mom and me hotel-ward, Goran remains on the tarmac, where my dad will try his best to explain the surreal wit inherent in decorating the interior of a space-age, multimillion-dollar aircraft to resemble the wattle yurt of a Stone Age caveman family. My dad will drone about the multivalent way in which our ersatz mud hut will resonate as smart and ironic with the well-educated literati, yet read as sincere and environmentally forward with the erstwhile younger fan base of my mother's films.

And, yes, I might be dreamy and preadolescent, but I know the meaning of *multivalent*. Kind of. I think. Pretty much.

On the notebook computer, I key Ctrl+Alt+J to spy on the interior of our jet. There, my dad is trying to tell Goran all about Marshall McLuhan while Goran simply glares at the security camera, scowling out of the computer screen directly at me.

Strictly by accident, mind you, one time—I swear, I'm no Miss Wanton McSlutski—but I toggled Ctrl+Alt+T and caught a gander of Goran taking a shower, naked. Not that I was peeking on purpose, but I did see that he already had some hair . . . *down there*. To understand my panting pursuit of Goran, he of the plush lips and frigid glare, you need to know my first baby picture appeared on the cover of *People* magazine. Personally, I've never served as a satisfactory mirror for my parents' success because luxuries were a given. From my birth, the world was already rendered deferential. At best I served as a souvenir—like drugs or grunge music—of my parents' long-gone younger selves. The adopted children were supposed to affirm my mom and dad's hard work and resulting rewards. You pluck some famished skeleton out of an Ethiopian dirt hole, hustle him aboard a Gulfstream, and serve him a selection of free-range Havarti baked in gluten-free, whole-grain tart shells, and it's way more likely that kid will bother to say thank-you. Here's some kid who had a life expectancy of around zero—the drooling vultures already circling overhead—and, no duh, he's going to get all excited about a dumb weekend house party with Babs Streisand in East Hampton.

But what do I know; I'm dead. I'm a dead brat. If I were way brilliant I'd be alive, like you. Nevertheless, if you ask me, most people have children just as their own enthusiasm about life begins to wane. A child allows us to revisit the excitement we once felt about, well . . . everything. A generation later, our grandkids bump up our enthusiasm yet again. Reproducing is a kind of booster shot to keep us loving life. For my parents, first having blasé me, then adopting a string of brats, ending with bored, hostile Goran, it truly illustrates the Law of Diminishing Margin of Returns.

My dad would tell you, "Every audience gets the performance it expects." Meaning: If I'd been a more appreciative child, maybe they'd have seemed like better parents. On a larger scale, maybe if I'd shown more gratitude and appreciation for the precious miracle of my life, then maybe life itself would've seemed more wonderful.

Maybe that's why poor people give thanks BEFORE they eat their nasty tuna casserole dinner.

If the living are haunted by the dead, then the dead are haunted by their own mistakes. Maybe if I hadn't been so flip and glib, maybe my parents wouldn't have looked to get their emotional needs met by corralling together so many other destitute kids.

As the chauffeur arrives at the hotel, and the doorman steps forward to open the car door, I hit Ctrl+Alt+B to search my bedroom closet in Barcelona, and there's my missing pink blouse. In an instant message to the Somali maid, I tell her where to overnight the blouse in time for my tryst with Goran. I almost tell her, "Thanks," except I don't know the exact word in her language.

And yes, I know the word *tryst*. I know an awful lot of things, especially for a thirteen-year-old, dead fat girl. But maybe I don't know as much as I think.

At that, my mom rips open another envelope and says, "And the winner is . . ."

XIV.

Are you there, Satan? It's me, Madison. I know what you're thinking . . . to you I'm just some spoiled, rich brat who's never had to work a day in her life. In my defense, I'm proud to say that I've obtained full-time employment. A genuine job. As of now I'm a regular working stiff—if you'll pardon the terrible pun. What follows might seem ragged, but please consider it an impressionistic slice o' death. A glimpse into a day in the death of me.

s far as I can tell, you have a choice between two types of careers in Hell. Your first option is to work for one of those Web sites which everyone assumes are run in Russia or Burma, where naked men and women stare unflinchingly into the webcams, a dazed look in their glassy eyes, while they lick their fingers and insert greasy plastic model airplanes or plantain bananas halfway into their shaved woo-woos or hoo-hoos. Either that, or they fake-smile while sipping their own urine out of champagne flutes. You see, Hell is responsible for about 85 percent of the Internet's total smut content. The demons just tack up some old, soiled bedsheet to serve as a backdrop, they throw a foam-rubber mattress on the ground, and you're expected to flop around, putting junk inside yourself and responding to the real-time webchat of alive perverts, worldwide.

Frankly, I've never been that desperate for attention. Do not mistake me for one of those troubled preteens who walk around practically wearing a T-shirt which says: ASK ME ABOUT MY RAPE. Or, ASK ME ABOUT MY ALCOHOLISM.

The dirty little secret about Hell is that the demons are always running tabs on you. If you breathe their air, if you loiter, the powers that be are constantly dinging you for the cost. No, it's not fair, but the demons charge you for your upkeep. The meter is always running, and you're piling up years of additional torture, according to Babette, who it turns out used to manage people's paperwork until she had to take a stress-related disability leave of absence and return to her cage for a little nonclerical R & R. Babette says most people are condemned for only a few aeons, but they accrue additional time simply by occupying space in Hell. It's like being over the limit on your charge cards, or accidentally flying your jet into French airspace; the clock starts ticking the moment you've gone too far. The bean counters are keeping track, and someday you'll be socked with a massive bill.

Jewels and cash are worthless here. The currency is candy, and marshmallow peanuts are accepted as payment for all bribes and debts. Root Beer Barrels are as valuable as rubies. The hellish equivalent of pennies are popcorn balls . . . black licorice . . . wax lips . . . and these are cast aside in disdain.

Probably I shouldn't even tell you this—the job market is tight enough as it is—but if you have any aspirations to earn your daily Junior Mints, you need to find a career and get working.

Not that you'll ever actually die—not *you*—not after all

the antioxidants you've choked down and all those laps around the reservoir. Ha!

But just in case you don't want to spend eternity giving yourself high colonics on some sleazy Web site, ogled by millions of men with serious intimacy problems, the other type of work which most people do in Hell is—telemarketing. Yes, this means sitting at a desk, elbow-to-elbow with fellow doomed telemarketing associates who stretch to the horizon in either direction, all of you yakking on headsets.

My job is: The dark forces are constantly calculating when it's dinnertime anywhere on earth, and a computer autodials those phone numbers so I can interrupt everyone's meal. My goal isn't actually to sell you anything; I just ask if you have a few seconds to take part in a market research study identifying consumer trends in chewing gum. In mouthwash. In dryer fabric-softener sheets. I get to wear my headset telephone and work from a flowchart of possible responses. Best of all, I get to talk to real-live people—like yourself—who are still living and breathing and have no idea that I'm dead and phoning them from the Afterlife. Trust me, the vast majority of telemarketing people who ring you up, they're dead. As are pretty much all Internet porn models.

Okay, it's not as if I'm practicing brain surgery or tax law, but it beats sticking crayons inside my hoo-hoo on a Web site called "Crazy Nympho Girly Plesures Self Using School Supply [sic]."

The autodialer connects me to somebody alive, and I say, "I'm conducting a market study to better serve the chewing gum consumers in your area. . . . Do you have a moment to answer a few questions?" If the alive person hangs up, the computer connects me to a new phone number. If the living person answers my questions, the flowchart instructs me to ask more. Each person seated at the phone bank has a laminated sheet of questions, more questions than you could count. The point is to impose on the respondent, always entreating to ask just *one more question, please* . . . until the would-be diner loses their composure, and their mood and evening meal are both ruined.

Once you're dead and in Hell your options are either to do something trivial, but in a very self-important manner, for instance, market research about paper-clip usage. Or you can do something serious in a very trivial manner, for instance, looking bored and disengaged while taking a poop into a crystal dish and eating it with a silver spoon—the poop, I mean, not the dish.

If you asked my dad about selecting any kind of professional career, he'd tell you, "Don't make a date with a heart attack." Meaning: You've got to pace yourself and not forget to slow down. No job is forever. So relax and have some fun.

With that goal in mind, I let my attention wander. While hungry alive people wheedle to end our conversation, begging that their pot roast is growing cold, I'm actually thinking, musing whether my mother would've acted differently had she known I had fewer than forty-eight hours to live. In hindsight, I wonder, if she'd known about my impending demise, would she still have cheaped out and planned to give me her swag bag of Academy Award luxury crap in lieu of a real birthday present? If she'd known the clock was ticking, I mean, and most of the sand had already run out from my hourglass.

Asking hungry people about their dental floss preferences, I remember how, when I was really young, I thought
the United States would just keep adding states, sewing
more and more stars to our flag until we owned the entire
world. I mean, why stop at fifty? Why stop with Hawaii? It
seemed natural that Japan and Africa would eventually be
absorbed into the starry part of our national flag. In the
past we'd pushed aside the pesky Navajos and Iroquois to
create Californians and Texans. We could do the same with
Israel and Belgium and finally achieve world peace. When
you're a little kid, you really do think that getting bigger—
growing tall, sprouting big muscles and breasts—will be
the answer to all of your problems. That's how my mom
still is: always acquiring new houses in other cities. Ditto
for my dad: always trying to collect appreciative kids from
awful places like Darfur and Baton Rouge.

The problem is, troubled kids never stay saved. The
Rwandan brother I had for about two hours, he ran off
with my debit card. My Bhutanese little sister of about a
day, she kept downing the Xanax my mom was happy to
offer . . . and spiraled into drug abuse. Nothing stays safe.
Even our homes in Hamburg and London and Manila sit
empty, tempting burglars and hurricanes and collecting
dust.

And Goran, well, the way that adoption ultimately
turned out, it's difficult to call his rescue a Big Success.

Yes, I can recognize my parents' faulty logic, but if I'm so
talented-and-gifted, why is it that the only authors I've ever
read are Emily Brontë and Daphne du Maurier and Judy
Blume? Why have I read *Forever Amber*, like, two hundred
times? Seriously, if I were truly-*truly* brilliant, I'd be alive

and skinny, and the structure of this story would be one epically long homage to Marcel Proust.

Instead, on my telephone headset, I'm asking some stupid alive person what colors of cotton swab would best complement her primary bathroom decorating scheme. On a scale of one to ten, I'm asking how she would rate the following flavors of lip gloss: warm honey . . . saffron breeze . . . ocean mint . . . lemon glow . . . blue sapphire . . . creamy rose . . . tangy ember . . . and douche-berry.

In regard to my polygraph test, Babette says not to hold my breath. Collating the results can take forever. Until we hear something back, she says I should just hang tight and do my telephone job. A few chairs away from me, Leonard asks someone about toilet paper. Beside him, Patterson sits in his football uniform, asking someone their opinion concerning mosquito repellent. Near them, Archer holds his headset to the side of his face, so it doesn't smash his blue Mohawk, while he seeks public opinions about a candidate for political office.

According to Babette, 98.3 percent of lawyers end up in Hell. That's in contrast to the 23 percent of farmers who are eternally damned. Some 45 percent of retail business owners are Hellbound, and 85 percent of computer software writers. Perhaps a trace number of politicians ascend to Heaven, but statistically speaking, 100 percent of them are cast into the fiery pit. As are essentially 100 percent of journalists and redheads. For whatever reason, people standing shorter than five-foot-one are more likely to be condemned. Also, people with a body mass index greater than 0.0012. Babette begins spouting these stats and you'd swear she was autistic. Just because she once worked processing paperwork for incoming souls, she can tell you that blondes outnumber brunettes three to one in Hell. People with at least two years of continuing education beyond high school are almost six times more likely to be damned. As are people earning more than a seven-figure annual income.

Bearing all of this in mind, I figure my parents have roughly a 165 percent likelihood of joining me forever.

And no, I have no idea how "douche-berry" is supposed to taste.

Over my own headset, some old-lady voice crackles, droning on and on about the flavor of something called "Beech-Nut" chewing gum, and over the telephone I swear I can smell the pee stink of her nine hundred cats. Her old-lady breathing sounds wet and full of static, popping and rasping from her old throat, the lisping effect of ill-fitted dentures, the shouted volume of age-related hearing loss, and she allows me to go deeper into the flowchart than anyone I've ever called. Already we're at the twelfth level, topic four, question seventeen: flavored toothpicks, for God's sake.

I'm asking, Would she consider purchasing toothpicks artificially treated to taste like chocolate? Like beef? Like apples? Then I realize how desperately lonely and isolated this old lady must feel. Probably I'm the only human contact she's enjoyed all day, and her meat loaf or rice pudding sits rotting on the plate in front of her because she's more starved for communication with another person.

Even as a telemarketer, it's best not to enjoy yourself too

much. If you don't look miserable, the demons will reseat you next to someone who whistles. Then next to someone who farts.

From the survey questions I've already asked, I know the old lady is eighty-seven years old. She lives alone in a freestanding home. She has three grown children who live more than five hundred miles distant from her. She watches seven hours of television each day; and in the past month, she's read fourteen romance novels.

Just so you know, before you decide to do telemarketing over doing Internet porn, the sleazy Pervy Vanderpervs who text you with one hand while they abuse themselves with their other—at least they're not going to break your heart. Not like the pathologically lonely oldsters and cripples you quiz about nonstreak glass cleaner.

Listening to this sad old lady, I want so much to reassure her that death isn't so bad. Even if the Bible is correct, and it's easier to push caramels through the eye of a needle than get to Heaven, well, Hell doesn't totally suck. Sure, you're menaced by demons and the landscape is rather appalling, but she'll meet new people. I can tell from her 410 area code that she lives in Baltimore, so even if she dies and goes straight to Hell and gets immediately dismembered and gobbled by Pszpolnica or Yum Cimil, it won't be a huge culture shock. She might not even notice the difference. Not at first.

Too, I yearn to tell her that—if she loves reading books—she's going to adore being dead. Reading most books feels exactly like you're a dead body. It's all so . . . finished. True, Jane Eyre is an eternal, ageless character, but no matter how many times you read that darned book, she always gets married to gross, burn-victim Mr. Rochester. She never enrolls at the Sorbonne to earn her master's degree in French ceramics, nor does she open a swanky bistro in New York's Greenwich Village. Reread that Brontë book all you want, but Jane Eyre's never going to get gender-reassignment surgery or train to become a kick-ass ninja assassin. And it's pathetic that she believes she's real. Jane's just ink stamped on a page, but she really, truly thinks she's a living-alive person. She's convinced she has free will.

Listening to this eighty-seven-year-old voice weep about her aches and pains, I yearn to encourage her to just give up and die. Kick the bucket. Forget toothpicks. Forget chewing gum. It won't hurt, I swear. In fact, death will make her feel way better. Look at me, I want to say, I'm only thirteen, and being deceased constitutes about the best thing that's ever happened to me.

As a word to the wise, I'd advise her just to make sure she's wearing some durable, low-heeled, dark-colored shoes before she croaks.

A voice says, "Here." And standing at my elbow is Babette with her fake Coach bag and straight skirt and breasts. In one hand, Babette holds a strappy pair of high heels. She says, "I got these from Diana Vreeland. I hope they fit. . . ." And she drops them into my lap.

On the phone, the old lady in Baltimore continues to sob.

The high heels are silver-colored patent leather, with ankle straps and rhinestone buckles across the toe, stilettos so tall I'll never have to wade through cockroaches. These are shoes like I've never worn before because they'd make me look too old, and thereby make my mom REALLY look too old. Ridiculous shoes. These silly shoes are uncomfortable and impractical and too formal, and way too grown-up.

With the old lady still yammering through my headset, I kick off my Bass Weejuns and slip my feet into the strappy high heels.

And yes, I'm well aware of all the valid reasons why I should politely but firmly refuse these shoes. . . . But instead, I LOVE THEM. And they fit.

XV.

Are you there, Satan? It's me, Madison. I hope this won't sound too confusing, but I do hereby and forever abandon abandoning all hope. Honestly, I give up on giving up. I'm just not cut out to be some hopeless, disillusioned wretch with no aspirations for the rest of eternity, sprawled catatonic in my own feces on a cold stone floor. In all probability the Human Genome Project will, someday, find that I carry some recessive gene for optimism, because despite all my best efforts I still can't scrape together even a couple days of hopelessness. Future scientists will call it the Pollyanna Syndrome, and if forced to guess, I'd say that mine has been a way-long case history of chasing rainbows.

ow come I click so well with Goran is that he's never been allowed to be a child, and I'm strictly forbidden to grow any older.

The day before my mom was supposed to appear at the Oscars, she took me to a day spa on Wilshire for a little industrial-strength pampering, mother-daughter style. While she and I got our hair highlighted, belted in identical fluffy white terry-cloth bathrobes, our faces caked with masks of Sonoran mud, my mom explained how Goran grew up as a refugee in one of those Iron Curtain orphanages where the babies all lie ignored and untouched in cavernous wards until they're old enough to vote for the current regime. Or to be conscripted.

There in the day spa, even as Laotian masseuses knelt to buff the dead skin from our feet, my mom told me that infants require a minimum amount of physical touch in order to develop any sense of empathy and connection with other human beings. Without such handling, a baby would grow up to be a sociopath, lacking any conscience or ability to love. More as a political gesture—not merely for publicity's sake—we're having all of our acrylic finger- and toenail overlays replaced. One of my mom's deepest political convictions is that, if people want so desperately to come to the United States, wading across the Rio Grande at great risk to their life and limb simply for the opportunity to pick our lettuce and iron our hair, well, we should allow them. Entire nations would enjoy nothing more than the opportunity to scrub our kitchen floors, she says, and to prevent them from doing so would be a violation of their most basic human rights.

My mom is adamant on the subject. At the moment, we're surrounded by various political and economic refugees as they crowd forward to scrape and wax and pluck at our imperfections.

After all the herbal high colonics I've endured, not to mention the electrolysis, the tortures of Hell hold little terror. It never fails to impress me how so many of the huddled masses and wretched refuse can flee the political oppression and torture of a foreign government, then arrive in America ready and eager to inflict largely the same tortures on the ruling classes here.

As my mom sees it, her dry, flaky skin is some immigrant's vocational opportunity. Plus, hurting her offers immigrants a nifty cathartic therapy for venting their rage.

Her chapped lips and split ends constitute someone's rungs up the socioeconomic ladder to escape poverty. Sliding into middle age complete with cellulite and scaly elbows, my mother has become an economic engine, generating millions of dollars which will be wired to feed families and purchase cholera medicine in Ecuador. Should she ever decide to "let herself go," no doubt tens of thousands would perish.

And no, I haven't overlooked the steadfast way in which my parents blame Goran's failure to adore them on everyone except themselves. To them, if Goran doesn't love them, that clearly indicates that Goran is damaged and incapable of loving anyone.

In the spa, the stylists and artists hover around us, those minions as dense as the worst Harpies of Hell, circling and offering the information—always credited to a way-inside source—that while Dakota makes a lovely girl, she was in fact born with superfluous male genitalia. My mom's personal assistant, Cherry or Nadine or Ulrike or whoever, she brays that Cameron is so dense that she bought the morning-after abortion pill and, instead of swallowing, stuck one up inside her woo-woo.

According to my mom, national boundaries must be adequately porous, and incomes must be redistributed to allow all people, regardless of race and religion and circumstances of birth, to be able to purchase her films. Her noble egalitarian philosophy holds that all human beings should be allowed to buy tickets to her movies AND to vacuum her pores. She insists neither Africa nor the Indian subcontinent will ever achieve technological and cultural parity with the Western world until their density of DVD players makes them a major consumer of her body of filmic work. And by that, she means her REAL work, marketed in its actual studio-designed packaging, not merely some crappy pirated, black-market unit which pays royalties to nobody except drug lords and child sex slavers.

Lecturing the assembled publicists and stylists, my mom says that if any aboriginal peoples or primitive tribe still does not celebrate her acting, that's only because those subjugated native cultures find themselves oppressed by an evil, fundamentalist form of religion. Their budding appreciation of her films is obviously being quashed by some devilish imam or patriarchal ayatollah or witch doctor.

Rallying the pedicurists and aestheticians around the white terry-cloth hem of her robe, my mother speechifies that they're not just grooming an actor in order to pimp a motion picture. In actuality, the team of us, my mom and her stylists and masseuses and manicurists, we're engaged in raising awareness around bold, cinematic narratives which model the possibility of truly equal standards of blah, blah, blah. . . . Instead of spending their lives as pregnant, dirt-eating, genitally mutilated victims of some crushing theocracy . . . now, third-world ladies can aspire to become cosmo-swilling, Jimmy Choo–wearing sexual predators. By our deft use of acrylic fingernails and bleached-blond hair extensions—here she flutters her outflung arms in an all-inclusive gesture—we're empowering the downtrodden, exploited peoples of the world.

Yes, my mom lacks even the remotest sense of irony, but she's certain that in a perfect world, any miserable little boy or girl should be able to grow up and become nothing less than . . . her. Best left unsaid was the fact that she and my dad were already brandishing glossy, gate-folded brochures for all-boys boarding schools in Nova Scotia. Military schools in Iceland. It was clear: Goran wasn't a success, and some impending dawn I'd find him packed up and gone, replaced by a four-year-old Bhutanese leper.

If I wanted to practice my feminine wiles on Goran, my time was running out.

As my mother would say, "You've got to strike while the flatiron is hot." Meaning: I needed to get pretty and make my move soon. Ideally, tomorrow night. Ideally, while my folks were onstage, doling out the Oscars.

The final straw that broke the camel's back was, this week, when Goran sold five of my mom's Emmys over the Internet for ten dollars apiece. Before that, apparently, he'd collected a bunch of her Palme d'Or awards from our house in Cannes and sold them all for five bucks a pop. After a decade of my parents insisting that movie-industry awards meant nothing, and amounted to little more than a crass gold-plated embarrassment, my mom and dad went ape shit.

The way my mom saw it, Goran's every transgression, his every misanthropic misbehavior was simply a result of his not receiving adequate love and cuddling.

"You must promise me, Maddy," my mom said, "that you'll show your poor brother an extra-special amount of patience and affection."

His deprived infancy is how come, when my parents rented out a Six Flags amusement park for his birthday, and trotted out a purebred Shetland pony as his gift, Goran assumed the animal was lunch. For Halloween, they'd dressed him up as Jean-Paul Sartre, with me as Simone de

Beauvoir, trick-or-treating up and down the hallways of the Ritz in Paris with copies of *La Nausée* and *The Second Sex*, and Goran didn't get the joke. More recently, Goran had hacked into my mother's bathroom security camera and sold Web subscriptions.

Of course, my dad wanted to introduce the concept of discipline and consequences into Goran's life, but a boy who's no doubt been tortured with electroshocks and waterboarding and intravenous injections of liquid drain cleaner, he's not going to be easily cowed by the threat of a spanking and a one-hour time-out.

By now my pink blouse had arrived from Barcelona. I planned to wear it with a skort and my cardigan sweater embroidered with the crest which represented my boarding school in Switzerland. That, and basic low-heeled Bass Weejun penny loafers. Soon enough Goran and I would settle ourselves in front of the television in our hotel suite. Alone, just him and me, we'd watch my parents arrive at the red carpet in the Prius arranged by the publicist. Frigid, reclusive Goran would be mine alone as we watched my mom and dad preen for the paparazzi. Once they were safely away, I planned to phone room service and request dinner *pour deux*, lobster and oysters and onion rings. For dessert, I'd procured five ounces of my parents' genetically enhanced Mexican sinsemilla. No, it's not especially logical: My parents constantly railed in opposition to irradiated, genetically spliced and engineered corn, but where marijuana was concerned plant scientists could never monkey with it too much. No matter how hybrid a Frankenstein skunkweed, they would pack the sticky resinous mess into a pipe and torch it.

In case you have yet to notice, my parents do nothing in moderation. On one hand, they mourn the fact that Goran spent his babyhood alone and untouched. While on the other hand they never cease touching me, hugging and kissing me, especially when the paparazzi are around. My mother limits my wardrobe to pink and yellow. My shoes are either cute Capezio ballet flats or Mary Janes. The only makeup I own is forty different shades of pink lipstick. You see, neither of my parents wants me to appear any older than seven or eight. Officially, I've been in the second grade for years.

When my baby teeth began to fall out, they went so far as to suggest I wear a set of the painful primary-teeth dentures that Twentieth Century Fox forced into little Shirley Temple's adolescent mouth. In times like these, being kneaded, probed, and polished by a team of beauty experts, I wished I had also been raised, untouched, in an Iron Curtain orphanage.

This year, the Academy Awards fell smack-dab on my thirteenth birthday. With stylists swarming around her, dressing and undressing her like a giant doll, makeup artists experimenting to decide which eye shadow worked best with what designer gown, hairdressers curling and straightening her hair, my mother suggests I get a small tattoo to mark the occasion. A little Hello Kitty or Holly Hobbie, she says, or a piercing in my navel.

My dad has a penchant for buying me stuffed animals. And, yes, I know the word *penchant*, although I'm still not certain what constitutes French-kissing.

God only knew what a cute Holly Hobbie or Hello Kitty tramp stamp would stretch and fade to become over the next sixty years. In the same way my parents imagined all the little boys and girls of the third world wanted to become them . . . my folks thought my childhood should be the childhood they'd wanted to have, resplendent with meaningless sex, recreational drugs, and rock music. Tattoos and body jewelry. All their peers feel pretty much the same, and it leads to children whom the public believes to be nine years old becoming pregnant. Thus the paradox of teaching nursery rhymes along with contraception skills. Birthday presents such as Hello Kitty diaphragms and Holly Hobbie spermicidal foam and Peter Rabbit crotchless panties.

Please don't imagine it's fun being me. My mom tells the stylist, "Maddy's not ready for bangs." She tells the wardrobe person, "Maddy's a little sensitive about her big bottom."

Don't imagine I even get to speak. On top of that, my mom complains that I never talk. My father would tell you that life is a game, and you need to roll up your sleeves and build something: Write a book. Dance a dance. To both my parents, the world is a battle for attention, a war to be heard. Perhaps that's what I admire about Goran: his distinct lack of hustle. Goran's the only person I know who's not negotiating a six-picture deal with Paramount. He's not staging a show of his paintings at the Musée d'Orsay. Nor is he having his teeth chemically bleached. Goran simply is. He's not secretly lobbying for the stupid Academy of stupid Motion Picture Arts and Sciences to give him a shiny statue while a zillion people stand and applaud. He's not campaigning to build his market share. Wherever Goran is at this moment—sitting or standing, laughing or crying—he's doing it with the clarity of an infant who knows that no one will ever come to his rescue.

While technicians blast her upper lip with lasers, my mom says, "Isn't this fun, Maddy? Just us two, together . . ." Whenever fewer than fourteen people are clutching at us, my mother considers that to be private mother-daughter "alone time."

No, whether he's alone or observed by millions, whether he's loved or loathed, Goran would be the same person. Maybe that's what I love most about him—that he's so much NOT like my parents. Or like anyone I know.

Goran absolutely, positively does NOT need love.

A manicurist with a Gypsy accent, something leftover from some country where brokers analyze the stock market by reading pigeon entrails, this woman buffs my nails, holding my hand cradled in her own. After a moment, she turns my hand palm up and looks at the new, red skin where I'd left my frozen skin stuck to the door handle in Switzerland. She doesn't say anything, this bug-eyed Gypsy manicurist, but she's clearly marveling at how my wrinkles have been erased. How both my lifeline and love line have not merely stopped—but vanished. Still cupping my red hand in her own coarse, rough fingers, the manicurist looks from my palm to my face, and with the fingers of her other hand, she touches her forehead, her chest, her shoulders, making a fast sign of the cross.

XVI.

Are you there, Satan? It's me, Madison. Over the phone today, I made a new friend. She's not dead, not yet, but I can tell we're going to be way-total best friends.

ccording to my wristwatch I've been dead for three months, two weeks, five days, and seventeen hours. Subtract that from infinity and you get some idea why loads of doomed souls abandon all their hope. Not to boast, but I've managed to stay reasonably presentable despite the overall grimy local conditions. Lately I've taken to scrubbing my telephone headset and giving my chair a good dusting before I make any calls. At the moment I'm talking with an elderly shut-in who lives, alone, in the Memphis, Tennessee, area code. The unfortunate lady is trapped at home for days at a time, debating whether to suffer through yet another round of chemotherapy despite the lessening quality of her life.

The poor infirm woman has answered nearly every question I've thrown at her about chewing gum preferences, about paper-clip buying habits, about her consumption of cotton swabs. I've long ago come out to her about being thirteen years old and dead and relegated to Hell. For my part, I'm pitching her that death is a breeze, and if she has any question about whether she'd go to Heaven or Hell, this lady needs to run out immediately and commit some heinous crime. Hell, I tell her, is the happening place.

"Jackie Kennedy Onassis is here," I tell her over the phone. "You *know* you want to meet her. . . ."

Really, all the Kennedys are hereabouts, but that larger fact might not be such a great selling tool.

Still, despite the pain from her cancer and the sickening side effects of her treatments, the Memphis lady has her reservations about abandoning her life.

I warn her that in no way do people simply arrive in Hell and achieve some instantaneous type of enlightenment. Nobody finds themselves locked within a grimy cell, then slaps a palm to their forehead and says, "No duh! I've been a total *asshole!*"

No one's histrionics are magically resolved. If anything, people's character flaws spin out of control. In Hell, bullies remain bullies. Angry people are still angry. People in Hell pretty much keep doing the negative behavior which earned them a one-way ticket.

And, I warn the cancer lady, don't expect any guidance or mentoring from the demons. Not unless you're palming them a constant supply of Chick-O-Sticks and Heath bars. The demonic bureaucracy, they might pretend to shuffle some papers in an officious manner, then promise to review your file, but their attitude is: Well, you're in Hell, so you must've done *something*. In that way, Hell is awfully passive-aggressive. As is earth. As is my mother.

If you believe Leonard, this is how Hell breaks people down—by permitting them to act out to greater and greater extremes, becoming vicious caricatures of themselves, earning fewer and fewer rewards, until they finally realize their folly. Perhaps, I muse over the telephone, that is the one effective lesson which one learns in Hell.

Depending on her mood, Judy Garland can still be more frightening than any demon or devil you might run across.

Sorry. I have not actually seen Judy Garland. Or Jackie O. Forgive me my small lie. After all, I am in Hell.

In a worst-case scenario, I tell the woman, if the Big C does kill her and she ends up in the Pit, she needs to look me up. I'm Maddy Spencer, phone bank number 3,717,021, position twelve. I'm four-foot-nine, wear eyeglasses, and sport the way-coolest new, silver, ankle-strap high heels anyone has ever seen.

The phone bank where I work is located at Hell headquarters, I instruct the dying woman. You just go past the Great Ocean of Wasted Sperm. Hang a left at the gushing River of Steaming-hot Vomit.

Out of the corner of my eye, I see Babette headed my way. In closing, I wish the cancer lady good luck with her chemo, and warn her not to smoke too much spliff for the nausea, since reefer is no doubt what got me express-mailed to my personal forever in the fiery pit. Before ending the call I say, "Now remember, ask for Madison Spencer. Everybody knows me and vice versa. I'll show you the ropes."

Just as Babette steps up beside me, I say, "Bye," and end the phone call.

Already the autodialer has another telephone ringing within my headset. On the filthy little screen reads a number with a Sioux Falls area code, where the window of dinnertime must just now be opening. In this fashion, we begin our shift by annoying people in Great Britain, then the Eastern United States, then the Midwest, the West Coast, etc.

Standing beside me, Babette says, "Hey."

Covering the mouthpiece of my headset, cupping one hand over it, I say, "Hey," in return. I mouth the words, *Thanks for the shoes. . . .*

Babette winks, saying, "No biggie." She folds her arms across her chest, leans back a smidgen, peering at me, and says, "I'm thinking maybe we should change your hair." Squinting, Babette says, "I'm thinking, maybe—bangs."

At merely the idea—bangs!—my butt's already bouncing little bounces in the seat of my chair. Within my earpiece, a voice answers the call, "Hello?" The voice sounds muffled and garbled with a mouthful of partially masticated dinner food.

To Babette, I nod my head enthusiastically. Into the phone, I say, "We're conducting a consumer survey to track purchase patterns for common household items. . . ."

Babette lifts her hand, taps the wrist with the index finger of her opposite hand, and mouths, *What's the time?*

In response, I mouth, *August.*

And Babette shrugs and walks away.

Over the next few hours, I run across an elderly man dying of kidney failure. A middle-aged woman apparently losing her battle against lupus. We talk for an hour, easy. I meet another man who's alone, trapped in a cheap apartment, dying of congestive heart failure. I meet a girl about my same age, thirteen, who's dying from AIDS. This last one, her name is Emily. She lives in Victoria, British Columbia, Canada.

All of these dying folks, I pitch them on relaxing, not being too attached to their lives, and not ruling out the possibility of relocating to Hell. No, it's not fair, but only the late-stage folks will allow me to harass them with thirty or forty questions, they're so strung-out from their treatments or they're so alone and frightened.

The AIDS girl, Emily, won't believe me at first. Either about being her same age or about being dead. Emily's been kept out of school since her immune system crashed, and she's so far gone that she's no longer even worried about flunking seventh grade. In response, I tell her that I'm dating River Phoenix. And, if she can hurry up, quick, and die, word is that Heath Ledger isn't dating anybody at the moment.

Of course, I'm not dating anybody, but what's my punishment for telling a little fib? Am I going to Hell? Ha! It's stunning how having nothing to lose will build your self-confidence.

And, yes, it ought to break my heart, talking to a girl my same age who's stuck alone, dying of AIDS in Canada with both her parents at work, while she watches television and feels weaker every day, but at least Emily's still alive. That alone puts her head and shoulders above me in the pecking order. If anything, it seems to brighten her spirits, meeting someone already dead.

Over the phone, all self-righteous, Emily announces that not only is she still alive, but she has no intention of ending up in Hell.

I ask if she's ever buttered her bread before breaking it? Has she ever used the word *ain't*? Has she ever fixed a fallen-down hem with either a safety pin or adhesive tape? Well, I've met mobs of people condemned to eternal hellfire for just those very slipups, so Emily had best not count her chickens before they're hatched. According to Babette's statistics, 100 percent of people who die of AIDS are consigned to Hell. As are all aborted babies. And all people killed by drunk drivers.

And all the people who drowned on the *Titanic*, rich and poor, they're here roasting away also. Every single soul. To repeat: This is Hell—don't ask for too much logic.

On the phone, Emily coughs. She coughs and coughs. At last, she catches enough breath to say the AIDS isn't her fault. Besides that, she's not going to die, not for a long, long time. She coughs once more, and her coughing ends in sobs, sniffing, and weeping, real way-genuine little-girl boo-hooing.

No, it's not fair, I reply. In reality, within my head, I'm still so excited. Oh, Satan, just imagine it: Me with Bangs!

On the phone it's silent except for the sound of crying. Then, Emily shrieks, "You're lying!"

Into my headset, I say, "You'll see." I tell her to look me up once she arrives. By then I'll probably be Mrs. River Phoenix, but we'll make a bet. Ten Milky Way bars says she's down here with me faster than she can imagine. "Ask anybody for directions," I tell her. "The name's Maddy Spencer," I say, and she needs to make sure and die with ten candy bars in her pocket so we can settle our bet. Ten! *Not snack-size!*

And, yes, I know the word *masticated*. It's not as dirty a word as it sounds. But no, I'm not way-totally surprised when this Canadian Emily girl hangs up.

XVII.

Are you there, Satan? It's me, Madison. I suspect that
my parents had an inkling about my covert plan to
seduce Goran. This night, while they're both out, I'll
profess my love as vehemently as Scarlett O'Hara
throwing herself at Ashley Wilkes in the library of his
Twelve Oaks plantation house.

ere hours prior to the Academy Awards,
my parents are fussing over which color
of political action ribbon to pin on themselves. Pink, for breast cancer. Yellow, for
Bring the Soldiers Home. Green, for climate change—
except my mom's gown arrived looking more orange than
crimson, so any symbolic protest against climate change
would clash. My mom folds a scrap of red ribbon, holding it against the bodice of her gown. Studying the effect
in a mirror, she says, "Do people still get AIDS?" She says,
"Don't laugh, but it just seems so . . . 1989."

The three of us, her, me, and my dad, are in the hotel
suite, waiting in the lull between the siege of the stylist
army and the launch of the Prius. My dad says, "Maddy?"
In one hand, he holds out a pair of gold cuff links.

I step closer to him, my own hand extended, palm up.

My father drops his cuff links into my cupped palm.
Then he shoots his shirt cuffs, French cuffs, extending both
hands, turned wrist-up, for me to insert and fasten the cuff
links. These are the teeny-tiny malachite cuff links some

producer gave everyone as a wrap gift after shooting ended on my mom's last film.

My dad asks, "Maddy, do you know where babies come from?"

Theoretically, yes. I understand the messy ordeal of the egg and the sperm, plus all the ancient tropes about finding infants beneath cabbage leaves or storks bringing them, but just to force what's obviously an uncomfortable situation, I say, "Babies?" I say, "Mommy, Daddy . . ." Canting my head in a not-unappealing manner, I widen my eyes and say, "Doesn't the *casting director* bring them?"

My father bends one elbow, pulls back the shirt cuff on that hand, and looks at his wristwatch. He looks at my mother. He smiles wanly.

My mom drops her evening bag into a hotel chair and heaves a deep, heavy sigh. She settles herself into the chair and pats her knees in a gesture for me to move closer.

My father steps to stand immediately beside her chair, then bends his knees to sit on the chair's arm. The two of them create a tableau of elegant good looks. So meticulously outfitted in their tuxedo and gown. Every hair assigned its perfect place. The pair of them, so beautifully blocked for a two-shot, I can't resist messing with their Zen.

Dutifully, I cross the hotel room and sit on the Oriental carpet at my mother's feet. Already, I'm wearing the tweedy skort, the pink blouse and cardigan sweater for my long-planned rendezvous with Goran. I gaze up at my parents with guileless terrier eyes. Wide-open Japanese-animation eyes.

"Now, when a man loves a woman very, very much . . ." my dad says.

My mother retrieves the evening purse from the seat beside her. Snapping open the clasp, she reaches out a pill bottle, saying, "Would you like a Xanax, Maddy?"

I shake my head, *No.*

With her perfectly manicured hands, my mom executes the stage business of twisting open the pill bottle, then shaking two of the pills into her own hand. My father reaches down from his perch on the arm of her chair. Instead of giving him one of the two pills she holds, she shakes two more pills out of the bottle into his hand. Both my parents toss back the pills they hold and swallow them dry.

"Now," my dad says, "when a man loves a woman very, very much . . ."

"Or," my mom adds, shooting him a look, "when a man loves a *man* or a woman loves a *woman.*" In the fingers of one hand, she still toys with the scrap of red grosgrain ribbon.

My father nods. "Your mother is right." He adds, "Or when a man loves two women, or three women, backstage after a big rock concert . . ."

"Or," my mom says, "when a whole cell block of male prisoners love one new inmate very, very much . . ."

"Or," my dad interjects, "when a motorcycle gang making a meth run across the Southwestern United States loves one drunken biker chick very, very much . . ."

Yes, I know their car is waiting. The Prius. At the awards venue, some poor talent wrangler is no doubt reshuffling their arrival time. Despite all of these stress factors, I merely furrow my preadolescent brow in a confused expression my Botoxed parents can only envy. I shift my gaze back and forth between my mom's eyes and my dad's even as the Xanax turns them glazed and glassy.

My mother looks up, casting her gaze over her shoulder so that her eyes meet my father's.

Finally, my dad says, "Oh, to hell with it." Reaching a hand into his tux jacket, he extracts a personal digital assistant, or PDA, from the inside pocket. He crouches next to the chair, bringing the tiny computer level with my face. Flipping the screen open, he keyboards Ctrl+Alt+P, and the screen fills with a view of our media room in Prague. He toggles until the wide-screen television fills the entire computer screen, then keys Ctrl+Alt+L and scrolls down through a list of movie titles. Tabbing down the list, my father selects a movie, and a keystroke later the computer screen fills with a tangle of arms and legs, dangling hairless testicles, and quivering silicone-enhanced breasts.

Yes, I may be a virgin, a dead virgin, with no knowledge of carnality beyond the soft-focus metaphors of Barbara Cartland novels, but I can well recognize a fake booby when I see one.

The camerawork is atrocious. Anywhere from two to twenty men and women grapple, frantically involved in violating every orifice present with every digit, phallus, and tongue available to them. Whole human bodies appear to be disappearing into other bodies. The lighting is abysmal, and the sound has obviously been looped by nonunion amateurs working without a decent final draft. What appears before me bears less resemblance to sexual congress than it does to the writhing, squirming, not-quite-dead-yet-already-partially-decomposed occupants of a mass grave.

My mom smiles. Nodding at the PDA screen, she says,

"Do you understand, Maddy?" She says, "This is where babies come from."

My dad adds, "And herpes."

"Antonio," my mother says, "let's not go down that road." To me, she says, "Young lady, are you absolutely sure you don't want a Xanax?"

In the center of the tiny pornographic movie, the hideous little orgy is interrupted. The words *Incoming Call* superimpose themselves over the grappling bodies. A red light blinks at the top of the PDA case, and a shrill bell rings. My dad says, "Wait," and he holds the PDA to his ear, where the gruesome assemblage of entwined limbs and genitals squirm against his cheek; videotaped penises erupt their vile sputum dangerously near his eye and mouth. Answering the call thus, he says, "Hello?" He says, "Fine. We'll be downstairs in a moment."

I shake my head again, *No. No, thank you*, to the Xanax.

Already, my mom starts poking around inside her evening purse. "This isn't your real birthday present," she says, "but just in case . . ." What she hands me is round, a rolled batch of shiny plastic or vinyl, printed with the repeating pattern of a cartoon cat face. The plastic or foil feels so slick that it could be wet, too slick to easily hold on to; thus when I reach to take it from her hand, the roll drops to the floor, unspooling itself to reveal a seemingly endless series of the same cartoon cat face. The long plastic strip, quilted into little squares, this trails from my hand to the floor. The length of it gives off a powdery, hospital smell of latex.

By then, my parents are gone; they've swept out the door of the hotel suite before I realize I'm holding a fifteen-foot-long supply of Hello Kitty condoms.

XVIII.

Are you there, Satan? It's me, Madison. Little by little, I forget my life on earth, how it felt to be alive and living, but today something happened which shocked me back to remembering—maybe not everything—but at least I realize how much I might be forgetting. Or suppressing.

he computerized autodialer in Hell makes it a top priority to call mostly numbers on the federal government's No Call List. I can practically smell the mercury-enhanced tuna casserole on the breath of people whose dinner I interrupt, even over the fiber-optic or whatever phone lines that connect earth and Hell, when they yell at me. Their dinner napkins still tucked into the collars of their T-shirts, flapping down their fronts, spotted with Hamburger Helper and Green Goddess salad dressing, these angry people in Detroit, Biloxi, and Allentown, they yell for me to, "Go to Hell . . ."

And yes, I might be a thoughtless, uncouth interloper into the savory ritual of their evening repast, but I'm way ahead of their hostile request.

This current day or month or century, I'm plugged into my workstation, getting shouted at, asking people their consumer preferences regarding ballpoint pens, when something new occurs. A telephone call comes through the system. An incoming call. Even as some meat loaf–eating moron shouts at me, a beep sound starts within my headset. Some kind of call-waiting sound. Whether this call's coming from earth or Hell, I can't begin to guess, and the caller identification is blocked. The instant the meat-loaf moron hangs up, I press Ctrl+Alt+Del to clear my line, and say, "Hello?"

A girl's voice says, "Is this Maddy? Are you Madison Spencer?"

I ask, Who's calling?

"I'm Emily," the girl says, "from British Columbia." The thirteen-year-old. The girl with the really bad case of AIDS. She's *69'd me. Over the telephone, she says, "Are you really and truly dead?"

As a doornail, I tell her.

This Emily girl says, "The caller ID says your area code is for Missoula, Montana. . . ."

I tell her, Same deal.

She says, "If I called you back, collect, would you accept the charges?"

Sure, I tell her. I'll try.

And—click—she hangs up on her end.

Granted, it's not entirely ethical to make personal calls from Hell, but everybody does it. To one side of me, the punk kid, Archer, sits with his leather-jacketed elbow almost touching my cardigan-sweatered elbow. Archer toys with the big safety pin which hangs from his cheek, while into his headset he's saying, ". . . No, seriously, you sound gnarly-hot." He says, "After your skin-cancer thing metasta-sizes, you and me need to totally hook up. . . ."

At my opposite elbow, the brainiac Leonard stares forward, his eyes unfocused, telling his headset, "Queen's rook to G-five . . ."

Even as I sit here, my head clamped in a headset, the ear-piece covering one ear and the microphone looped around to hang in front of my mouth, at the same time, Babette hovers over me, circling and snipping at my hair with the cuticle scissors from her purse, shaping me the most way-perfect pageboy haircut with straight-across bangs. Even she doesn't care that I'm socializing on Hell's dime.

My line rings again, and a mechanical voice says, "You have a collect phone call from . . ."

And the Canadian AIDS girl adds, "Emily."

The computer says, "Will you accept the charges?"

And I say, Yes.

Over the phone, Emily says, "I only called because this constitutes a way-terrible emergency." She says, "My parents want me to see a new shrink. Do you think I should go?"

Shaking my head, I tell her, "No way."

Babette's hand grips the back of my neck, her white-painted fingernails digging in until I hold still.

"And don't let them feed you full of Xanax, either," I say into the phone. From my personal experience, nothing feels as awful as pouring your heart out to some talk therapist, then realizing this so-called professional is actually vastly stupid and you've just professed your most secret secrets to some goon who's wearing one brown sock and one blue sock. Or you see an Earth First! bumper sticker on the rear of his diesel Hummer H3T in the parking lot. Or you catch him picking his nose. Your precious confidant you expected would sort out your entire twisted psyche, who now harbors all your darkest confessions, he's just some jerk with a master's degree. To change the subject, I ask Emily how it was that she contracted AIDS.

"How else?" Emily says. "From my *last* therapist, of course."

I ask, Was he cute?

Emily shrugs audibly, saying, "Cute enough, for a sliding-scale therapist."

Toying with a strand of my hair, looping it around my finger, then pulling it to where my teeth can nibble the tips, I ask Emily what it's like to have AIDS.

Even over the phone, her eye roll is audible. "It's like being Canadian," she says. "You get used to it."

Trying to sound impressed, I say, "Wow." I say, "I guess people can get used to pretty much anything."

Just to make conversation, I ask if Emily has gotten her first period yet.

"Sure," Emily says, "but when your viral loads are this sky-high, menstruation is less like a big celebration of attaining womanhood, and more like a way-biologically hazardous toxic spill in your pants."

Without realizing it, I must still be biting my hair, because Babette slaps my hand away. She waves the little scissors in my face and gives me a stern look.

Over the phone, Emily says, "I figure that once I'm dead I can start dating." She says, "Is Corey Haim seeing anybody?"

I don't answer, not right away, not that instant, because a herd of new Hell inductees is crowding past my work-station. A regular flood of people has just arrived, still not entirely certain they're dead. Most of them wear leis made of silk flowers looped around their necks. The ones not wearing sunglasses have a stunned, worried look in their eyes. A mob that could easily be the entire population of some country, it's usually proof that something terrible has just befallen folks on earth.

Over the phone, I ask Emily if something awful just occurred. A major earthquake? A tidal wave? A nuclear bomb? Did a dam burst? Of the milling, stunned newcomers, most appear to be wearing vivid Hawaiian-print shirts, with cameras slung on cords hanging around their necks. These people all boast roasted-red sunburns, some with white stripes of zinc oxide smeared across the bridge of their nose.

In response, Emily says, "Some big cruise-ship disaster, like, a jillion tourists died of food poisoning from eating bad lobsters." She says, "Why do you ask?"

I say, "No reason."

Deep in this crowd, a familiar face floats. A boy's face, his eyes glowering beneath the overhang of a heavy brow. His hair, too thick to comb flat.

In my ear, Emily asks, "How did you die?"

"Marijuana," I tell her. Still watching the boy's face in the middle distance, I say, "I'm not altogether certain." I say, "I was so way stoned."

Around me, Archer flirts with dying cheerleaders. Leonard checkmates some alive dweeb. Patterson asks somebody on earth how the Raiders are ranked this season.

Emily says, "Nobody dies from marijuana." Pressing the subject, she says, "What's the last detail you remember about your life?"

I say, I don't know.

Beyond this new flood of the damned, the boy's face turns. His eyes meet mine. He of the moody, wrinkled forehead. He of the snarling Heathcliff lips.

Emily says, "But what killed you?"

I say, I don't know.

The boy in the distance, he turns and begins to walk away, dodging and weaving to escape through the crowd of poisoned tourists.

By reflex, I stand, my headset still tethering me to my workstation. And with a sharp shove against my shoulder, Babette sits me back down in my chair and continues to snip at my hair.

"But what do you remember?" Emily asks.

Goran, I tell her. I remember watching the television, lying on the carpet on my stomach, propped on my elbows, next to Goran. Arrayed on the carpet around us, I recall half-eaten room-service trays containing onion rings, cheeseburgers. My mom appeared on the television screen. She'd pinned the pink breast cancer ribbon to her gown, and—as the applause died down—she said, "Tonight is a very special night, in more ways than one. For it was on this night, eight years ago, that my precious daughter was born. . . ."

Sprawled on the hotel carpet amid cold food and Goran, I remember seething.

It was my *thirteenth* birthday.

I remember the television cameras cutting to show my dad, seated in the audience, beaming with a proud smile to show off his new dental implants.

Even now, dead and in Hell, way-totally ready to get busted for accepting a collect call from Canada, I ask Emily, "In second or third grade . . ." I ask, "did you play the French-kissing Game?"

Emily says, "Is that how you died?"

No, I tell her, but that game is all I remember.

And, yes, I might be forgetful or in denial or five years older than my mother would like me to be, but as I stare across the landscape of Hawaiian shirts and fake-flower leis, some of those loud shirts and silk flowers still splashed with food-poisoning vomit, the face I see receding into the distance of Hell is that of my brother, Goran. In contrast to the garish tropical cruise apparel, Goran wears a pink jumpsuit, bright pink, with some sort of multidigit number stitched across one side of his chest.

On the phone, her voice still in my earpiece, Emily says, "What's the French-kissing Game?"

And then Goran, he of the kissable, lusciously full lips and bright pink jumpsuit, he's vanished into the crowd.

XIX.

Are you there, Satan? It's me, Madison. Please don't get the impression that I've always boasted a brilliant intellect. On the contrary, I've made more than my share of mistakes, not the least of which was my misconceived idea of what constituted French-kissing.

t was some Miss Whorey Von Whoreski girls at my school who taught me the French-kissing Game. At my boarding school in Switzerland, where I almost froze to death but only lost all the skin off my hands instead, a bunch of these same snotty girls always spent time together, three of them, but they were all way-total Trollopy McTrollops and Slutty Vandersluts and Harley O'Harlots who spoke English and French in the same flat accent as the Global Positioning System of my dad's Jaguar. They walked on the outside edge of their feet, each step slightly crossing in front of the last, to prove they'd taken too many years of ballet. These three girls were always together, usually cutting themselves or helping one another to vomit; within the insular sphere of the boarding school, they were infamous.

I was in my room one day, reading Jane Austen, when these three knocked on the door and asked to enter.

And no, I may display occasional antisocial tendencies brought about by years of witnessing my parents pander to the film-going public, but I'm not so rude that I would tell three classmates to beat it. No, I politely set aside *Persuasion* and invited these three Miss Tarty Tartnicks to enter, and bade them sit a moment on my austere-yet-comfortable single bed.

Upon entering, the first of them asked, "Do you know the French-kissing Game?"

The second asked, "Where's your bathrobe?"

The third said, "Do you promise not to tell?"

Of course I feigned curiosity. In all honesty I was not intrigued, but at their request I presented said bathrobe and watched as one of the Miss Slutty O'Slutskis withdrew the white terry-cloth belt from the robe's belt loops. Another of the Whorey Vanderwhores requested I lie back until I was prone on the bed, gazing up at the distant ceiling. The third Miss Harlot MacHarlot threaded the terry-cloth belt behind my neck and tied the two ends across my tender throat.

More out of politeness and an innate courtesy than any actual interest, I asked if these preparations were part of the game. The French-kissing Game. We were, all of us present in my small room, wearing the same school uniform of dark skorts and long-sleeved cardigan sweaters, kiltie tassel loafers, and white ankle socks. We were all either eleven or twelve years of age. The particular day was, I believe, a Tuesday.

"Just wait," said one Skanky Von Skankenberg.

"It feels . . . *si bon*," said another Miss Vixey Vandervixen.

The third said, "We won't hurt you; we promise."

Mine has always been an open, vulnerable nature. Where the motives and agendas of others come into play, I am perhaps too trusting. To suspect three of my own schoolmates struck me as a tad unseemly, so I merely consigned myself to their instruction as these girls arrayed themselves around me on the bed. A girl sat at each of my shoulders. The third girl gently lifted the eyeglasses from my face, folded them shut, and held them as she seated herself on the bed near my feet. The two flanking me each took one end of the cloth belt which was knotted loosely about my neck. The third instructed them to pull.

May this episode demonstrate the hazards inherent in being the offspring of former-hippie, former-Rasta, former–punk rock parents. Even as the belt constricted more snugly, restricting my breathing, collapsing not only my air supply but also the flow of blood to my precious brain, as all of this occurred I made no vehement protest. Even as shooting stars flooded my view of the ceiling, and I felt my face flushing deeper and deeper red, and the pulse of my heartbeat throbbed beneath my collarbone, I offered no resistance. After all, what was transpiring was nothing more than a game, being taught to me by members of my peer group in an enormously exclusive girls' boarding school located deep in the safe bosom of the Swiss Alps. Despite their current status as Miss Whorey Whorebergs and Miss Trampy Vandertramps, these girls would one day graduate to take positions as the chief editor of British *Vogue* or, failing that, first lady of Argentina. Etiquette and protocol and decorum were drummed into us daily. Such genteel young ladies would never attempt anything untoward.

Under their assault, I imagined myself the innocent governess in *Frankenstein*, hung from the gallows, the noose tightening unjustly around my neck for the murder of my charge by the reanimated monster of a mad scientist. Suffocating, I imagined tightly laced whalebone corsets. A lingering death by consumption. Opium dens. I envisioned fainting and swooning and massive overdoses of laudanum. I became Scarlett O'Hara, feeling Rhett Butler's powerful hands as they tried to choke away my love for the dashing, chivalrous Ashley Wilkes, and in that moment, even as my own red, raw fingers clutched at the bedclothes, my voice hoarse with effort, I cried out as Katie Scarlett O'Hara, "Unhand me, you vile cad!"

Even as the shooting stars filled my vision, stars and comets of every color, red and blue and gold, the ceiling of my room seemed to drift more and more near. Within moments, my heartbeat seemed to have ceased, and my nose was almost touching this, the bedroom ceiling which had only moments before soared so high above me. My awareness seemed to be hovering, floating, gazing down upon the occupants of the bed.

A girl's voice said, "Hurry and give her the kiss." The voice, coming from somewhere behind me. Turning, I saw myself still laid out on my bed, the cloth belt still knotted tightly around my neck. My face looked pasty and pale white, and the two girls seated beside my shoulders still pulled at the ends of the cloth belt.

The girl seated to my right said, "Stop pulling, and give her the kiss."

Another girl said, "Yuck." Their voices sounded muffled and foggy and miles away.

The third girl, seated near my feet, she unfolded my eyeglasses and slipped them onto her own smug face. Batting her eyelashes and cocking her head from side to side coquettishly, she said, "Look at me, everyone . . . I'm the fat, ugly daughter of a stupid-ass movie star. . . . My picture was on the cover of *People* stupid magazine. . . ." And all three Miss Bimbo Von Bimbos, they giggled.

If you'll permit me a moment of self-indulgent embarrassment, I did look terrible. The skin of my cheeks had swollen slightly, becoming puffy, similar to a soufflé d'apricot. My eyes, open only as slits, appeared as glazed as the glassy surface of an overly caramelized crème brûlée. Worse yet, my lips were gaping, and my tongue pushed forward—green as a raw oyster—as if attempting to escape. My face, from forehead to chin, varied in hue from alabaster white to light blue. The put-aside copy of *Persuasion* lay on the bedspread beside my blue hand.

As I hovered there, observing, as detached as my mother keyboarding to spy on the maids and adjust the lighting via her notebook computer, I felt neither pain nor anxiety. I felt nothing. Below me, the three girls untied the cloth belt from my neck. One girl slid a hand behind my head and tilted my face back slightly, and another drew a deep breath and leaned over. Her lips covered my own blue lips.

And yes, I know what constitutes a near-death experience; however, I was more concerned about my prescription eyewear. The girl seated at my feet, still wearing my reading glasses, she said, "Blow. Hard."

The girl leaning over me . . . even as she blew air into my mouth, I seemed to fall from the ceiling and land into my body. Even as the girl's lips pressed my lips, I found myself, once more, occupying the body which lay upon my bed. I coughed. My throat ached. The three girls laughed. My tiny bedroom, my tattered copies of *Wuthering Heights* and

144

Northanger Abbey and *Rebecca* sparkled and glowed. All of my body felt so electric, as thrumming and vibrant as I'd felt naked in the snow at night. My every cell swelled so full of newfound vitality.

One of the Hussey Vanderhusseys, the one who'd blown her breath into my mouth, said, "That's called 'the kiss of life.'" Her breath tasted like the wintergreen of her chewing gum.

Another girl said, "It's the French-kissing Game."

The third said, "You want to go again?"

And raising my weak hands, lifting my cold, trembling fingers to touch my throat where the terry-cloth belt still lay across the throbbing of my brand-new heartbeat, I nodded my head, faintly but repeating, whispering, "Yes." As if to Mr. Rochester himself, I whispered, "Ye gods!" Whispering, "Edward, please. Oh, yes."

XX.

Are you there, Satan? It's me, Madison. People say the world is a small place . . . well, in Hell this must be Old Home Week. Really, everyone seems to know me and vice versa. It's like alumni week at my boarding school, when all the old mossbacks would totter around campus all misty-eyed. Everywhere that you look, it seems as if a familiar face is looking back.

y dad would tell you, "When you're shooting on location, be ready for rain." Meaning: You never know what fate will throw your way. One minute, I'm luring some Canadian AIDS girl to come join me in Hell, and the next minute I'm staring down my beloved Goran, now wearing a hot-pink jumpsuit with what looks like a Social Security number embroidered on his chest. My telephone headset still clamped around my smart new pageboy haircut, I jump to my feet and begin swimming, stroking my arms through a veritable ocean of chubby, newly deceased holiday cruisers, all of them bespeckled with their own noxious lobster vomitus. Within moments, my hands tangle in camera straps and sunglasses bungee cords and artificial floral leis. Drowning and slimy in the coconut-smelling miasma of budget suntan lotions, I'm calling out, screaming, "Goran!" Gasping, I'm bobbing and flailing amid the tide of food-poisoned tourists, shouting, "Wait, Goran! Please wait!" Unfamiliar with walking in my new

high heels, netted in the wires of my telephone setup, I stumble and begin to sink beneath the surface of the teeming mob.

Suddenly, an arm wraps around me from behind. An arm encased in the sleeve of a black-leather jacket. And Archer rescues me, towing me from the sluggish riptide of wandering bovine dead.

With Babette looking on, Leonard watching, I say, "My boyfriend . . . he was just here."

Patterson untangles the headset from me.

"Calm down," says Babette. She explains that we need to slip Tootsie Pops or Oh Henry! bars to the right demons. If Goran's only recently been damned, his files ought to be easy to find. Already she's leading me in the other direction, exiting the telephone marketing hall, her hand wrapped around mine. Babette's dragging me along corridors, up and down stone stairways, navigating hallways past doorways and skeletons, under archways with black fringes of sleeping bats hanging overhead, across lofty bridges and via dripping, dank tunnels, but always staying within the vast hive of the netherworld headquarters. Finally, arriving at a bloodstained counter, Babette elbows aside the souls already waiting in line. She digs an Abba-Zaba from her purse and dangles it toward some demon who sits at a desk, some sort of half-man, half-falcon monster with a lizard's tail, engrossed in doing a crossword puzzle. Addressing him, Babette says, "Hey, Akibel." She says, "What do you have on a new arrival named . . ." And Babette looks at me.

"Goran," I say. "Goran Spencer."

The falcon-lizard-monster-man looks up from the folded page of his newspaper; wetting the tip of his pencil against the wet point of his forked tongue, the demon says, "What's a six-letter word for 'power failure'?"

Babette looks at me. She brushes her fingernails to stroke my new bangs so they fall straight across my forehead, and says, "What's he look like, honey?"

Goran of the dreamy vampire eyes and jutting caveman brow. Goran of the surly, fleshy lips and unruly hair, he of the sneering disdain and abandoned-orphan demeanor. My wordless, hostile, walking skeleton. My beloved. Words fail me. With a helpless sigh, I say, "He's . . . swarthy." Quickly, I say, "And brutish."

Babette adds, "He's Maddy's long-lost boyfriend."

Blushing, I protest, saying, "He's only kind of my boyfriend. I'm only thirteen."

The demon, Akibel, swivels in his desk chair. Turning to face a dusty computer screen, the demon keyboards Ctrl+Alt+F with the talons of his falcon claws. When a blinking green cursor appears on the screen, the demon keys in "Spencer, Goran." With a stab of his index talon, he hits Enter.

At that same instant, a finger taps me on the back of my shoulder. A human finger. And a frail voice says, "Are you little Maddy?" Standing behind me, a stooped old lady asks, "Would you happen to be Madison Spencer?"

The demon sits, his face propped in his hands, both his elbows leaned on his desk, watching his computer screen and waiting. Tapping a talon, impatiently, on the edge of his keyboard, the demon says, "I hate this fucking dial-up. . . ." He says, "Talk about glacial." A beat later, the demonic Akibel picks up his crossword once more. Studying it, he says, "What's a four-letter word for 'cribbage props'?"

The old woman who tapped my shoulder, she continues to look at me, her eyes shining bright. Her hair fluffy and bunched into wads as white as tufts of cotton, her voice flickering she says, "The telephone people said you might be here." She smiles a mouthful of pearly, bright dentures and says, "I'm Trudy. Mrs. Albert Marenetti . . . ?" her intonation lifting into a question.

The demon whacks a falcon claw against the side of his computer monitor, swearing under his breath.

And yes, I am wildly invested in tracking down my adored Goran, denizen of my most romantic dreams, but I am NOT totally oblivious to the emotional needs of others. Especially those recently dead after prolonged terminal illness. Throwing my arms around this stooped, stunted little shrub of an old lady, I squeal, "Mrs. Trudy! From Columbus, Ohio! Of course I remember you." Giving her powdery, wrinkled cheek a little peck, I say, "How's that little pancreatic cancer thing?" Realizing our present situation, both of us dead and doomed to the straits of Hell for all eternity, I add, "Not good, I guess."

With a twinkle in her sky-blue eyes, the old lady says, "You were so kind and generous, talking to me." Her old-lady fingers pinch both my cheeks. Cupping my face between her hands, gazing at me, she says, "So, just before my last trip into the hospice I burned down a church."

We both laugh. Uproariously. I introduce Mrs. Trudy to Babette. The demon, Akibel, hits his Enter key, again and again and again.

While we wait, I compliment Mrs. Trudy on her choice of footwear: black low-heeled mules. Otherwise, she wears an iron-gray tweed suit and a very smart Tyrolean hat of gray felt, with a red feather tucked into the band at a jaunty angle. Now, here's an ensemble which will stay fresh-looking despite aeons of hellish punishment.

Babette waves a Pearson Salted Nut Roll, baiting the demon to work faster. Badgering him, she calls, "Hey, step it up! We don't have forever!"

The people already here, already waiting, they give up a weak laugh.

"This here is Madison," Babette says, introducing me to everyone present. Throwing an arm around my shoulders and steering me to the counter, she adds, "Just in the past three weeks, Maddy, here, is responsible for a seven-percent increase in damnations!"

A murmur passes through the crowd.

In the next moment, an elderly man approaches our tiny group. Clasping his hat in both hands and wearing a striped silk bowtie, the old man says, "Would you happen to be Madison Spencer?"

Says Mrs. Trudy, "She is." Beaming, Mrs. Trudy slips her wrinkled hand around my hand and gives my fingers a bony squeeze.

Looking at this man, with his cloudy cataract eyes and pinched, trembling shoulders, I say, "Now, don't tell me . . ." I say, "Are you Mr. Halmott from Boise, Idaho?"

"In the flesh," the old man says, "or whatever I am, these days." So apparently pleased that he blushes.

Congestive heart failure, I recite. I shake his hand and say, "Welcome to Hell."

On the far side of the counter, at the demon's desk, a dot-matrix printer grinds to life. Sprocket wheels pull continuous-feed paper from a dusty box. The paper, yellowed and brittle. The printer carriage roars back and forth as each page advances, line by line, pulled along by its perforated tracks.

With Babette's arm draped across the back of my neck, her hand hangs near the side of my face. There, the cuff of her blouse has pulled back to reveal dark red lines on the inside of her wrist. Running from the sleeve to the base of her palm, gouged scars gape, raw as if they'd been recently cut.

And yes, I know suicide is a mortal sin, but Babette has always insisted she was damned for wearing white shoes after Labor Day.

With old Mr. Halmott and Mrs. Trudy smiling at me, I myself am staring point-blank—first, at Babette's suicide scars—then at her sheepish grin.

Removing her arm from my shoulders, sliding the sleeve to conceal her secret, Babette says, "Girl really, really, *really* interrupted . . ."

The demon tears the page from the printer and slaps it on the countertop.

XXI.

*Are you there, Satan? It's me, Madison. My last sight-
ing of my beloved Goran had been the night of the
Academy Awards. If Hell is—as the ancient Greeks
claimed—the place of remorse and remembering, then
I am slowly accomplishing those tasks.*

olling about amid the cold remains of
our room-service meals, Goran and I
sprawled on the carpet in front of the
suite's wide-screen television. I torched a
spliff of my parents' best hybrid skunkweed, took a toke,
and handed the stinking doobie to the object of my preteen
adoration. For a Judy Blume instant, our fingers touched.
Barely our fingertips brushed, sprawled as we were on the
carpet, not dissimilar to God and Adam on the ceiling of
the Sistine Chapel, but a spark of life—or merely static
electricity—snapped and jumped between us.

Goran took the joint and puffed. He tapped the ash onto
a dinner plate, next to a half-eaten cheeseburger and an
array of stale potato chips. We both sat, silent, holding the
smoke in our lungs. Romantic anarchists that we are, we
ignored the fact that this was a nonsmoking suite. On television, someone accepted an Oscar for something. Somebody thanked someone. A commercial pitched mascara.

Exhaling, I coughed. I coughed and coughed, a genuine
fit, finally reaching for a glass of orange juice which sat on
a tray with a cold plate of buffalo wings. The air in the

suite smelled like every wrap party my parents had ever hosted on the final day of principal photography. Stinking of cannabis and French fries and scorched rolling paper. Cannabis and congealed chocolate fondue. On television, a European luxury sedan raced across desert salt flats, swerving between orange traffic cones, driven by a movie star, and I'm not certain whether this is another commercial or something sampled from a nominated movie. Next, a famous actress drinks a major brand of diet soda in what could be either an advertisement or a feature film. Even the fast cars seem to drag along in slow motion. My hand reaches out toward a plate of cold garlic toast, and Goran slips the smoldering roach between my fingers. I take another hit, and hand it back. I reach toward a plate heaped with steaming, buttery, mouthwatering prawns, but my fingertips touch only smooth glass. My fingernails scratch at this glass barrier.

Goran laughs, blasting out great clouds of sour dope stench.

My prawns, so enticing and delicious-looking, are merely a television commercial for a franchised seafood restaurant. Tasty and crunchy and completely beyond my reach. They're only a teasing mirage of savoriness on the high-definition screen.

On television, gigantic hamburgers rotate slowly, their grilled meat so hot it still bubbles and spits with grease. Slices of cheese collapse, molding themselves over the contours of searing-hot beef patties. Molten rivers of fudge flow through a mountainous landscape of vanilla soft-serve ice cream under a cruel hail of chopped Spanish peanuts. Blizzards of powdered sugar bury frosted doughnuts. Pizza drips dollops of tomato sauce and trails gooey whitish strings of mozzarella.

Goran takes the smoking roach from between my fingers. He takes another hit, chasing the smoke with a swig of chocolate milk shake.

Once more mouthing the damp butt of the shared marijuana cigarette, I attempt to discern the flavor of my beloved's saliva. Tonguing the moist folds of paper, I taste chocolate-chip cookies purloined from the minibar. I taste the tang of artificial fruit, lemons, cherries, watermelon, stolen candies, forbidden to us because of their tooth-decaying qualities. At last, beneath it all, my taste buds locate something earthy, fecund, the spit of my primitive rebel man-boy, the foreign pong of my stolid Heathcliff. My rustic rude savage. I relish this, the appetizer to a banquet of Goran's moist tongue kisses. In the scorched ganja I taste the residue of his chocolate milk shake.

On television, a basket of nachos, heavily laden with sliced olives and gory salsa, this vision dissolves to take the shape of a beautiful woman. The woman wears a red gown—in hindsight, more orange than red—a scrap of grosgrain ribbon pinned to her bodice. The ribbon as pink as diced tomatoes. The woman says, "The nominees for this year's best motion picture are . . ."

The woman on screen is my mom.

At this, I climb to my feet, towering above the hotel carpet, swaying high above the discarded food and Goran. I stumble into the suite's bathroom; there, I unroll an awful lot of toilet paper, miles of toilet paper, making two lumps of roughly equal size which I proceed to stuff into the front of my sweater. In the bathroom mirror, my eyes look red-rimmed and bloodshot. I stand sideways to the mirror and study my new busty profile. I pull the tissue from inside my sweater and flush it down the toilet—the tissue, not the sweater. I am *so high*. It seems as if I've been in this bathroom for years. Decades have passed. Aeons. I pull open a drawer next to the sink and retrieve the long strip of Hello Kitty condoms. I reemerge from the bathroom, presenting myself before Goran with the strip of condoms looped around the back of my neck like a feather boa.

On television, the camera shows my dad sitting in the audience, midway down the main floor, right on the aisle, his favorite seat, so he can sneak out and drink martinis during the awards for boring foreign crap. Only scant moments have actually gone by. Everyone applauds. Still standing in the bathroom doorway I bow, deeply.

Goran looks from the television to me. His eyes almost glow red, and Goran coughs. Crimson seafood sauce is smeared on his chin. Gooey dabs of tartar sauce trail down the front of his shirt. The air in the suite hangs misty, foggy with dope smoke.

I knot the strip of condoms around my neck and pull the knot tight, saying, "You want to play a game?" I say, "You only need to blow into my mouth." I step forward, slinking toward my beloved, and say, "It's called the French-kissing Game."

XXII.

Are you there, Satan? It's me, Madison. Please don't take this as a criticism, but you really ought to upgrade your word-processing equipment. The readability of your dot-matrix printer especially way sucks, not to mention those perforated tracks that hang off the edges of every printed page.

y mom would tell you, "Two lips and a tongue can promise you anything." Meaning: Get all your deals in writing. Meaning: Always preserve a paper trail.

Across the top of the printed form, the faint dot-matrix words read: *Hell Induction Report for Goran Metro Spencer. Age 14.*

Under "Site of Death" it says: *Los Angeles River Detention Center for Violent Juvenile Offenders.*

That would explain his hot-pink getup, complete with the prison number sewn to his chest. While somewhat fashion-forward, still not an obvious choice for the moody, imperious Goran I know.

Under "Cause of Death" the report says: *Stabbed by fellow inmate during riot.*

Under "Reason for Damnation" it says: *Manslaughter conviction for the strangulation of Madison Spencer.*

XXIII.

Are you there, Satan? It's me, Madison. Unpleasant as
death might seem, the upside is that you only suffer it
once. Subsequent to that, the sting is gone. The memory
might be enormously traumatic, but that's all it is:
a memory. You won't be asked to perform an encore.
Unless, just possibly, you're a Hindu.

Probably I shouldn't even tell you this next part. I know how self-righteous alive people are.

Face it, every time you scan the obituary pages in the newspaper and you see somebody younger than yourself who died—especially if the obit features a photograph of them smiling, sitting on some mown lawn beside a golden retriever, wearing shorts—admit it, you feel so damned superior. It could be you also feel a smidgen lucky, but mostly you feel all smug. Everybody alive feels so superior to the dead, even homosexuals and American Indians.

Probably when you read this you'll just laugh and make fun of me, but I remember gasping for breath, choking there on the carpet of the hotel suite. The crown of my head was wedged against the bottom of the television screen, the remains of our room-service banquet arrayed on plates around me. Goran knelt astride my waist, leaning over me, his face looming above my face; his hands gripped the two ends of the Hello Kitty condoms which were knotted around my neck, and he was yanking the noose tight.

The stink of our every exhaled breath hung heavy, clouding the suite with its skunkweed reek.

Above me on television, so real she seemed to be standing there, rose the figure of my mother. She seemed to tower up to the distant ceiling of the suite. The full length of her, glowing, radiant in the stage lights. Luminescent in her perfect beauty. A glorious vision. An angel garbed in a designer gown. On the television, my mom stands, gracious and patient in silence, waiting for the applause of her adoring world to subside.

In contrast, my arms and legs flail and thrash, scattering the nearby plates of jumbo prawns. My desperate convulsions upset the bowls of leftover buffalo wings. Spill ranch dressing. Strew old egg rolls.

On television, the cameras cut to show my dad seated in the audience, beaming.

As the applause fades to quiet, my serene, lovely mother, smiling and enigmatic, says, "Before presenting this year's Oscar for best feature film . . ." She says, "I'd like to wish my dear, sweet daughter, Madison, a happy eighth birthday. . . ."

As of today, the truth is—I'm thirteen. My pulse pounds in my ears, and the condoms cut into the tender skin of my neck. The stars and comets of red and gold and blue begin to fill my vision, obscuring Goran's grim face, obscuring my view of the room's ceiling and my radiant mother. In my school uniform of sweater and skort, I'm sweating. My kiltie tassel loafers, kicked off my feet.

As my vision narrows to a smaller and smaller tunnel, edged by a growing margin of darkness, I can still hear my mother's voice say, "Happy birthday, my dearest baby girl. Your daddy and I love you very, very much." A beat later, muffled and far away, she adds, "Now, good night, and sleep well, my precious love. . . ."

In the hotel suite, I hear panting, gasping, someone drawing great inhales of breath, but it's not me. It's Goran panting with the effort to suffocate me, to strangle me in exactly the manner I'd dictated according to the rules of the French-kissing Game.

By then I'm floating up, my face drifting closer to the painted plaster of the ceiling. My heartbeat, silent. My own breathing, stilled. From the highest point in the room, I turn and look back at Goran. I'm shouting, "Kiss me!" I'm screaming, "Give me the kiss of life!" But nothing makes a sound except for the rush of televised applause for my mother.

Splayed there on the carpet, I'm reduced to the status of the cooling food which surrounds me: my life only partially consumed. Wasted. Soon to be consigned to the garbage. My swollen, livid face and blue lips, they're merely a conglomerate of rancid fats, so like the old onion rings and stale potato chips. My precious life, rendered nothing more than congealing and coagulating liquids. Desiccating proteins. A rich banquet only nibbled at. Barely tasted. Rejected and discarded and alone.

Yes, I know I sound quite cold, insensitive to the pathetic sight of a thirteen-year-old Birthday Girl dead on the floor of a hotel suite, but any other attitude would overwhelm me with self-pity. Floating here, I want nothing more than to go back and to fix this hideous error. In this moment, I've lost both my parents. I've lost Goran. Worst of all, I've lost . . . myself. In all my romantic scheming, I've ruined everything.

On television, my mom puckers her lips. She presses the fingers of her manicured hand to her mouth, then blows me a kiss.

Goran drops the ends of the condom strip and gazes down on my body, a stricken look on his face. He leaps to his feet, dashing into the bedroom, then reemerges wearing his coat. He doesn't take the room key. He doesn't intend to return. Nor does he call 911. My beloved, the object of my romantic affection, simply races from the hotel suite without so much as a single look back.

XXIV.

Are you there, Satan? It's me, Madison. Ask me the square root of pi. Ask me how many pecks are in a bushel. Ask me anything about the truncated, tragic life of Charlotte Brontë. I can tell you exactly when Joyce Kilmer died in the Second Battle of the Marne. I can tell you the combination of keys, Ctrl+Alt+S or Ctrl+Alt+Q, which will access the security cameras or manipulate the lighting and window treatments of my sealed bedrooms in Copenhagen or Oslo, those rooms my mother has air-conditioned down to meat locker . . . down to archival temperatures, where the electrostatic air filters prohibit a speck of dust to ever settle, where my clothes and shoes and stuffed animals wait in the darkness, locked away from sun fade and humidity, patient as the alabaster jars and gilded toys which accompanied any boy pharaoh into his eternal tomb. Ask me about the ecology in Fiji and the amusing personal habits of tony Hollywood gadabouts. Ask me to describe the political machinations embedded in the all-girls culture of a très-reserved Swiss boarding school. Just do NOT ask me how I'm feeling. Do not ask if I still miss my parents. Don't ask if I still cry from being so homesick. Of course the dead miss the living.

Personally, I myself miss sipping Twinings English Breakfast Tea and reading Elinor Glyn novels on rainy days. I miss smelling the citrus tang of Bain de Soleil, cheating at backgammon against our Somali maids, and practicing the gavotte and the minuet.

But on a larger scale, to be brutally honest, the dead miss everything.

n my desperation to talk, for the comfort of a little chat therapy, I telephone Canadian Emily, and a woman answers the phone. When she asks my name I tell her that I'm Emily's friend from long distance and ask if Emily can please come talk, just for a minute. Please.

At this, the woman begins to sniff, then sob. Over the telephone, she's drawing deep shuddering breaths, choked with guttering sobs. Keening. "Emily," she says, "my baby . . ." Her words dissolving into cries, she says, "My baby girl's gone back into the hospital. . . ." The woman rallies, sniffing, asking if she can relay a message from me to Emily.

And yes, despite all my considerable Swiss training in decorum, regardless of my hippie training in empathy, over the telephone I ask, "Is Emily about to die?"

No, it's not fair, but what makes life feel like Hell is our expectation that it should last forever. Life is short. Dead is forever. You'll find out for yourself soon enough. It won't help the situation for you to get all upset.

"Yes," the woman says, her voice hoarse, deep with emotion. "Emily is about to die." Her voice flat with resignation, she asks, "Would you like me to tell her something for you?"

And I say, "Never mind."

I say, "Don't let her forget to bring my ten Milky Way candy bars."

XXV.

*Are you there, Satan? It's me, Madison. It's not true
that your life flashes before your eyes when you die. At
least, not all of it. Some of your life might flash. Other
portions of your life it might take you years and years
to recall. That, I think, is the function of Hell: It's a
place of remembering. Beyond that, the purpose of Hell
is not so much to forget the details of our lives as it is to
forgive them.*

*And, yes, while the dead do miss everything and
everybody, they don't hang around the earth forever.*

his one time, my dad flew our Learjet
to attend some stockholder meeting in
Prague, except that same day, my mom
needed to be in Nairobi to collect some
harelip-and-cleft-palate orphan or a film-festival award or
some dumb *something*, so she leased a jet to fly her and
me, except the leasing time-share jet people . . . they sent
the exact diametrically WRONG kind of jet from what my
mother had ordered, thoughtlessly dispatching one with
gold-plated bathroom fixtures and hand-painted frescoes
on the ceilings, exactly the sort of jet which younger members of the Saudi royal family would hire to fly a harem of
Miss Coozey Coozerbilt call girls to Kuwait, and it was too
late to send a different jet, and my mom went nuts, she was
just so way-aesthetically freaked out.

Well, walking into the hotel suite after the Academy

Awards and stepping into about a billion half-eaten plates of old club sandwiches, then finding me dead and strangulated by a strip of Hello Kitty condoms—let's just say my mom freaked out even worse.

At that time my spirit was still hovering in the room, crossing my spiritual fingers that somebody might bother to call the paramedics, and they'd rush in and perform some resuscitation miracle. Needless to say Goran was long gone. He and I had hung the Do Not Disturb sign so the maid hadn't performed the turndown service. No chocolates rested on the bed pillows. All the lights were turned off, plunging the suite into total pitch-darkness. My parents enter, tiptoeing because they think Goran and I are fast asleep. It wasn't pretty.

No, it's never a special treat to watch your mom just scream and scream your name, then fall to her knees in a mess of ketchupy onion rings and cold prawn cocktails, grabbing at your dead shoulders, shaking you and yelling for you to wake up. It was my dad who called 911, but that was really, really way too late. The EMTs who came did more to treat my mom's hysterics than to rescue me. Of course the police came; they took as many photographs of me dead as *People* magazine had taken of me as a newborn baby. The homicide detectives lifted about a million of Goran's fingerprints off the strip of condoms. My mom took about a million Xanax, one after another. During all of this, my dad stalked over to the closet where Goran's new clothes were stored, threw open the closet door, and ripped the Ralph Lauren sportswear from the hangers, rending, shredding without a word shirts and trousers, buttons popping and ricocheting around the suite.

All that time, all night, I could merely watch, as detached and distant as my mother accessing security cameras on her laptop. Maybe I drew the hotel curtains closed, or turned on a light, but nobody seemed to notice. At best, a sentry. At worst, a voyeur.

It's power, but a kind of pointless, impotent power.

No one is discriminated against more than alive people discriminate against the dead. Nobody is as badly marginalized. If the dead are portrayed in popular culture it's as zombies . . . vampires . . . ghosts, always something threatening to the living. The dead are depicted the way blacks were in 1960s mass culture, as a constant danger and menace. Any dead characters must be banished, exorcised, driven from the property like Jews in the fourteenth century. Deported like illegal-alien Mexicans. Like lepers.

That said, go ahead and laugh at me. You're still alive, so apparently you're doing something right. I'm dead, so go right ahead and kick sand in my fat, deceased face.

In the prejudiced, bigoted modern world, alive is alive. Dead is dead. And the two factions must not interact. This attitude is entirely understandable when you consider what the dead would do to property values and stock prices. Once the dead informed the living that material possessions were a big joke—ARE a big joke—well, the De Beers people could never sell another diamond. Pension funds would truly wither.

In reality, the dead are always around the living. I hung around with my parents for a week; seriously, it beat tagging along to watch the Mr. Skeazy Vanderskeaze mortuary guy pump out my blood and monkey with my naked thirteen-year-old corpse. My environmentalist parents chose a biodegradable casket of pressed-wood pulp guaranteed to rapidly break down and encourage bacterial subsoil life-forms. This is typical of how little respect you get once you're dead. I mean, the well-being of earthworms gets a higher priority.

Consider that as proof positive that you're never too young to record a final directive.

It was like being buried inside a piñata.

If I'd managed to call the shots I'd have been buried in an all-bronze, hermetically sealed casket studded with rubies, not even buried but laid to rest in a crypt of carved white marble. On a tiny wooded island in the center of a lake. In the Italian Alps. However, my parents pursued their own vision. Instead of something elegant, they chose a caterwauling gospel choir from some church that needed to garner national exposure for an album they were ready to launch. Somebody reworked that Elton John song about the candle so it went, "Good-bye, Madison Spencer, though I never knew you at all. . . ." They even released about a zillion white doves. Talk about clichéd. Talk about derivative.

Among the loitering dead, even JonBenet Ramsey felt sorry for me. Even the Lindbergh baby was embarrassed on my behalf.

Here I was, dead, and all the little Miss Skanky Von Skankenbergs at my boarding school were still alive and attending my memorial service. The three Slutty MacSluts stood there, all pious, heads bowed, not saying a word about how they'd taught me the French-kissing Game. Those three Whorey Vanderwhores took their printed funeral programs to my mom and asked her to autograph them. The president of the United States helped carry the papier-mâché, eco-friendly biotainer to my grave. So did the prime minister of Great Britain.

Movie stars were in somber attendance. Some famous poet said some crap flowery poem that didn't even rhyme. World leaders were there to pay their vaunted respects. Connected by satellite, the entire planet was there to say, "Good-bye."

Except Goran, my beloved, my one true love . . .

Goran wasn't.

XXVI.

Are you there, Satan? It's me, Madison. It dawns on me that I've never adequately thanked you for sending the car, and I ought to; it was an extremely sensitive, thoughtful gesture on your part. You acted very kindly toward me at a time when I desperately needed such courtesy, and I want you to know that I'll always appreciate that generosity.

t's no easier to be a just-dead spirit than it is to be a just-born infant, and I'm pathetically grateful for any modicum of care and nursemaiding. Clustered around my grave site at Forest Lawn, everyone was crying: my mom and dad were crying, the president of Senegal was crying. Everyone was just boo-hooing with the notable exception of me, and that's because me crying at my own funeral strikes me as awfully egocentric. It goes without saying that no one can see the real me, the spirit me, standing in their grieving midst. I know, I know, in that totally archetypal *Tom Sawyer* scenario it's supposed to be way satisfying to attend your own funeral and witness how everyone secretly loved and adored you, but the sad truth is that most people are just as fakey-fake to you after you're dead as when you're alive. If there's even a thin margin of profit in it, everyone who hated you will rend their garments and flop around like phony crybabies. Case in point: the trio of Miss Trampy McTramptons station their skeazy preteen

selves around my bereft mother and tell her how much they loved me, even as their spidery anorexic fingers and French manicures toy with bejeweled rosaries all lumpy with Tahitian black pearls and fat rubies and emeralds designed by Christian Lacroix for Bulgari that they ran off and bought on Rodeo Drive just for today's funeral. These three Miss Slutty Sluttenheimers keep whispering to my bereft mom that they've each been receiving psychic messages from me, that I keep visiting them in their dreams and begging them to pass along words of love and support to my family, and my poor mom seems traumatized enough to listen to these three horrid harpies and take their lies seriously.

In greater numbers, a bevy of blond production assistants glom onto my dad, all of them wearing sexy black stripper gloves and trying to out-leg one another by letting their black miniskirts ride up too far on their tanned-and-waxed thighs while they clutch little brand-new, black leather-bound Bibles the same way they would Chanel pocket-books, and all told it's obvious they're all sleeping with him—my father, with all his noble-sounding, high-minded, left-wing platitudes—but he can't expense their various salaries to any project's shooting budget if he admits that the only job they ever perform is blow jobs. This weepy media circus centers around my earthly remains, which are wadded deep inside an organic shroud of unbleached bamboo fiber with some bullshit Asian-looking calligraphy scribbled all over it, resembling nothing so much as a gigantic off-white turd covered with Chinese gang tags, situated next to my own freshly hewn tombstone. Such are the myriad indignities foisted upon the dead: The stone is chiseled with my full ridiculous name of Madison Desert

Flower Rosa Parks Coyote Trickster Spencer, a monstrous personal secret I've been vigorously covering up for all my thirteen years and which the three Miss Coozy Coozenburgs clearly can't wait to share with all my old classmates back in Switzerland, not to mention the fact that the birth and death dates carved into the granite will forever fix me at an erroneous nine years old. To add insult to injury, the epitaph says: *Maddy Rests Now, Cupped and Suckling at the Sacred Breast Milk of the Eternal Goddess.*

This, all of this asinine crap is what you justly deserve if you die without a legally binding final directive. I'm dead and standing a decent distance apart from this mad crush, but I can still smell all their makeup and hair spray.

And if I didn't know the meaning of *asinine* before, I certainly do now. As for the definition of *erroneous*, I only have to look around.

And if you can stomach knowing one more fact about the afterlife, here it is: Nobody grieves more at funerals than does the newly deceased. That's why I'm so pathetically grateful when I avert my gaze from this dismal tableau to see, parked at the curb, just idling at the edge of a graveyard lane, a black Lincoln Town Car. The shiny waxed-and-polished black of it reflects the army of mourners . . . the blue sky . . . the gravestones of Forest Lawn . . . really, it reflects everything except for me, because the dead don't have reflections. On earth, the dead don't cast a shadow or show up in photographs. Best of all, standing beside the car is a uniformed chauffeur, his hair hidden beneath a visored cap and half his face blocked behind mirrored sunglasses. In his black-driving-gloved hand he holds a white clipboard with, written across it in blocky handwriting, *Madison Spencer*. This driver wears a little chrome name tag on his lapel, his name engraved there, but it's not worth the bother to read, because I know from long habit that I'll forget it a millisecond from now and just start calling him George.

Having spent half my life tooling around in these car-service cars, I know the drill. I take a step, another step, a third step toward the car, and the driver wordlessly opens the rear door and steps aside for me to enter. He makes a slight bow and touches the edge of the clipboard to the edge of his visored hat in a little salute. Once the legs of my skort are safely ensconced in the seat, the driver swings the door closed with a thud, the solid sound of a quality-made American land yacht, so heavy and muffled that it ends any suggestion of the living, breathing world outside. The windows are so darkly tinted that I find myself in a cradling cocoon of black leather, the smell of leather polish, the cold feel of air-conditioning, and the soft gleam of murky glass windows and brass interior trim. The only sound comes from behind the old-school partition that separates the front and rear seats. Submerged under the overall smell of leather is another, fainter smell; it's as if someone has recently peeled and eaten a hard-boiled egg in this car, a tiny stink of sulfur or methane. And there's the smell of popcorn . . . popcorn and caramel . . . popcorn balls. The little window in the center of the partition is shut, but I can hear the driver take his seat and click his seat belt. The engine starts and the car moves forward in slow, languid motion. After a long moment the front of the car tilts upward. It's the same sensation one associates with the long climb up the first hill of a roller coaster or the impossibly steep ascent needed for a Gulfstream to achieve take-off from the little alpine airport of Locarno, Switzerland.

The padded and upholstered leathery womb that is the backseat of a Town Car . . . anytime one finds oneself in such a place she ought to assume she's en route to Hades. In the magazine pocket sits the usual assortment of trade rags, including the *Hollywood Reporter, Variety*, and a copy of the *Vanity Fair* with my mom grinning on the cover and spouting her Gaia, Earth First! gibberish on the inside. She looks Photoshopped almost beyond recognition.

And yes, my parents have taught me well about the Power of Context and Marcel Duchamp, and how even a urinal becomes art when you hang it on the wall of a classy gallery. And pretty much anyone could pass as a movie star if you put their mug shot on the cover of *Vanity Fair* magazine. But that's how come I so, so, so appreciate crossing into the afterlife aboard a Lincoln Town Car as compared to a bus or a pole barge or some other cattle-car, steerage form of sweaty mass transit. So I again thank you, Satan.

The steep rising angle of the car's trajectory and the resulting g-forces settle me deeper into the leather upholstery. The little window in the driver's partition slides aside to reveal the chauffeur's sunglasses framed in the rearview mirror. Speaking to me via his reflection, the driver says, "If you don't mind my asking . . . are you related to the movie producer Antonio Spencer?" Of his features, all I can see is his mouth, and his smile stretches to become a spooky leer.

I retrieve the copy of *Vanity Fair* and hold the cover photo of my mother beside my own face, saying, "See any resemblance? Unlike my mom I have pores. . . ." Already,

I'm falling asleep, drifting off. Sadly, I sense where this conversation is going.

The driver says, "I do some screenwriting, myself."

And yes, of course, I saw this reveal coming from the moment I first saw the car. Every driver is named George, and every driver in California has a screenplay ready to fob onto you, and since the age of four—when I came home from Halloween trick-or-treating, my pillowcase loaded with spec screenplays, I've been trained to manage this awkward situation. As my dad would say, "We're not reading for new projects at this time. . . ." Meaning: "Go peddle your spec script to some other sucker for financing." But despite a childhood of arduous training in how to gently and politely dash the hopes and dreams of moderately gifted, earnest young talents . . . maybe just because I'm exhausted . . . maybe because I realize that the eternal afterlife will seem even longer without the distraction of even low-quality reading material . . . I say, "Sure." I say, "Get me a clean copy, and I'll give it a read."

Even as I'm drifting off to sleep, my hands still gripping the *Vanity Fair* with my mom's face on the cover, I sense that the front of the car is no longer climbing into the sky. It's leveled off, and, as if we've crested a mountain, we're slowly beginning to tilt downward in a slow, perilous, straight-down plunge.

From the rearview mirror, still leering, the driver says, "You might want to buckle up, Miss Spencer."

That said, I release my magazine and it falls down, through the partition hole, and lies flattened against the inside of the windshield.

"Another thing is," the driver says, "when we get to our destination, you don't want to touch the cage bars. They're pretty dirty."

The car plummeting, plunging, diving impossibly fast, in ever-accelerating free fall, I quickly and sleepily fasten my seat belt.

XXVII.

Are you there, Satan? It's me, Madison. By their nature,
stories told in the second person can suggest prayers.
"Hallowed be thy name . . . the Lord is with thee . . ."
With this in mind, please don't get the idea that I'm
praying to you. It's nothing personal, but I'm simply
not a satanist. Nor, despite my parents' best efforts, am
I a secular humanist. In light of finding myself in the
afterlife, neither am I any longer a confident atheist
nor agnostic. At the moment, I'm not certain in what
I believe. Far be it from me to pledge my faith to any
belief system when, at this point, it would seem that
I've been wrong about everything I've ever felt was real.

In truth, I'm no longer even certain who I, myself, am.

y dad would tell you, "If you don't know
what comes next, take a good long look at
what came before." Meaning: If you allow
it, your past tends to dictate your future.
Meaning: It's time I retrace my footsteps. With that in mind,
I abandon my job at the telemarketing phone bank and set
off on foot, carrying my new high heels, wearing my trusty,
durable loafers. Clouds of black houseflies hover, buzzing,
dense and heavy as black smoke. The Sea of Insects continues to boil in eternal rolling, gnashing chaos, its shimmering, iridescent surface stretching to the horizon. The
prickly hillocks of discarded finger- and toenail parings
continue to grow and slough in scratchy avalanches. The

desert of broken glass crunches underfoot. The noxious Great Ocean of Wasted Sperm continues to spread, engulfing the hellish landscape around it.

And yes, I find myself a thirteen-year-old dead girl gaining a fuller knowledge of her own trust issues, but what I'd really rather be is an Eastern Bloc orphan abandoned and alone in my misery, ignored, with no possibility of rescue until I become indifferent to my own horrid circumstances and unhappiness. Or, as my mother would tell me, "Blah, blah, blah . . . *shut up, Madison*."

My point is, I've made my entire identity about being smart. Other girls, mostly Miss Slutty Vandersluts, they chose to be pretty; that's an easy enough decision when you're young. As my mom would say, "Every garden looks beautiful in May." Meaning: Everyone is somewhat attractive when she's young. Among young ladies, it's a default choice, to compete on the level of physical attractiveness. Other girls, those doomed by hooked noses or ravaged skin, settle on being wildly funny. Other girls turn athletic or anorexic or hypochondriac. Lots of girls choose the bitter, lonely, lifetime path of being Miss Snarky Von Snarkskis, armored within their sharp-tongued anger. Another life choice is to become the peppy and upbeat student body politician. Or possibly to invent myself as the perennial morose poetess, poring over my private verse, channeling the dreary weltschmerz of Sylvia Plath and Virginia Woolf. But, despite so many options, I chose to be smart—the intelligent fat girl who possessed the shining brain, the straight-A student who'd wear sensible, durable shoes and eschew volleyball and manicures and giggling.

Suffice it to say that, until recently, I had felt quite

satisfied and successful with my own invention. Each of us chooses our personal route—to be sporty or snarky or smart—with the lifelong confidence that one can possess only as a small child.

However, in light of the truth: that I did not die of a marijuana overdose . . . nor did Goran reveal himself as my romantic ideal . . . my schemes have brought nothing except heartache to my family. . . . Thus, it would follow that I am not so smart. And with that, my entire concept of self is undermined.

Even now, I hesitate to use words such as *eschew* and *convey* and *weltschmerz,* so thoroughly is my faith in myself shaken. The actual nature of my death reveals me to be an idiot, no longer a Bright Young Thing, but instead a deluded, pretentious poseur. Not brilliant, but an impostor who would craft my own illusory reality out of a handful of impressive words. Such vocabulary props served as my eye shadow, my breast implants, my physical coordination, my confidence. These words: *erudite* and *insidious* and *obfuscate,* served as my crutches.

Perhaps it's better to recognize this degree of personal fallacy while still young, rather than lose one's fixed sense of self in middle age as beauty and youth fade, or strength and agility fail. It might be worse to cling to sarcasm and contempt until one finds herself isolated, loathed by all her peers. Nevertheless, this extreme form of psychological course correction still feels . . . devastating.

With that crisis fully realized, I retrace my route, returning to the cell where I first arrived in Hell. My arms swinging, the diamond ring which Archer gave me, the finger ring, flashes heavy and stolen. No longer can I present myself as an authority on being dead, so I retreat to my enclosure of filthy bars, the comfort provided inside a lock, the rust and grime scratched by the pointed safety pin of a dead punk rocker. Doomed within their own cells, my neighbors slump, gripping their heads between their hands, so long frozen and catatonic in attitudes of self-pity that spiderwebs envelop them. Or they pace, punching the air and babbling.

No, it's not too late for me to devote myself to being funny or artsy, energetically flopping my body around on some gymnastics mats or painting moody masterpieces; however, having failed at my initial strategy, I'll never again have such faith in a single identity. Whether I channel my future into being the sporty girl or stoner girl, the smiling cover on a Wheaties cereal box, or an absinthe-guzzling auteur, that new persona will always feel as phony and put-on as plastic fingernails or a rub-on tattoo. The rest of my afterlife, I'll feel as counterfeit as Babette's Manolo Blahniks.

Nearby, oblivious souls sprawl within their cages, so sunken in their shock and resignation they fail to shoo the houseflies that crawl along their soiled arms. These flies freely roam across their smudged cheeks and foreheads. Black flies, fat as raisins, walk across the glassy surface of people's staring, dazed eyes. Unnoticed, these houseflies wander into slack, open mouths, then emerge from nostrils.

Behind their own jail bars, other condemned souls tear at their hair. Enraged souls, they rend and shred their own togas and vestments, ripping their ermine robes, their shrouds and silk gowns and tweed Savile Row suits. Some of them, Roman senators and Japanese shoguns, dead and damned to Hell since long before I was even born. These tormented wail. Their specks of raving slobber mist the fetid air. Their sweat runs in rivulets down their foreheads and cheeks, glowing orange in the ambient Hellish fire-light. The denizens of Hades, they flail and cower, shake fists at the flaming sky, pound their heads into the iron bars until their blood blinds them. Others claw at their own countenances, raking their skin raw, scratching out their own eyes. Their broken, hoarse voices keening. In adjacent cells . . . in cages beyond cages . . . trapped, they stretch to the burning horizon in every direction. Countless billions of men and women yammer, despairing, shouting their names and status as kings or taxpayers or persecuted minorities or rightful property owners. In this, the cacophony of Hell, the history of humanity fractures into individual protest. They demand their birthrights. They insist on their righteous innocence as Christians or Muslims or Jews. As philanthropists or physicians. Do-gooders or martyrs or movie stars or political activists.

In Hell, it's our attachments to a fixed identity that torture us.

In the distance, following the same route on which I've so recently returned, a bright blue spark floats. The spot of blue, vivid against the contrasting blaze of orange and red fire, the blue nimbus bobs along, edging between faraway cages and their shrieking occupants. The blue speck passes the dead presidents gnashing their teeth, ignores the forgotten emperors and potentates. This blue spot disappears behind heaps of rusted cages, vanishing behind crowds of lunatic former popes, obscured behind the iron hives of imprisoned, sobbing deposed shamans and city fathers and exiled, scowling tribesmen, only to appear a little more blue, a little larger, closer, a moment later. In this manner, the bright blue object zigzags, coming nearer, navigating the labyrinth of despair and frustration. The bright blue, lost within clouds of flies. The blue, cloaked in occasional pockets of dense, dark smoke. Still, it emerges, larger, closer, until the blue becomes hair, a dyed-blue Mohawk haircut atop an otherwise shaved head. The head bobs, perched upon the shoulders of a black leather motorcycle jacket, supported and borne along by two legs clad in denim jeans, and two feet shod in black boots. With each step, his boot clanks with a bicycle chain which is looped about his ankle. The punk-rock kid, Archer, approaches my cell.

Clamped under one leather-clad arm, Archer carries a brown manila envelope. His hands stuffed into the front pockets of his jeans, the envelope pinned between his elbow and his hip, Archer tosses his pimpled chin in my direction and says, "Hey."

Archer throws a look at the people who surround us, sunk in their addictions and righteousness and lust. Each person cut off, isolated from any future, any new possibility, withdrawn and isolated within the shell of their past life. Archer shakes his head and says, "Don't you be like these losers . . . ."

He doesn't understand. The truth is I'm prepubescent and dead and incredibly naive and stupid—and I'm consigned to Hell, forever.

Archer looks directly into my face and says, "Your eyes look all red . . . is your psoriasis getting worse?"

And I'm a liar. I tell him, "I don't actually have psoriasis."

Archer says, "Have you been crying?"

And I'm such a big liar that I say, "No."

Not that being damned is entirely my fault. In my own defense, my dad always told me that the Devil was disposable diapers.

"Death is a long process," Archer says. "Your body is just the first part of you that croaks." Meaning: Beyond that, your dreams have to die. Then your expectations. And your anger about investing a lifetime in learning shit and loving people and earning money, only to have all that crap come to basically nothing. Really, your physical body dying is the easy part. Beyond that, your memories must die. And your ego. Your pride and shame and ambition and hope, all that Personal Identity Crap can take centuries to expire. "All people ever see is how the body dies," Archer says. "That Helen Gurley Brown only studied the *first* seven stages of us kicking the bucket."

I ask, "Helen Gurley Brown?"

"You know," Archer says, "denial, bargaining, anger, depression . . ."

He means Elisabeth Kübler-Ross.

"See," Archer says, and he smiles. "You are smart . . . smarter than me."

The truth is, Archer tells me, you stay in Hell until you forgive yourself. "You fucked up. Game over," he says, "so just relax."

The good news is that I'm not some fictional character trapped in a printed book, like Jane Eyre or Oliver Twist; for me anything is now possible. I can become someone else, not out of pressure and desperation, but merely because a new life sounds fun or interesting or joyful.

Archer shrugs and says, "Little Maddy Spencer is dead . . . now maybe it's time for *you* to get on with the adventure of your existence." As he shrugs, the envelope slips from under his arm and drifts to the stony ground. The manila envelope. The brown paper is stamped CONFIDENTIAL in red block letters.

I ask, "What's that?"

Stooping to retrieve the fallen envelope, Archer says, "This?" He says, "Here's the results of the salvation test you took." A dark crescent of dirt shows beneath each of his fingernails. Scattered across his face, the galaxy of pimples glow different shades of red.

By "salvation test" Archer refers to that weird polygraph test, the lie-detector setup where the demon asked my opinion about abortion and same-sex marriage. Meaning: the determination of whether I should be in Heaven or Hell, possibly even my permission to return to life on earth. Reaching spontaneously, compulsively for the envelope, I say, "Give it." The diamond ring, the one Archer stole and gave to me, the stone flashes around one finger of my outstretched hand.

Holding the envelope outside of my cell bars, beyond my reach, Archer says, "You have to promise you'll stop sulking."

Stretching my arm toward the envelope, carefully avoiding contact with the smutty metal bars of my cell, I insist that I'm not sulking.

Dangling the test results near my fingertips, Archer says, "You have a fly on your face."

And I wave it away. I promise.

"Well," Archer says, "that's a good start." Using one hand,

Archer unclips the oversize safety pin and withdraws it from his cheek. As he did before, he pokes the sharpened point into the keyhole of my cell door and begins to pick the ancient lock.

The moment the door swings open, I step out, snatching the test results from his hand. My promise still fresh on my lips, still echoing in my ears, I tear open the envelope.

And the winner is . . .

XXVIII.

Are you there, Satan? It's me, Madison. Please consider amending the famous slogan currently synonymous with the entrance of Hell. Rather than "Abandon all hope, ye who enter here . . ." it seems far more applicable and useful to post, "Abandon all tact . . ." Or perhaps, "Abandon all common courtesy . . ."

f you asked my mom, she'd say, "Maddy, life isn't a popularity contest."

Well, in rebuttal, I'd tell her that neither is death.

Those of you who have yet to die, please take careful note.

According to Archer, dead people are constantly sending messages to the living—and not just by opening window curtains or dimming the lights. For example, anytime your stomach is rumbling, that's caused by someone in the afterlife who's attempting to communicate with you. Or when you feel a sudden craving to eat something sweet, that's another means the dead have of being in touch. Another common example is when you sneeze several times in rapid succession. Or when your scalp itches. Or when you jolt awake at night with a savage leg cramp.

Cold sores on your lips . . . a bouncing, restless leg . . . ingrown hairs . . . according to Archer, these are all methods that dead people use to gain your attention, perhaps in order to express their affection or to warn you about an impending hazard.

184

In all seriousness, Archer claims that if you, as a living, alive person, hear the song "You're the One That I Want" from the musical *Grease* three times in a single day— seemingly by accident, whether in an elevator, on a radio, a telephone hold button, or wherever—it indicates that you'll surely die before sunset. In contrast, the phantom odor of scorched toast merely means that a deceased loved one continues to watch over you and protect you from harm.

When stray wild hairs sprout from your ears or nostrils or eyebrows, it's the dead trying to make contact. Even before legions of dead people were telephoning the living during the dinner hour and conducting polls about consumer preferences regarding brands of nondairy creamer, before the dead were providing salacious Web site content for the Internet, the souls of the expired have always been in constant contact with the living world.

Archer explains all of this to me while we trudge across the Great Plains of Broken Glass, wading the River of Steaming-hot Vomit, trekking across the vast Valley of Used Disposable Diapers. Pausing a moment, atop a stinking hill, he points out a dark smudge along the horizon. A low ceiling of buzzards, vultures, carrion birds soar and hover above that distant, dark landscape. "The Swamp of Partial-birth Abortions," Archer says, nodding his blue Mohawk in the direction of the shadowy marshes. We catch our breath and move on, skirting said horrors, continuing our foray toward the headquarters of Hell.

It's Archer's assertion that I ought to abandon being likable. My entire life, he's willing to wager, my parents and teachers have taught me to be pleasant and friendly. No doubt I was constantly rewarded for being upbeat and peppy.

Plodding along beneath the flaming orange sky, Archer says, "Sure, the meek might inherit the earth, but they don't get jack shit in Hell. . . ."

He says that since I spent my entire life being nice, maybe I should consider some alternative demeanor for my afterlife. Ironic as it seems, Archer says nobody nice gets to exercise the kind of freedom a convicted killer enjoys in prison. If a formerly nice girl wants to turn over a new leaf, maybe explore being a bully or a bitch, or being pushy or simply being assertive and not just smiling bright toothpaste smiles and listening politely, well, Hell's the place to take that risk.

How Archer found himself damned for all eternity is, one day, his old lady sent him to shoplift some bread and diapers. Not old lady meaning wife, but old lady referring to his mother; she needed the diapers for his baby sister, except they didn't have the funds to pay, so Archer stalked around a neighborhood grocery store until he thought nobody was watching.

As the two of us walk along, shuffling through the flaky, waxy dead skin of the Dandruff Desert, we approach a small group of doomed souls. They stand in a cluster roughly the size of a cocktail party in the VIP lounge of a top-tier nightclub in Barcelona, every person turned to face the center of the crowd. There, raised above the core of the group, a man's fist waves in the air. Muffled within the people, a man's voice shouts.

At the edge of the crowd, Archer ducks his head near mine and whispers, "Now's your chance to practice."

Seen through the listening figures, filtered between their standing forms, their filthy arms and ratty heads of hair, there's no mistaking the center of their attention: a man with narrow shoulders, his dark hair parted so that it falls across his pale forehead. He thrashes the fetid air with both hands, gesticulating wildly, punching and slashing while he shouts in German. Dancing atop his upper lip is a boxy brown mustache no wider than his flared nostrils. His audience listens with the slack expressions of the catatonic.

Archer asks me, What's the worst that can happen? He says I ought to learn how to throw my weight around. He says to elbow my way to the front of a crowd. Push people out of my path. Play the bully. He shrugs, creaking the black leather sleeves of his jacket, saying, "You choose. . . ." At that, Archer places one hand flat against the small of my back and shoves me forward.

I stumble, jostling the crowd, falling against their woolen coat sleeves, treading on the polished brown uppers of their shoes. Honestly, everyone present wears the type of sensible clothes best suited to Hell: loden coats of deep green and gray flannel, thick-soled shoes and boots of leather, tweed hats. The only ill-chosen fashion accessory present is an abundance of armbands worn around everyone's biceps, red armbands emblazoned with black swastikas.

Archer tosses a look at the speaker. Still whispering to me, he says, "Little girl . . . if you can't be rude to Hitler . . ."

He urges me to go pick a fight. Stomp some Nazi ass.

I shake my head no. My face blushing. After a lifetime of being trained never to interrupt, I couldn't. I can't. The skin of my face flushes hot, feeling as deep red as Archer's pimples. As red as the swastika armbands.

"What?" Archer whispers, his mouth pulled into a sideways smirk, his skin bunched around the stainless-steel lance of the safety pin which skewers his cheek. He chides me, saying, "What? Are you afraid Mister Herr Hitler might not *like* you?"

Within me, a tiny voice asks, What's the worst that can happen? I lived. I suffered. I died—the worst fate any mortal person can imagine. I'm dead, and yet something of me continues to survive. I'm eternal. For better or worse. It's obsequious little nicety-nice girls like me who allow assholes to run the world: Miss Harlot O'Harlots, billionaire phony tree huggers, hypocrite drug-snorting, weed-puffing peace activists who fund the mass-murdering drug cartels and perpetuate crushing poverty in dirt-poor banana republics. It's my petty fear of personal rejection that allows so many true evils to exist. My cowardice enables atrocities. Under my own steam, I step away from Archer's pushing hand. I'm shouldering my way through woolen coat sleeves, elbowing between the swastikas, clawing and swimming a path toward the center of the crowd. With each step I'm actively stomping on strangers' feet, wedging myself, plunging deeper into the tightly packed mass of the damned, until I burst into the eye of the mob. Tripping over the front row of feet, I tumble, falling with my effort, only to land on my hands and knees, face-first in the loose dandruff, my eyes level with the polished toes of two black boots. Reflected in the buffed, glossy leather, I see myself close-up: a pudgy girl dressed in a cardigan sweater and tweedy skort, a dainty watch strapped around one chubby wrist, my face blazing with bug-eyed, flushed embarrassment. Above me, Adolf Hitler looms with his hands clasped behind his back. Rocking on his boot heels, he looks down and laughs. My glasses have flown from my nose and lie half-buried in dead skin, and without them the world looks distorted. Everyone bleeds together to form a solid mass entrapping me; unfocused, their faces look smeared and melted. His head thrown back, towering monstrously over me, Hitler directs his tiny mustache at the flaming sky and roars with laughter.

Encircling us, Hitler and me, the crowd follows his cue until I'm buried in their laughter. They stand so densely that Archer and his blue Mohawk hair are lost, walled off behind so many dead bodies.

Climbing to my feet, I brush the loose flakes of sticky dandruff from my clothes. I open my mouth to tell everyone to be quiet, please. My hands scrabbling in the layered dermis of greasy dandruff, I feel around in search of my eyeglasses. Even blind, I beg for silence so I can ridicule their leader, but the mob merely bellows with sadistic glee, their blurred faces reduced to their gaping mouths and teeth.

Perhaps it's due to some post-traumatic stress reaction, but in that instant I'm transported to the afternoon at the Swiss boarding school when the trio of Miss Slutty Vandersluts took turns choking me to death, mugging with my eyeglasses and ridiculing me before bringing me back to life. I feel a hand descend to clutch at my arm, a huge, coarse hand, cold as the mortician's table; the calloused fingers wrap my elbow, as tightly as a swastika armband, and something lifts me to my feet. Perhaps it's due to some suppressed memory of some skeezy undertaker's fondling touch, the reek of formaldehyde and men's cologne, but I pull backward. The entire thirteen-year-old weight of me falls backward, pushing my fist and skinny arm forward in a rocketing arc, a pinwheel swing which connects with something solid. This . . . something . . . crunches against the bony impact of my knuckles. Again, I collapse into the soft carpet of dandruff flakes, only this time something heavy lands in the dead skin beside me.

The crowd's laughter goes silent. My hands unearth my glasses. Even through the dirty lenses, fogged with dead flakes of scalp, I can see Adolf Hitler crumpled beside me. He moans softly, a purple doughnut of a bruise already forming around one closed eye.

The ring, the diamond ring which Archer had stolen from a groveling, slobbering, doomed soul trapped in a cage near my own grimy cell, this ring around my finger has collided with Hitler's face. Like a bulbous, seventy-five-carat brass knuckle, the fat diamond has knocked him cold. My fist vibrates. My wrist thrums like a tuning fork, so I shake my fingers to regain full feeling in that hand.

A man's voice shouts. Archer's voice, behind the stunned wall of onlookers, shouts, "Take a souvenir!"

As Archer would explain later, all great bullies have taken totems or fetish objects in order to steal the power of the enemies they have vanquished. Some warriors took scalps they could display on their belts. Others took ears, genitals, noses. Archer insists that taking a souvenir has always been crucial to assuming an enemy's power.

There I stood with Hitler lying prone at my feet. To be honest, I really didn't want his boots. Nor did I feel the slightest desire to lay claim to his necktie or silly armband. His belt? His gun? Some little piece of Nazi costume jewelry, a tin-plate eagle or a skull? No, good taste seemed to preclude taking any readily apparent portion of his costume.

And, yes, I might be a formerly nicety-nice girl with no qualms about using the words *preclude* or *qualms*, and no hesitation to coldcock a fascist tyrant, but I continue to be very particular about the manner in which I accessorize my very bland wardrobe.

From the far edge of the crowd, Archer's voice shouts, "Don't be a pussy!" He shouts, "Take the damned mustache!"

Of course, it's the one talisman which bears the entire identity of this madman. His mustache—a tiny scalp to hang from my belt—it represents something without which Hitler would no longer be Hitler. Bracing the heel of one sensible loafer firmly against his neck, I lean over and entwine my fingers through the coarse, pubic-feeling fringe of the tiny lip hairs. His breathing feels warm and damp against my hands. Even as I brace myself for one gigantic pull, one herculean yank, Hitler's eyelashes flutter and his eyes pin me with their focused rage. Stomping my foot into his throat, I jerk, pulling the short hairs with all of my strength—and Hitler screams.

The crowd recoils, retreating a step.

Once again, I fall backward, my arms pinwheeling but still clutching my prize.

Adolf Hitler holds his face wrapped in both hands, blood pouring from between his fingers; his bellowing words sound garbled and choked, the sleeves of his uniform running with blood, so soaked that the vivid red erases the dull swastika banded around his arm.

Cupped within the palm of my hand curls the warm little mustache, torn away, still attached to a pale, thin crescent of upper lip.

XXIX.

Are you there, Satan? It's me, Madison. My taste for
power continues to grow, as does my ability to accrue it.

he diamond ring, Archer explained, came from Elizabeth Bathory, a Hungarian countess who died and has been imprisoned within her own grimy, hellish cage since 1614. Always a beauty, the Countess Bathory had once struck a servant girl, who bled from the assault, and where the spilled blood accidentally splashed on the countess it seemed to rejuvenate her royal skin. Based on this clearly anecdotal evidence, Elizabeth Bathory went nuts for this new skin-care ritual, immediately hiring and exsanguinating some six hundred servant girls at a lightning pace, so that she might continually bathe in their warm blood. These days, the countess looks terrible; she sits slobbering and comatose with frustration and denial, unable to transition from a bloodthirsty Miss Whorey Von Whoreski.

Armed with the ring of vampirish Elizabeth, I could more easily knock out Adolf Hitler. And now, armed with his tiny fascist mustache, I banished the Nazi superman. Of course, once someone is sentenced to Hell, it becomes nearly impossible to discard him further. My solution was to send him someplace where I myself never planned to venture. My initial selection was the Sea of Insects; however, with additional consideration I revised my choice to the Swamp of Partial-birth Abortions. There it is, in the hell of Hell, that boggy landscape of nightmares where stewed infants simmer beneath an enormous movie screen, an inescapable billboard, upon which *The English Patient* plays in a never-ending Technicolor loop, that's where Herr Hitler resides, shorn of mustache and identity.

Deprived of their demagogue, Hitler's mindless drones inevitably fell into step behind Archer and me, traversing the Dandruff Desert in our footsteps while we continued our journey. Of course, I requested they discard their distasteful armbands, and to underscore my demands I did brandish the tiny profane mustache.

We'd ventured no farther than the Lake of Tepid Bile— Archer and I and our band of newfound sycophants—when we encountered a statuesque woman holding court amid a retinue of bowing, scraping attendants. A great ill-gotten heap of Almond Joys served as her throne, and the members of her court formed concentric circles surrounding the hem of her brocaded and embroidered gown. The woman, while mad with a manic, eye-rolling hysteria, wore a coronet or a diadem of pearls perched atop the nest of her elaborately plaited hair. Even as her court kowtowed at her feet, her wan smile fell upon Archer and me and promptly vanished.

As our traveling party neared this new sight, Archer leaned close to my ear. His Ramones concert T-shirt pungent with the stench of his perspiration, he whispered, "Catherine de Médicis . . ."

If you asked my father for advice he'd tell you, "The secret to being a successful comedian is to never stop talking until you hear someone laugh." Meaning: Persevere. Meaning: Be determined. Make just one person laugh;

then leverage that person and that joke into more laughter. As some people decide you're funny, increasing numbers of people will begin to agree.

The tiny Hitler mustache secreted safe within the pocket of my skort, I listened to Archer's counsel.

"She's some queen of someplace," Archer whispers.

Of Renaissance France, I reply. The consort and queen of Henry II, she died in 1589. Most likely she's condemned to eternal hellfire for instigating the St. Bartholomew's Day Massacre, in which Parisian mobs slaughtered thirty thousand French Huguenots. As we draw nearer and nearer, the queen's eyes become fixed upon me, perhaps sensing my newfound power and my growing lust for more. In the same manner that Hitler was trapped in the persona of a ranting blowhard, and the Countess Bathory was fixated on being a permanent youthful beauty, Catherine de Médicis seems far too attached to her imperious noble station of birth.

Stopping, Archer allowed me to continue my approach, my every step narrowing the distance between me and my new adversary. From behind me, standing at a safe distance, Archer called, "Go for it, Madison. Kick her royal candy ass. . . ."

Admittedly, my battle charge might've appeared somewhat crudely juvenile, consisting of racing full-tilt at the object of my attack, shouting a litany of playground curses such as, "Prepare to die, dirty butt-face, you stinky, skuzzy dumb-ass snotty stuck-up wop queen . . . !" before shoving Catherine de Médicis bodily from her candy-bar throne and pummeling her with a rain of toe kicks, fingernail scratches, hair pulls, savage tickles, and cruel pinches. Yet despite this schoolyard barbarism, I did manage to compel the lofty de Médicis to consume a mouthful of soil after successfully positioning Her Highness to lie facedown upon the ground. Thence, it took only my modest body weight directed through the point of my crooked elbow, driven between her shoulder blades, to motivate her royal Cathyness to recite, under duress, "*Sì! Sì!* I am a skuzzy Miss Skuzzyski and a Douchey MacDouche Bag and I smell like stale cat pee. . . ." It goes without saying that neither Catherine nor her parasitic courtiers could understand a syllable of what she recited, but her compulsory speech occurred as highly comic to Archer, who erupted in a veritable volcano of surly guffaws.

Yes, now it's power I want. Not affection. I don't want that kind of pointless, impotent power, as earlier discussed. Mark my words: Being dead isn't all sitting around in remorseful reflection and bitter self-recrimination. Death, like life, is what you make of it.

Fortified with the Hitler mustache and the Bathory diamond, I made quick, brutal work of this cutthroat religious bigot. Once she's sent packing to join Adolf in the mucky swamp, I resume my journey with Archer, the coronet of pearls now balanced upon my own head, and the ragged retinue of Renaissance ladies and gentlemen fall into step among my growing legion of followers. Traipsing along behind us, Archer and me, our army swells with Nazi zombies . . . plus these de Médicis hangers-on . . . later, Caligula's camp followers.

You may attribute my new boldness to a sort of placebo effect, but by carrying the mustache of a loudmouthed despot, my own words began to sound more eloquent to my ear. My every statement carries the force and authority of a speech blasted over amplifiers to a rally of goose-stepping, torch-bearing, book-burning minions. In order to balance the pearl crown of a righteous, sadistic queen, I'm forced to stand taller, my spine, my bearing, my entire carriage stretched to a nobler height. Casting aside my sensible Bass Weejun loafers, I place my feet in the high heels provided by Babette, further increasing my stature.

Before we reached the next horizon, I'd vanquished yet another foe—Vlad III, alias Vlad the Impaler, a prince of the Dracul family, who died in 1476 after torturing some hundred thousand people to death—a man who formed the flesh-and-blood basis of the Dracula vampire legend. From him, I claimed a jeweled dagger, a dusty clique of corrupt knights, and a treasure chest brimming with Charleston Chews.

Subsequent to him, I utilize said dagger to obtain the testicles of the corrupt Roman emperor Caligula. And his mighty cache of Reese's Peanut Butter Cups.

After we'd resumed walking, at present shadowed by half the obedient idiots from world history, I ask Archer, "So you're in Hell because you shoplifted bread?" I say, "How . . . Jean Valjean."

Archer merely stares at me.

"How Number 24601 . . ." I say, fluttering my hand in a flourishing Gallic gesture. "How *Les Misérables*."

In response, Archer says, "There's more to it than just stealing bread."

Farther along on our journey, we enter the Thicket of Amputated Limbs, a grotesque bramble of severed arms and legs, tangled hands and feet, which filters the smoky, sooty breeze. The path is paved with a litter of disembodied fingers, all of the limbs and digits lost and separated from their rightful owners, all the battlefield amputations and hospital leftovers which were perfunctorily discarded and never arrived at an appropriate grave site. Plus the ubiquitous, worthless popcorn balls. There, I lay claim to the belt of King Ethelred II, the English monarch responsible for the deaths of twenty-five thousand Danes in the St. Brice's Day massacre. It's from this belt that I hang the dangling, severed testicles; the jeweled dagger; and the tiny scalp of the mustache. The spoils of my ongoing campaign to prove myself a badass. Soon these talismans are joined by the ceremonial *rumal*, or handkerchief, used by cult leader Thug Behram to strangle his 931 victims. This belt, becoming the grisly charm bracelet that proclaims my progress from nicety-nice boarding-school girl to way-impolite warrior princess with no regard for decorum. I am the Anti–Jane Eyre. Barely breaking my stride, I vanquish the infamous Bluebeard, Gilles de Rais, adding his braquemard—the rod with which he'd suffocated six hundred children while sodomizing them—to the grotesque trophies which dangle and sway from my waist. As with each victory, a new troop of lieutenants falls into step in my shadow.

Throughout my pilgrimage of transformation, the manila envelope containing the results of my salvation polygraph test, folded carefully, remains tucked deep into one hip pocket of my skort. Seldom do we break stride in our relentless campaign across the burning landscape, beneath the sky scorched with orange flames.

"After I got the bread and diapers," Archer says, "I took them home to my old lady. . . ."

I say, "Please tell me that you're *not* a school shooter, like you originally claimed."

And Archer says, "Just listen, okay?"

He delivered the bread and diapers to his mother, only to discover that he'd nervously stolen the exact wrong type of diaper. Instead of swiping the brand with adhesive plastic tabs to hold them in place, Archer had brought home a less expensive product which required safety pins. To compensate, he'd offered the pins he normally wore pierced through his cheeks and nipples. It was one of these poorly sanitized punk accessories which, no doubt, pricked his infant sister. The frail child fell ill from a blood infection and, almost overnight—died.

Sensing the awkwardness of his admission, I deliberately did not seek to make eye contact. Instead, I continued to march at Archer's side, our army streaming along in our wake. Directing my eyes straight ahead, I felt the bump and jostle of talismans, fetishes, power objects swaying from my waist and colliding with my striding hips. I stood upright, balancing the weight of my new pearly crown. Keeping the tone of my voice nonchalant, offhand, I asked if that was his reason for being eternally damned . . . because he'd killed his baby sister.

"That was pretty shitty, the way she died," Archer says, keeping pace at my side. He says, "But there's more to it. . . ."

It's with our next step that the towers, the turrets and battlements of the Hell headquarters first poke above the far horizon. At our heels, the numbers of our marching army, the most vile scofflaws and thugs and criminals of all human history, the number of our legions has grown to become almost infinite. The combined tread of our marching feet shakes the ground, crushing discarded toffees to dust. We parade, a grand pageant, underlings prancing ahead to sprinkle our path with a fragrant carpet of Red Hots, Skittles, peanut M&M's, and gumballs. Our spoils of Boston Baked Beans and Jolly Ranchers are nearly beyond measure.

The young lady who expired in the glow of a hotel television . . . she is not the same young woman who now presents herself before the gates of Hell. Hannibal should've presented such a fearsome sight. The hordes of Genghis Khan would appear as nothing compared to my own. The Spartans. The legions of the Caesars. The armies of the pharaohs. None could hope to survive a battle with these, my hollow-eyed blackguards, their corroded cutlasses and scimitars clashing against the dirty sky.

Behold, my name is Madison Spencer, child of Antonio and Camille Spencer, citizen of Hell, and my army is as numberless as the stars. As is the wealth of my candy. I bid all the demons and devils of Hades immediately to open their stout fortress unto me.

XXX.

Are you there, Satan? It's me, Madison. Whether you are or you are not, it hardly matters . . . because I am here. The prodigal daughter. Little Maddy Spencer has come home to roost.

ven as we approach the precipice walls of underworld headquarters, the stout gates of Hell—oaken beams blackened with age and bound in iron—are already swinging shut to block our entry. Stretched to the horizon on either hand, these crumbling battlements rise lofty as thunderheads, rearing back as if braced against our assault. Standing black against the orange sky. Here, the Great Plains of Discarded Razor Blades, a vast, baked continent paved miles deep with every dull and rusted razor blade cast off by humanity, this glittering field ends at the base of these ominous stone walls.

A sole demon stands guard as the gates are made fast, rattling from within with the telltale rasp of bars sliding into place, chains being wrapped and locked, bolts shot. This demon, its skin pebbled with infected sores, its hide running with pus and corruption, the snout of a monstrous boar dominates its rubbery face. Its eyes are those black stones through which a killer shark surveys its cold, watery victim. Here presents itself Baal, deposed deity of the Babylonians, receiver of generations of sacrificial children slaughtered in tribute. Thundering with the voice of these screaming millions, the demon demands, "Halt and approach no closer!" The demon, Baal, commands, "Disperse your menacing armies! And relinquish your delicious stores of Nestlé Crunch bars!"

Thus blocking the path, this demon hybrid of pig and shark and pedophile demands to know my name.

As if, at this newest moment, I knew what to call myself.

Who I am is no longer the plump girl who'd smile winningly, bat her eyelashes, and say, "Pretty please, with sugar on top." My voice speaks with the rage of the Hitler mustache. My head stands unbowed beneath the weight of the garish de Médicis crown. My chunky loins, girded with the belt of a murderous king, swagger and display the spoils of my campaign. My hips bristle with totems and talismans, proof that I am not simply a character in a fixed book or film. I am no single narrative. As neither Rebecca de Winter nor Jane Eyre, I am free to revise my story, to reinvent myself, my world, at any given moment. Advancing beside Archer, I am resplendent in my savage finery of seized power. In my service charge the collected blackguards of a dozen tyrants now dispatched to a lesser oblivion. My fingers, stained crimson with the blood of despots, are not the fingers which paged through the paper lives of helpless romantic heroines. No more am I a passive damsel who waits for circumstance to decide her fate; now have I become the scalawag, the swashbuckler, the Heathcliff of my dreams bent on rescuing myself. For now do I embody all the traits I had so hoped to find in Goran. Meaning: No longer am I limited.

I am my own rakish seducer. I do serve as my own surly, brutish bounder.

As we advance upon the gates of Hell, not slowing our pace, that cadence of our billion-upon-billion marching feet, Archer whispers to me, "The greatest weapon any warrior can carry into battle is absolute certainty of her eternal soul."

No slippery, wet heart beats within the damp hollow of my chest. Blood courses not beneath the delicate skin of my limbs. At this point, I am no longer anything which can be killed.

Archer whispers, "Your death offers you a golden opportunity."

The demon pig Baal bares its fangs, its palate brimming with the ruptured fluids and gore of countless foes, a jagged nightmare of toothy torture and suffering—but only to those still wedded to their past lives. As kings or beauties. As rich men or celebrated artists. No, such gnashing, clashing fangs would frighten only those who have yet to accept the fact of their immortality. The demon beast snorts flame, hacking the scalding air with great, slashing claws. The monster roars laughter so greedy, so guttural with hunger that even the scoundrels and knaves marching in my wake, my rapscallions and lowlifes, even they begin to fall back in fear. Even Archer, his head bent against the onslaught of venomous, sulfurous exhalations, even my blue-haired lieutenant slacks in his brave charge.

Yet I do not venture here to be well liked. Nor do I seek any tribute of sweet, smiling affection. My objective is not to flirt and curry favor; and in my mind's eye, my hair streaming, my knees thrown high, dagger unsheathed, I appear quite Byronic.

Upon arrival within arm's length of the heinous demon,

if truth be told, I am not surprised to find myself standing alone. The entire lot of them, my legions of cads and gladiators, despite their machetes and bravado, do tremble and withdraw. Even my second in command, the punk Archer, falters in his bold attack. The whisper of his sage advice no longer hissing in my ear.

Pity the poor demon with but its single strategy to win. In the same handicapped way Jane Eyre must remain meek and stoic, this demonic Baal knows only one way to exist: by being fearsome. While I exist plastic to change and adapt, tailoring my battle plan to each new moment, Baal can never dissolve an enemy into helpless laughter, nor charm a foe by using extraordinary beauty. Therefore, when we neglect to fear such a brittle monstrosity, we render it powerless.

Issuing a war whoop far more Grace Poole than Jane Eyre, I launch myself boldly and squarely toward Baal's porcine thorax. In accordance with my long-ago, school-mandated rape-prevention training, I execute a two-pronged offensive against the demon's stony eyes and tender pork genitals, gouging the former and stomping my stiletto heels upon the latter. Paying no heed to the until-now careful preservation of my neat and clean appearance, I snatch up a handful of the corroded razor blades which pave the ground and commence to slash and claw, my efforts bringing forth a flood of piggish blood. The stench of the demon's exposed, ruptured viscera is the reek of the charnel house. A fog of spouting slaughterhouse blood and killing-floor screams ensues. The offal flies in wide arcs, Grand Guignol style, and even the Hellish orange sky is racked by Baal's squealing protest.

It's a little-known fact, but demons are only slightly more difficult to defeat than despots or tyrants. Despite their immense size and fearsome appearance, demons lack any actual self-confidence. All of their advantage lies in bluster, hideous deformity, and putrid stink, and once those defenses are breached a demon has very little with which to back them up. The great pride of a demon is also its weakness. Like all bullies, at the point where it finds itself losing face, a demon most often takes flight.

What little that was left of Madison Spencer, movie-star scion, is lost in the subsequent savage flurry. Battling alone against the evil Baal, I am not unaware of the sullied hordes who, from a distance, witness my bold savagery. Assaulted with the unrelenting volley of my infantile slaps and girlish pokes, my churlish vocal taunts, the infuriating rain of my wet willies and Indian burns, this fiercest of demons cries in panicked frustration. Subjected to my fearsome barrage of painful noogies, then my lightning-fast attack of titty twist-ers, my entire arsenal of grade-school insults, Baal wrestles to free himself. Following a particularly violent wedgie, the demon unfurls his wrinkled, leathery wings and flees the scene of battle. Those batlike wings beating, beating the black smoke and clouds of houseflies, Baal races to vanish over the far orange horizon.

Thus I'm left standing alone at the sealed gates of head-quarters but for only a moment. I savor the glory of being bathed, soaked, drenched with warm blood which is not my own.

Even before said blood can cool, a sole voice calls down from a window placed high in the locked battlements. A woman's voice calls, "Maddy? Is that you?" Little larger than the face which fills it, the window is situated so high that it takes a moment for my eyes to locate it, but there hovers the visage of an old woman, Mrs. Trudy Marenetti, most recently from Columbus, Ohio, who arrived in Hell by way of pancreatic cancer. She calls, "Hurray for little Madison!"

From another distant window, another face, that of Mr. Halmott, victim of congestive heart failure and Boise, Idaho, echoes the shout, "Hurray for little Maddy!"

From other windows, other battlements and turrets, a multitude of faces trumpet the name of Madison Spencer. Of these, some I recognize, but others I do not, for I've spoken to them only over the telephone, counseling them not to fear their imminent deaths. During my absence, these souls have been arriving in droves, transforming Hell into a veritable Ellis Island of new arrivals, shocked but not devastated by their demise, more curious than frightened, in fact eager to shed their former failing lives and embark upon some new enterprise. It would seem that I've recruited them. All of them, every one of these faces lauds me from their far-flung windows in the walls of Hell. They demand the gates be thrown open so that they might embrace me . . . their new hero.

Suddenly the very air is filled with sweetness as dead people shower me with Sugar Babies and malted-milk balls. In tribute they toss a sugary blizzard of Pez and Root Beer Barrels.

My army coalesces once more, and the unmistakable sounds of bolts and chains can be heard from within the barred doors. By fractions of a degree, by hairbreadths, the two ponderous gates begin to swing aside, offering a glimpse of the headquarters within. Behind me, the thunderous troops rush forward to convey me upon their burly, murderous shoulders and carry me, victorious, into the besieged city. My hordes begin to plunder the candy coffers of Hades. Looting that treasury of Pixy Stix, Atomic Fire-Balls, and York Peppermint Patties.

With the gates not yet a shoulders' width apart, a figure appears from the interior, a young woman with nice breasts and good hair; wearing beat-up fake Manolo Blahnik shoes, dime-size cubic zirconium earrings, a counterfeit Coach bag slung over one arm, there stands—Babette.

Looking at me, with Caligula's shriveled balls worn on my belt, next to that Hitler's nasty mustache hanging like a tiny scalp, my assorted bloodstained daggers and bludgeons, then wrinkling her button nose, Babette says, "You never could accessorize for shit."

No doubt she still wants to transform me into some Whorey Vanderwhore version of an overly made up Ally Sheedy.

Stepping forward, I say, "Do me a favor?"

The multitudes surrounding us wait in pensive silence while I withdraw the folded polygraph test from the hip pocket of my bloodied skort. That cryptic report concerning my views on gay marriage and stem cell research and women's rights, I place this, the final scored version of my test, into Babette's outstretched hand and say, "Did I pass, or what?"

And with the chipped white nail polish of her manicure, Babette slides the test results from their manila envelope and begins to read.

XXXI.

Are you there, Satan? It's me, Madison. My mom used to say, "Madison, you're a worrier." Meaning: I fret over everything. Meaning: EVERYTHING. Now I'm worried that I've won. My ascent to power seems to have been too easy. In my life, in my parents' lives, the rewards have come with so little struggle. The homes in Dubai and Singapore and Brentwood. The afterlife goes on; however, it's not quite death as usual. Something seems fishy, but I can't put my finger on it.

one is the previous Maddy Spencer, she of the sterling posture and finishing-school manners. That winsome me has been declared extinct. True, once more I am seated before the console of my telemarketing station, but the headset rests canted atop my head to allow for the pearl-studded de Médicis crown, and my demeanor is forever altered, for the better or not.

Instead of wheedling the chronically ill, diplomatically and nonthreateningly, with my assurance about the livability of Hades—is there such a word as "die-ability"?—espousing all the wonderful opportunities offered by the afterlife, the new me browbeats those who procrastinate, those lollygaggers who postpone their deaths. Rather than nurture and assure, the aggressive new me harangues the dying who have the misfortune to engage me in telephone conversation. Yes, I'm thirteen years old and dead and doing child labor in Hell—but at least I'm not whining and crying about my situation. In contrast, the people to whom I talk are so endlessly attached to their wealth and achievements, their homes and loved ones and physical bodies. So attached to their stupid *fear*. These failing strangers with their stage-four brain tumors and kidney failure, they've put a lifetime into perfecting themselves, practicing and fine-tuning every nuance of their identity, and now all of this effort is about to be wasted. In all honesty, they irk the bejesus out of me.

The previous Madison Spencer would bother to hold their frightened hand, to calm and comfort them. Who I am now, however, I tell them to cry me a stinking shit river and fall down dead, already.

On occasion, a division or company of my stained hordes, the armies I've inherited from Gilles de Rais or Hitler or Idi Amin will stop by, begging for a work assignment, some large-scale task to perform on my behalf.

More often, the people I've coached into Hell stop by to pay their respects. The just-arrived dead still smelling of funeral carnations and formaldehyde, these immigrant souls sport the troweled-on cosmetics and overly primped hairdos that only an undertaker would inflict, and only a corpse would tolerate. These new arrivals, they all feel compelled to talk through their terrible death experience, and I just let them chatter away. More often than not, I direct them to one of the numerous talk-therapy sessions I've launched, my new hope-aholics recovery groups, a twelve-step peer-supported cliché. But with our high graduation rate and low recidivism it would do Dante

Alighieri proud. After a couple weeks of complaining and self-mourning—the usual railing over lost luxury items and surviving enemies and wrongs left unavenged, plus the typical gloating about past awards and accomplishments—most people get their fill and decide to move forward with their eternal existence. Crude as my methods might appear, my dead friends are not among those people who linger for centuries in their soiled cages cursing their new reality. The dead whom I coach prove to be remarkably well-adjusted and productive. Among them, Richard Volk—who died of blunt-force trauma caused by an automobile accident last week in Missoula, Montana; this week he's leading the former battalions of Genghis Khan in their current campaign to collect all the discarded cigarette butts which inevitably end up here. Here also is Hazel Kunzeler, who succumbed to hemophilia two weeks ago in Jacksonville, Florida; she's now commanding former Roman legions in their latest me-assigned mission to propagate a billion flowering rose-bushes in the space now occupied by the Lake of Tepid Bile. Obviously this constitutes a blatant make-work project—so sue me—but the effort keeps everyone occupied for contented aeons, and even a small measure of success improves the overall atmosphere of the underworld. What's of most importance is how these assignments deflect would-be hangers-on and allow me to focus on my own projects.

Yes, I might be a dead child strangled in a poorly understood sex game, but to me the glass is most times half-full. Despite my optimism there remains no sign of Goran—not that I've been scouring the afterlife searching for him in a desperate, lonely stalker way.

At the limits of my peripheral vision, Babette comes walking in my direction, my salvation polygraph test clasped in her chipped white fingernails.

Into my telephone headset, I ask a middle-aged woman dying in Austin, Texas, "Are you familiar with the old Reno-style divorces?" I explain how, decades ago, one simply took a six-week vacation to establish residency in Nevada in order to file for a no-fault dissolution of marriage. Well, I tell her to catch the next flight to Oregon, where they have legalized assisted suicide. She won't even have to buy a round-trip plane ticket, and she can be dead by this coming weekend. "Book yourself into some luxury hotel in downtown Portland," I say, "get a massage, and call room service for an overdose of phenobarbital. *It's that easy*. Make a real junket out of it. . . ."

Sitting here, talking on the telephone, my fingers crossed, I swear all of this is true. Honest Injun. My workstation, what would pass as my office cubicle on earth, is arrayed with my power souvenirs, the various murder weapons and body parts and symbols of imperial power. Staring me in the face, pinned to my cork bulletin board, the dried monkey patch of the Hitler mustache does not inspire honesty.

In my peripheral vision, Babette proceeds ever closer, bearing the inevitable results of my test.

Into my telephone, I assure this dying Texas person that her permanent record is open on the desk in front of me, and it shows she's been pretty much on the fast track to Hell since the age of twenty-three, when she committed adultery. Despite the fact that she'd been married to her husband for barely two weeks, she engaged in sexual intercourse with a local mail carrier, largely because he reminded her of a former beau. Upon the heels of that revelation, the woman gasps. She convulses into racking coughs, struggling to ask, "How'd you know that?"

In addition, it would appear that she honked her automobile horn one too many times. According to divine law, I explain, each human being is allowed to honk no more than five hundred times over the course of a lifetime. One honk beyond that number, regardless of circumstances, results in an automatic condemnation to Hell—suffice to say all taxicab drivers are Hellbound. A similar unbreakable law applies to discarded cigarette butts. The first hundred are permitted, but any dropped butts beyond that number result in eternal damnation with no hope for recourse. It seems she's also in violation of this regulation. It's all spelled out, here, printed in almost illegible dot-matrix black and white in her personal file.

By now Babette has arrived at my elbow, where she stands, tapping the toe of one faux Blahnik, twisting her wrist to look pointedly at the time on her long-dead Swatch.

To stall for time I hold up one straightened index finger, mouthing the word *wait*, while into the telephone I tell the Texas lady there's nothing she can do in the brief time she has left on earth which will earn her a place in Heaven. She needs to consider her loved ones, to stop hogging the spotlight and allow the people who love her to go back to their own precious, brief, messed-up lives. Yes, she should warn them about not honking their automobile horns and not discarding cigarette butts, but then she ought to move on.

I tell her, "Die already." My finger hovering above the control board, I say, "Hold, please . . . ," and punch the button. I twist in my seat to face Babette, my eyebrows arched in expectation. My entire face a silent, begging, *Please*.

Babette offers the report. She taps a chipped fingernail on a number at the bottom of a long column of faint dot-matrix numbers, saying, "Just from your overall culpability score . . ." She says, "This number, here." Handing me the sheet of paper, Babette says, "You need to file for an appeal." With that, she turns on one battered high heel and begins to walk away.

My latest Hell recruit, the horn-honking, cigarette-strewing gal slowly dying in Texas, she's still blinking, blinking on hold.

Calling after Babette, I ask what she means by *appeal*.

In response, without looking back, Babette shouts, already four . . . five . . . six workstations away; still receding, she says, "You shouldn't even be here. . . ."

From even farther gone, Babette shouts, "There's been an official screwup." Loud enough for everyone to overhear, she shouts, "Double-check the numbers yourself." She shouts, "Because, right this minute, you ought to be in Heaven."

Up and down the infinite row of telemarketers, faces twist to see mine. A lingering crowd of mercenaries and fresh-off-the-boat Hell newbies wait within earshot, their faces slack with confusion. One of their small group steps forward, not a dastardly blood-drenched pirate, nor an aged person attired in her best funeral suit of clothes. No, this stranger stands approximately my height. A reasonable guess would place her age at thirteen. This stranger could almost pass as the earlier me, the pristine, well-behaved Madison wearing sensible shoes and a tweedy ensemble carefully chosen to mask future soiling. In contrast to my current self, this small stranger presents herself with no dried demonic blood on her hands and face, her hair neatly combed and meticulously arranged. Offering a dainty hand of nicety-nice pink fingernails, this girl says, "Madison Spencer?" She meets my gaze with calm, unblinking eyes, her perfect double row of white teeth bound in stainless-steel braces, saying, "You win. . . ."

At that, the girl's dainty hands dip into the pockets of her tweed skirt, and then the pockets of her cardigan sweater, and she brings forth candy. Seven, eight, nine candy bars. Ten full-sized Milky Way bars, my new best friend—*my first best friend ever, Emily*—this dead girl offers these sweet chocolaty prizes to me.

XXXII.

Are you there, Satan? It's me, Madison. How miserably hypocritical, you might say, but no sooner am I offered a chance to flee Hell than I yearn to stay. Few families hold their relations as closely as do prisons. Few marriages sustain the high level of passion that exists between criminals and those who seek to bring them to justice. It's no wonder the Zodiac Killer flirted so relentlessly with the police. Or that Jack the Ripper courted and baited detectives with his—or her—coy letters. We all wish to be pursued. We all long to be desired. At this point I've been in Hell for a longer period of time than I've ever spent in any of my earthly homes, in Durban, in London, in Manila. Worse than feeling merely conflicted, I'm miserable at the thought of leaving.

n order to keep the various bloodthirsty armies occupied and out of my hair, I've ordered them to capture and paint all the noxious bats of Hell red and blue, to pass for cardinals and bluebirds. The industrious butchers previously employed by Pol Pot and Madame Defarge, I've dispatched them to fabricate bright butterfly wings out of colorful construction paper and glitter, then glue these false wings to the real wings of our ever-present houseflies. Not only does this spruce up the normally dismal atmosphere of the underworld, it also prevents what would be the inevitable clashes between Mongolian hordes and Nazi

storm troopers and Egyptian charioteers. Most important, it keeps them all busy and allows me to spend my time touring Emily around, eating Milky Ways, and discussing boys.

Throughout our relaxed amble, I remark on possible improvements to the landscape, a flowering dogwood here, a reflecting pool there, perhaps an aviary of colorful parrots, each of which Emily dutifully makes note of on a clipboard she carries.

The potentially needy mobs of newly dead, those anxious souls I've enrolled in dying and relocating to Hell, I've delegated those folks to various other reclamation projects. Really, I could pass as no less than the FDR of the afterlife, what with all the dams I've decreed be built across rivers of scalding blood. I've ordered other work teams to dig channels and drain expansive marshes of rank perspiration; thanks to me the ancient Sweat Swamps of Hell no longer exist. Lost souls who logged entire lifetimes in the study and practice of civil and structural engineering, those people are thrilled for the opportunity to put their existing skills to use. The rolling hills of semicoagulated mucus have been leveled. And an entire gulag of happily damned slave laborers does nothing except fashion false water lily blossoms from crepe paper and float their products on the surface of Shit Lake.

More and more I see that Hell isn't so much a punitive conflagration as it is the natural result of aeons of deferred maintenance. Frankly put: Hell amounts to nothing more than a marginal neighborhood allowed to deteriorate to the extreme. Picture all the smoldering, underground coal mine fires expanding to rub elbows with all the burning tire dumps, throw in all the open cesspools and hazardous-waste landfills, and the inevitable result would be Hell, a situation hardly improved by the self-absorbed tendency of the residents to focus on their own misfortune and neglect to lift a dead finger in defense of their environment.

From our vantage point, strolling along the shore of the Sea of Insects, Emily and I survey the slow but certain improvements in the dismal landscape. I point out areas of interest: the roiling River of Hot Saliva . . . the buzzards circling Hitler and his distant colleagues relegated to their unspeakable place. I explain the seemingly arbitrary rules of which people run afoul, how each living person is allowed to use the F-word a maximum of seven hundred times. Most living persons haven't the slightest idea how easy it is to be damned, but should anyone say *fuck* for the 701st time, he or she is automatically doomed. Similar rules apply to personal hygiene; for example, the 855th time you fail to wash your hands after voiding your bowels or bladder, you're doomed. The 300th time you use the word *nigger* or the word *fag*, regardless of your personal race or sexual preference, you buy yourself that dreaded one-way ticket to the underworld.

Walking along, I tell Emily how the dead may send messages to the living. In the same way that living people send each other flowers or e-mails, a dead person may send a living person a stomachache or tinnitus or a nagging melody which will occupy the alive person's attention to the point of madness.

The pair of us walking along, idly examining the putrid, boiling landscape, apropos of nothing, Emily nonchalantly says, "I talked to that girl Babette, and she says you have a boyfriend. . . ."

I do not, I insist.

"His name," says Emily, "is Goran?"

I insist Goran is not my boyfriend.

Her eyes remaining fixed upon the notes she's jotted on her clipboard, Emily asks if I miss boys. What about prom? Do I miss the opportunity to date and get married and have my own children?

Not particularly, I reply. A crew of sinister Snarky Miss Snarky-pants girls at my old boarding school, the infamous three who taught me the French-kissing Game, they once professed to educate me about human reproduction. As they told it to me, the reason boys desire so desperately to kiss girls is because, with each kiss, the activity makes the boy's wanger grow larger. The more girls a boy can kiss, the larger a wanger he'll eventually possess, and the boys boasting the largest are awarded the best-paying, highest-status jobs. Really, it's all very simple. All boys devote their lives to amassing the most elongated genitals, growing the nasty things so that when they eventually wedge them inside some unfortunate girl, the distant end of the enlarged wanger actually breaks off—yes, the wanger flesh becomes so hardened that it shatters—and the broken portion remains lodged within the girl's hoo-hoo. This natural event is much like those lizards that live in arid deserts and can voluntarily detach their squirming tails. Any amount, from the pointed tip to almost the entire wiener, can literally snap off inside a girl, and she's fully unable to remove it.

Emily stares at me, her face distorted in far more disgust

than she registered even when first witnessing the Lake of Tepid Bile or the Great Ocean of Wasted Sperm. The clipboard hangs, ignored, between her hands.

Continuing, I explain that the embedded portion of the fractured wanger grows to become the resulting baby. In the event the wanger has broken into two or three portions, each of these evolves to become twins or triplets. All of this factual information comes from a very legitimate source, I assure Emily. If anyone at my Swiss boarding school knew anything about boys and their ridiculous genitals it would be those three Miss Coozy O'Cooznicks.

"Knowing the facts of life as I do," I tell Emily, "no, I certainly do *not* miss having a boyfriend. . . ."

The two of us continue walking along in silence. My array of fetishes and power objects dangle and sway from my belt. They clang and knock against each other. On occasion I suggest a lovely birdbath be placed here or there. Or a sundial surrounded by a picturesque bedding scheme of red and white petunias. Eventually, to break an extended silence, I ask what she misses about being alive.

"My mother," Emily says. Good-night kisses, she says. Birthday cake. Flying kites.

I suggest tinkling wind chimes might improve the black smoke that swirls and billows around us.

Emily fails to write down my idea. "And summer vacation from school," she says. "And I miss swing sets. . . ."

Ahead of us, a figure comes walking down the path in the opposite direction. It's a boy, passing in and out of the drifting clouds of smoke. In turns, he's revealed and occluded. Apparent and hidden.

She misses parades, says Emily. Petting zoos. Fireworks.

The figure, a boy, approaches us holding some sort of pillow cradled to his chest. His eyes are rakish, his brow surly and moody, his lips twisted into a sensuously puckered sneer. The pillow he carries is colored bright orange, textured such that it appears simultaneously soft and vivid. The boy wears a hot-pink jumpsuit with a long number stitched across one side of his chest.

"I miss roller coasters," Emily says. "And birds . . . *real birds*, I mean. Not just red-painted bats."

The boy, now blocking our path, he's Goran.

Looking up from her clipboard, Emily says, "Hello."

Nodding to her, he speaks to me. "I am sorry I choked you into dead," says Goran in his vampire accent, and he moves his orange pillow toward me. "At present, you see now I am dead as well," Goran says, placing the pillow in my arms. He says, "I found this for you."

The pillow feels warm. It hums in short pulses. Bright orange, soft, it looks at me with flashing green eyes, fully alive and purring, nestled against my bloodstained sweater. It swats a paw, its tiny claws batting at the Caligula testicles.

No longer dead and stuffed in the plumbing of some luxury hotel, no longer a pillow, it's my little kitten. Alive. It's Tiger Stripe.

XXXIII.

Are you there, Satan? It's me, Madison. I have my kitty.
I have my boyfriend. I have my best friend. I have more
dead than I ever did while alive. Except for my mom
and dad.

o sooner had I made my peace with Goran
than another crisis occurred.

No sooner had I accepted the warm,
cuddly fuzz ball of my beloved kitty,
Tiger Stripe, than my emotional equilibrium was again
knocked askew. Goran, I assured him, did not kill me. Yes,
in some sense, he accidentally killed the person identified as
Madison Spencer; he forever destroyed that physical mani-
festation of me, but Goran did not kill . . . me. I continue
to exist. Furthermore, his actions were precipitated by my
own fallacious concept of French-kissing. What transpired
in that hotel suite was a gross comedy of errors.

Graciously, I accepted Tiger Stripe, then introduced
Goran to Emily. The trio of us continued to stroll until
obligation required I resume my telemarketing duties. My
beloved kitty curled and snoozing in my lap, happily purring away, my headset firmly in place, I began to field survey
calls as the central computer connected me to households,
to breathing people alive in time zones where the evening
meal was set to commence.

In one such residence, someplace with a familiar Californian area code, a man's voice answered the telephone, "Hello?"

"Hello, sir," I said, following by rote the script which dictated my every statement and response. Petting the cat at rest in my lap, I say, "May I have a few minutes of your time for an important consumer study concerning buying habits in relation to several competing brands of adhesive tape . . . ?"

If not adhesive tape, the topic would be something else just as mundane: aerosol furniture polish, dental floss, thumbtacks.

In the background, almost lost in the distance behind the man's voice, a woman's voice says, "Antonio? Are you ill?"

The woman's voice, like the telephone number, feels strangely familiar.

Still petting Tiger Stripe, I say, "This will only take a few moments. . . ."

A beat of silence follows.

I say, "Hello?" I say, "Sir?"

Another beat of silence occurs, broken by a gasp, almost a sob, and the man's voice asks, "Maddy?"

Double-checking the telephone number, the ten-digit number which reads on my little computer screen, I recognize it.

Over my headset, the man says, "Oh, my baby . . . is that you?"

The woman's voice in the background says, "I'll grab the bedroom extension."

The telephone number is our unlisted line for the house in Brentwood. By sheer coincidence, the autodialer has connected me with my family. This man and woman are the former beatniks, former hippies, former Rastas, former anarchists—my former parents. A loud click sounds, someone lifting another receiver, and my mother's voice says, "Darling?" Not waiting for an answer, she begins to weep, begging, "Please, oh, my sweetness, please say something to us. . . ."

At my elbow, brainiac Leonard sits at his workstation plotting chess moves against some alive adversary in New Delhi. On my opposite side, Patterson conspires with living football enthusiasts, keeping track of teams and quarterbacks, marking their statistics in the blank spaces of a fantasy spreadsheet. The business of Hell continues unabated, spread to either horizon. Elsewhere, the afterlife continues as usual, but within my headset, my mother's voice begs, "Please, Maddy . . . Please tell your daddy and me where we can come find you."

Sniffing, his voice choked and his breath exploding into the telephone receiver, my father sobs, "Please, baby, just don't hang up. . . ." He sobs, "Oh, Maddy, we're so sorry we left you alone with that evil bastard."

"That . . ." my mother hisses, "that . . . assassin!"

My guess is that they're referring to Goran.

And yes, I've vanquished demons. I've deposed tyrants and taken command of their conquering armies. I'm thirteen years old, and I've shepherded thousands of dying people into the next life with relatively little upset. I never finished junior high school, but I'm overhauling the entire nature of Hell, on schedule and under budget. I deftly toss off words such as *absentia* and *multivalent* and *convey*, but I'm caught completely off guard by the sound of my parents' tears. For help lying, I finger the dried scrap of the Hitler mustache. For coldness, to quell the tears already building in my burning eyes, I consult the de Médicis crown. Over the telephone I tell my weeping mother and father to hush. It's true, I assure them: I am dead. In the icy voice of child killer Gilles de Rais, I tell my family I have passed out of fragile mortal life and now dwell in the eternal.

At this, their weeping subsides. In a hushed, hoarse whisper, my father asks, "Maddy?" In a voice weighted with awe, he asks, "Are you seated with the Buddha?"

In the lying voice of serial murderer Thug Behram, I tell my parents that everything they taught me about moral relativism, about recycling, about secular humanism and organic food and expanded Gaia consciousness—it's all turned out to be absolutely true.

A joyous, shrill cry of laughter escapes my mother's mouth. A pure gasp of relief.

And yes, I assure them, I am thirteen and still their precious baby girl and dead . . . but I reside forevermore in serene, peaceful Heaven.

XXXIV.

*Are you there, Satan? It's me, Madison. My dead posse
and I are planning a little pilgrimage back to hobnob
among the living. And to plunder the earth for its
wealth of candy.*

eonard goes after the candy corn, those
faux kernels of gritty sugar striped in
colors of white, orange, and yellow. Patterson craves the chocolate-flavored caramels better known as Tootsie Rolls. Archer covets the
overly sweet blend of peanuts and toffee marketed as
Bit-O-Honey. For Babette, it's peppermint Certs.

As Leonard explains, Halloween is the only regular
occasion on which the dead of Hell can revisit the living
on earth. From dusk until midnight, the damned may
walk—fully visible—among the living. The fun ends with
the stroke of midnight; and like Cinderella, missing that
curfew merits a special punishment. As Babette describes
it, any tardy souls are forced to wander the earth for a year,
until dusk of the next Halloween. Thanks to the melted
plastic of her dead Swatch, Babette missed the deadline
once and was banished to loitering, invisible and unheard,
among the self-obsessed living for twelve boring months.

In preparation for our Halloween foray, we sit in a group,
sewing, gluing, cutting our costumes. Chess-champion,
brain-trust Leonard rips the hem from a pair of pants; with
his teeth, he bites and frays the pant legs. Scooping a

handful of cinders and ash from the ground, Leonard rubs these into the pants. He soils a tattered shirt and wipes his dirty palms to blacken his face.

Watching, I ask if he's supposed to be a hobo? A tramp?

Leonard shakes his head no.

I ask, "A zombie?"

Leonard shakes his head no and says, "I'm a fifteen-year-old slave copyist who died in the fire which destroyed the great library of Ptolemy the First in Alexandria."

"That was my next guess," I say. Exhaling breath onto the blade and polishing my jeweled dagger, I ask why Leonard chose that particular costume.

"It's not a costume," Patterson says, and laughs. "That's what he was. It's how he died."

Leonard might look and act like a contemporary kid, but he's been dead since the year 48 B.C. Patterson, with his football uniform and all-American fresh-faced good looks, he explains this while polishing a bronze helmet. Removing his football helmet, he fits the bronze one over his curly hair. "I'm an Athenian foot soldier killed doing battle with the Persians in 490 B.C."

Drawing a comb through her hair, the red scars clearly showing on her wrists, Babette explains, "I am the great Princess Salome, who demanded the death of John the Baptist and was punished by being torn apart by wild dogs."

Leonard says, "You wish."

"Okay," Babette confesses, "I'm a lady-in-waiting to Marie Antoinette, and ended my own life rather than face the guillotine in 1792. . . ."

Patterson says, "Liar."

Leonard adds, "And you aren't Cleopatra, either."

"Okay," Babette says, "it was the Spanish Inquisition . . . I think. Don't laugh, but it's been so long I don't really remember."

On Halloween, custom requires the dead to not merely revisit the earth, but to do so in the guise of their former lives. Thus, Leonard becomes once more an ancient dweeb. Patterson, a Bronze Age jock. Babette, a tortured witch or whatever. That some of my newfound friends have been dead for centuries, some for millennia, this makes the present moment we're seated together, stitching and polishing, seem all the more fragile and fated and precious.

"Forget that," says little Emily. She's clearly sewing an elaborate skirt of tulle, decorating it with gems she's gathered from comatose and distraught souls. Stitching away, she says, "I'm not trick-or-treating as a dumb Canadian girl with AIDS." Emily says, "I'm going to be a fairy princess."

In secret, I dread the thought of roaming among the alive. Due to the fact that this is the first Halloween since my demise, I can only shudder at the idea of how many Miss Skuzzy Vanderskuzzies will be out wandering with Hello Kitty condoms looped around their necks, their faces anoxic with blue makeup in a cheap parody of my own tragic end. Walking in those few hours, will I be continually confronted by insensitive revelers as they make fun of me? Like Emily, I consider appearing as some stock character: a genie or angel or ghost. Another possible option is to take my evil armies back to earth and compel them to carry me around in a golden sedan chair while we hunt down my various Snarky Miss Snarky-pants enemies and terrorize them. I could carry Tiger Stripe and present myself as a witch accompanied by her familiar.

Perhaps sensing my reluctance, Leonard asks, "You okay?"

To which I simply shrug. It doesn't help my mood, remembering how I lied to my parents over the telephone.

The only thing that makes Hell feel like Hell, I remind myself, is our expectation that it should feel like Heaven.

"This might cheer you up," says a voice. Unbeknownst to me, Archer has entered our company, and instead of a costume, he carries a thick file folder. Holding the folder in one hand, he uses his other to pinch a sheet of paper from the contents and withdraw it. Holding the sheet aloft for everybody to see, Archer says, "Who says you only live once?"

Stamped on the sheet of paper, in red block letters, is the single word APPROVED.

XXXV.

Are you there, Satan? It's me, Madison. If you'll forgive me, I need to jump backward for a moment.

Funny . . . me asking for the Devil's forgiveness.

The sheet of paper Archer held aloft, it's my appeal. It's the blah, blah, blah form for reconsideration, which Babette filed on my behalf in response to the results of my polygraph-y salvation test. It could be that my soul has actually been found innocent, and the powers that be are righting their mistake. More likely, what's happened is more political, and my growing political strength—the newly dead recruits I've garnered from earth, and the armies I've gathered—poses such a threat that the demons are willing to release me if that means retaining their overall power. What it all boils down to is . . . I no longer have to stay in Hell. I no longer even have to be dead.

I can go back to earth, to be with my parents, to live whatever lifetime I have allotted. I'll be able to menstruate and have babies and eat avocados.

The only problem is, I told my parents we'd be together for all time. Yes, of course, I told them we'd all be in Heaven with the Buddha and Martin Luther King Jr. and Teddy Kennedy smoking hashish or whatnot . . . but I WAS only trying to spare their feelings. Honestly, my motivation was fairly noble. Really, I just wanted them to stop crying.

No, I'm not completely unrealistic about my parents'

slim chances of attaining Heaven. To that end, talking over the telephone, I'd made my father promise to honk his car horn at least a hundred times each day. I'd sworn my mother to constantly use the word *fuck* and to always drop her cigarette butts outdoors. With their existing track record, these behaviors would way guarantee their assured damnation. Forever in Hell is still forever, and at least we'd all be together as an intact nuclear family.

Even as he wept, I forced my father to promise that he'd never pass up an opportunity to break wind in a crowded elevator. My mom I made promise to urinate in every hotel swimming pool she'd ever enter. Divine law allows each person to pass gas in only three elevators, and to urinate in the shared water of only two swimming pools. This is regardless of your age, so most people are already relegated to Hell by the age of five.

I told my mom she looked way beautiful giving away those dumb Academy Awards, but that she should hit Control+Alt+D and unlock the doors of my bedrooms in Dubai, London, Singapore, Paris, Stockholm, Tokyo, and everywhere, all of my rooms. By keystroking Control+Alt+C she ought to open all my curtains and allow sunlight into those sealed, shadowy places. I made my dad promise to give all my dolls and clothes and stuffed animals to the Somali maids we had in every household—and to give them all a sizable raise in their wages. On top of all those demands I asked my parents to adopt all our Somali maids, to really legally adopt them, and make certain those girls get college degrees and become successful cosmetic surgeons and tax attorneys and psychoanalysts—and that my mom can't lock them in bathrooms anymore, even as a joke—and both my parents yelled in unison over the telephone: "Enough! Madison, we promise!"

In my effort to comfort my parents, I said, "Keep your promises, and we'll be one big, happy family, forever!" My family, my friends, Goran, Emily, Mister Wiggles, and Tiger Stripe . . . we'll all spend eternity together.

And now, ye gods . . . it seems as though *I'm the one who won't be in Hell.*

XXXVI.

Are you there, Satan? It's me, Madison. But I guess you
already knew that. If you're to be believed I guess you
know more about me than I do. You know everything,
but I suspected that something was not right. At last we
meet face-to-face. . . .

e're all dressed in our Halloween cos-
tumes, which aren't really costumes, with
the exception of Emily's fairy-princess
outfit. Babette refuses to accept the possibility that she's some dead nobody; instead, she's dolled
herself up as Marie Antoinette, with jagged, black-thread
stitches going around her neck, and at present we're loitering around the shore of the Lake of Tepid Bile, waiting to
hitch a ride back to Real Life and hustle ourselves some
sweet, sweet candy riches.

Just when it appears that we'll be compelled to take some
nasty-dirty cattle-car leftover from commuting the Jews to
the Holocaust, a familiar black Lincoln Town Car drifts
to a slow-motion stop beside us. It's the same car as from
my funeral, and the same uniformed chauffeur wearing a
visored cap and mirrored sunglasses steps from the driver's
seat and approaches our group. In one driving-gloved hand
he holds an ominous-looking sheaf of white paper. Along
one edge, three Chicago screws bind the pages together.
Clearly, it's a spec screenplay, and from even a few steps'
distance it stinks of hunger and naively high expectations

231

and absurd outsider optimism—more outsider than I could possibly dream.

Holding the thickness of pages out in front of him, obviously waiting for me to take it, the driver says, "Hey." His mirrored glasses twitch between the pages and my face, baiting me to see the screenplay and acknowledge it. "I found my script for you to read," he says. "On your trip back to earth."

In this taut moment, one corner of the driver's mouth twitches into a possible leer, some expression either shy or snide, showing a tangle of browned rodent teeth sprouting from his gums. His exposed cheeks flush crimson red. He twists and ducks his head, hunching his shoulders. With the toe of one foot, shod in gleaming black riding boots— very old-school for a chauffeur, almost like hooves—he draws a five-pointed star in the dust and ash. He's holding his breath, his vulnerability so tangible you can taste it, but I know from vast experience that the moment I touch his cinematic pipe dream I'll be expected to attach bankable talent to it, secure financing for principal photography, and land a fat distribution deal for him. Even in Hades, such moments are excruciatingly painful.

Nevertheless, I want to ride back to Halloween trick-or-treating in style, not in some typhus-stinking, lice-ridden Nazi boxcar, so I acquiesce to actually looking at the proffered title page. There, centered in boldface all-caps letters—the first dreaded sign of an amateur's precious, self-important work—I read the script's title:

THE MADISON SPENCER STORY
Authored by and Copyright Belonging to Satan

First off, I read the title again. And again. Second, I look at the name tag pinned to the lapel of his chauffeur's uniform, the engraved silver, and it does, indeed, read: SATAN.

With his free hand, the driver removes his cap, revealing two bone-colored horns that poke up through his mop of ordinary brown hair. He slips off his mirrored sunglasses to show eyes cut with side-to-side irises, like a goat's. Yellow eyes.

My heart . . . instantly, my heart is in my throat. At long last, it's you. Without thinking I step forward, ignoring the offered screenplay, and throw my arms around the driver, asking, "You want me to read that?" Burying my face in his tweedy uniform—in *your* tweedy uniform. The cloth smells of methane and sulfur and gasoline. A hug later, I step away. Nodding at the pages, I ask, "You wrote a movie about me?"

There it is again, that leering smile, as if he sees me naked. As if he knows my thinking. He says, "Read this? My little Maddy, *you've lived it.*" Satan shakes his horned head, saying, "But, technically speaking, there is no 'you.'"

His gloved hands flip open the manuscript and shove it toward me, demanding, "Look!" He says, "Every moment of your past is here! Every second of your future!"

Madison Spencer does not exist, Satan claims. I am nothing but a fictional character he invented aeons ago. I am his Rebecca de Winter. I am his Jane Eyre. Every thought I've ever had, he wrote into my head. Every word I've said, he claims he scripted for me.

Baiting me with the screenplay, his yellow eyes flashing, Satan says, "You have no free will! No freedom of any kind. You've done nothing I didn't plot for you since the beginning of time!"

I've been manipulated since the day I was born, he insists, steered as gracefully as Elinor Glyn would position a heroine on a tiger-skin rug for a tryst with an Arab sheik. The course of my life has been channeled as efficiently as pressing Ctrl+Alt+Madison on a laptop keyboard. My entire existence is predestined, decreed in the script he holds out for my inspection.

I step back, still not accepting that dreck script. Not accepting any of this new concept. If Satan is telling the truth then even my refusal is already written here.

Arching his thorny eyebrows, he says smugly, "If you have courage and intelligence it's because I willed for you to have them. Those qualities were my gift! I demanded that Baal surrender to you. Your so-called 'friends' work for me!"

Hitler, Caligula, Idi Amin, he claims that they each threw the battle to me. That's why my ascent to power happened so quickly. It's why Archer egged me to fight in the first place.

But I refuse. "Why should I believe you?" I stammer. I scream, "You're the Prince of Tides!"

Satan throws his head back, stretching his stained teeth at the orange sky and shouting, "I am the 'Prince of Lies'!"

Whatever, I say. I say that—if he's really and truly responsible for my every quote—then HE fucked up my last line of dialogue.

"I gave your mother movie fame! I gave your father a fortune!" he bellows. "If you want proof, just listen . . . ," and he flips the script open, reading aloud: "'Madison suddenly felt confused and terrified.'"

And I did. I did feel confused and terrified.

He reads, "'Madison looked around anxiously for reassurance from her clique of friends.'"

And at that moment I had, indeed, been craning my neck, trying to catch sight of Babette and Patterson and Archer. But they'd already climbed into the waiting Town Car.

And yes, I know the words *panic* and *racing pulse* and *anxiety attack*, but I'm not certain whether I even exist to experience them. Instead of a fat, smart thirteen-year-old girl . . . I might be a figment of Satan's imagination. Just ink stains on paper. Whether reality actually shifted in that instant . . . or only my perception of it changed . . . I can't tell. But everything seems undermined. Everything good seems spoiled.

In his nerdy way, Leonard had tried to warn me. It's possible that reality was exactly the way he'd described: Demon = Daimon = Muse or Inspiration = My Creator.

Perusing the pages of his script, chuckling over his work, Satan says, "You are my best character." He beams. "I'm so proud of you, Madison. You have such a natural talent for luring souls to perdition!" With more than a smidgen of wistfulness, he says, "People hate me. No one trusts me." He looks at me almost lovingly, tears trembling in his goat eyes, and Satan says, "That's why I've created you. . . ."

XXXVII.

Are you there, Satan? It's me, Madison, and I'm not
your Jane Eyre. I'm nobody's Catherine Earnshaw. And
you? You're certainly no writer. You're not the boss
of me; you're just messing with my head. If anybody
wrote me it would be Judy Blume or Barbara Cartland.
I have confidence and determination and free will—at
least, I guess I do. . . .

n a whim, I didn't take any of my storm troopers or Mongol hordes with me trick-or-treating. If I can trust them—if I won them fair and square—I don't know anymore. Besides, there are only so many people you can fit into a Lincoln Town Car, and despite what my mom says, an entourage *can* be too large. At the last minute, I couldn't even wear the Hitler mustache because Tiger Stripe ate it; and then I didn't want to take my kitty and risk his coughing up some big Nazi hairball on somebody's front stoop. In the end it was just us, Archer and Emily, Leonard, Babette, Patterson, and me, going door-to-door. The Dead Breakfast Club.

That said, I did wear the belt of King Ethelred II, the dagger of Vlad III, the rod with which Gilles de Rais murdered so many children. Emily, dressed as a fairy princess, wears the diamond ring of Elizabeth Bathory. Leonard trades everyone for their candy corn. First we went to the town where Archer had last lived, someplace with houses lined up along streets brimming with alive children. Maybe some are dead children, returned like us for a few hours of nostalgia. For one millisecond I could swear I saw JonBenet Ramsey wearing sequined tap shoes and waving hi to us.

Surrounded as we are by the marauding packs of costumed urchins, it's unsettling to know that some of these diminutive living goblins will die in drunk-driving accidents. Some little cheerleaders and angels will develop eating disorders and starve to death. Some geishas and butterflies will marry alcoholic husbands who beat them to death. Some little vampires and sailors will stick their necks through nooses or get shanked in prison riots or be poisoned by jellyfish while on dream vacations snorkeling the Great Barrier Reef. Of the lucky superheroes and werewolves and cowgirls, old age will bring them diabetes, heart disease, dementia.

On the porch of one brick house, a man answers the doorbell, and the group of us shout, "Trick or treat!" in his face. As he gives us chocolate bars, this man effuses over Emily's fairy costume . . . Babette's bejeweled Marie Antoinette outfit . . . Patterson as a Greek foot soldier. As his eyes settle on me, the man scans the strip of Hello Kitty condoms twisted around my neck. Placing a candy bar in my bloodstained hand, the man says, "Wait, don't tell me. . . ." He says, "You're supposed to be that girl, the movie star's kid, who got choked to death by the psycho brother, right?"

Standing beside me on the man's porch, Goran wears a turtleneck sweater and a beret. Goran smokes an empty pipe. Even shielded behind heavy, horn-rimmed spectacles, Goran's sultry eyes look wounded.

It's possible that Satan scripted this moment. Or it might really be happening.

"No, sir," I tell the man. "I happen to be Simone de Beauvoir." Motioning to Goran, I add, "And this, of course, is the much-celebrated Monsieur Jean-Paul Sartre."

Even now I'm lost. Was I just being clever and compassionate, or was I reading smart-ass dialogue written by the Devil? Leaving the porch, our group continues down the street. Almost without notice, Archer has veered away in a different direction, so I sprint after him to collect him and herd him along with the rest of us. Catching him by one black leather sleeve, I tug for him to follow me, but Archer only continues to walk in the opposite direction, clearly on his own mission, putting more and more distance between the two of us and the larger group of our peers. Abandoning the Breakfast Clubbers. Without further words, I follow until the streetlights occur only irregularly, then not at all. We continue until the concrete sidewalk ends, until the houses end and the two of us are walking along the gravel shoulder of an empty, dark road.

Archer looks at me and asks, "Maddy? Are you okay?"

Is he being concerned, or is he playing a role? Is Satan writing our walk? I don't know, so I don't respond.

A wrought-iron gateway rises near us in the shadows, and Archer turns into it. We pass through a wrought-iron fence, and we're instantly surrounded by tombstones, treading on mown grass, listening to crickets chirp. Even in near-total darkness, Archer marches without a false step. Only by clutching the sleeve of his leather jacket can I follow, and even with such guidance I'm stumbling over grave markers.

I'm kicking aside bouquets of cut flowers, my high-heeled shoes wet from the damp.

Archer comes to an abrupt stop, and I collide with his legs. Not saying a word, he stands looking down on a grave, the stone carved with a picture of a sleeping lamb, engraved with two dates only a year apart. "My sister," Archer says. "She must've gone to Heaven, because I ain't ever seen her."

Beside the grave a second stone bears the name Archibald Merlin Archer.

"Me," says Archer, tapping the second stone with the toe of his boot.

We stand there, silent. The moon hovers, throwing a weak light over the scene around us, countless headstones spread in every direction. Moonlit grass covers the ground. Uncertain how to respond, I study Archer's face for clues. The moonlight glows blue in his Mohawk and glints silvery off his safety pin. Finally, I say, "Your name was *Archie Archer*?"

Archer says, "Don't make me punch your lights out."

The night after his baby sister was buried, Archer explains how he'd returned to the grave site. That night a storm was rolling in, pushing along thunderclouds, so Archer had hurried to shoplift a spray bottle of herbicide, the aerosol kind used to kill weeds and grass. He'd spritzed his motorcycle boots until the leather was sodden, and then walked to the newly mounded grave. Once there, his boots squishing and squirting poison with every step, Archer had done a primitive shuffle, a rain dance in the last hour before the storm would hit. He'd pirouetted and leaped. His leather jacket flapping, he'd cursed, craning his neck and rolling his eyes. Stomping his toxic feet, Archer had ranted and bellowed, bounding and capering in the growing onslaught of wind. With the storm building, he'd pranced and cavorted and gamboled. He'd raved and howled. As the first raindrops touched his face, Archer had felt the air surrounding him crackle with static electricity. His blue hair had stood to its full, straight-up height, and the safety pin in his cheek had sparked and vibrated.

A white finger of light had zigzagged down from Heaven, Archer says, and his whole body had cooked around the oversize safety pin. "Right here," he says, standing beside his sister's tombstone, on the spot which would become his own grave. He smirks and says, "What a rush."

In that swath of mown grass extending over a dozen graves in either direction, that allée, a ghost of Archer's dance steps still lingers. There, a new generation of grass, greener, softer, like the first fresh blades grown to cover a battlefield, this new grass traces every toxic footstep Archer left before being struck down by lightning. Everywhere he'd stomped his poisoned boots, he says, the grass had died, and it was only now growing back, reseeded, to erase his late-night choreography.

There, only days after he'd been rendered a giant heretical, sacrilegious shish kebab skewered around his own red-hot piercing, in time for his own funeral, his final words had already surfaced as poisoned yellow letters clearly legible in the manicured green. Even as the pallbearers bore his casket to the grave, they marched across these last angry dance steps, this shuffling, stumbling path which spelled— in dead-yellow letters too tall for anyone except a deity to read: *Fuck Life.*

"Two kids in one week . . ." says Archer, ". . . my poor mom."

In the silence which follows, I begin to hear my name streaming on the nighttime breeze, as thin as the distant smell of candle flames cooking carved pumpkins from the inside. From somewhere over the nighttime horizon, a chorus of three faint voices seems to call me. In the distant, faraway dark, three different voices chant repeatedly: "Madison Spencer . . . Maddy Spencer . . . Madison Desert Flower Rosa Parks Coyote Trickster Spencer . . ." With this siren's song entrancing, captivating, luring me into the unknown, I stagger in pursuit of the bait. I'm edging between tombstones, hypnotized, listening. Thoroughly pissed off.

Behind me, Archer calls, "Where are you going?"

I have an appointment, I call back. I don't know where.

"On Halloween?" Archer shouts. "We've all got to be back in Hell by midnight."

Not to worry, I shout to reassure him. Still drifting, dazed, in pursuit of the mysterious voices, drawn along by the sound of my own name, I call back to Archer, "Don't worry." Distracted, I shout, "I'll see you in Hell. . . ."

XXXVIII.

Are you there, Satan? It's me, Madison Desert Flower
Rosa Parks Coyote Trickster Spencer.

You've thrown down the gauntlet. You've brought
my wrath down upon your house. Now, to prove that I
exist I must kill you. As the child outlives the father, so
must the character bury the author. If you are, in fact,
my continuing author, then killing you will end my
existence as well. Small loss. Such a life, as your puppet,
is not worth living. But if I destroy you and your dreck
script, and I still exist . . . then my existence will be
glorious, for I will become my own master.

When I return to Hell, prepare to die by my hand.
Or be ready to kill me.

y worst fears have been realized. In the
Swiss boarding school where I found
myself locked out-of-doors, naked in the
snowy night, I have become the ghost
rumored into being by silly rich girls.

Why is it that I occur as a story to everyone except
myself?

Crowded into the small residence hall room I once
occupied, the various classes of students—these giggling,
nervous girls—spend this Halloween around my former bed. Seated upon the bed in approximately the same
positions in which they held me and suffocated me and
baited me back to life, there are the three Miss Whorey

Vanderwhores. It is their trio of little Miss Skanky Von Skankenberg voices that recite, "We summon the everlasting soul of the late Madison Spencer."

In unison, they say, "Come to us, Madison Desert Flower Rosa Parks Coyote Trickster Spencer. . . ." And they all three snicker over my ludicrous name. They intone, "We demand the ghost of Maddy Spencer come and do our bidding. . . ."

Skanks or Satan. Why am I always called to do someone's bidding?

Centered on the bed, a plate stolen from the dining hall holds a few burning candles, but otherwise my former room is dark. The curtains are open, revealing the ragged trees and wintry night. The door to the hallway is closed.

One Miss Slutty MacSlutski leans off the side of the bed. She reaches under the mattress and retrieves a book. A dog-eared book. "With this personal object," the Skanky Skankerpants says, "We exercise our power to control you, Maddy Spencer. . . ."

The book? It's my beloved copy of *Persuasion*. A collection of characters who've long outlived their author.

At the sight of my personal possession, my favorite book, the other giggling, wide-eyed witnessing girls fall silent. Their eyes flicker with candlelight.

It's on that cue, just as I'd press Ctrl+Alt+C on my mother's laptop computer, that I begin to slowly draw the curtains closed, and with the first hint of movement the assembled girls scream. The smaller girls scramble and tumble over one another in their hurry to escape the room. As easy as pressing Ctrl+Alt+A, I increase the air-conditioning, dropping the room temperature until the remaining girls can see their breath hang, hazy, in the candlelight. In the same way I'd toggle Ctrl+Alt+L, I flash the room's overhead lights on and off, on and off, strobing the lights as fast as lightning. Filling the room with the equivalent of every flash photograph of every *People* magazine photographer who'd ever snapped my picture. I blind the assembled girls as would an army of mercenary paparazzi.

With this, the remaining girls claw their way to the open door, spilling out into the hallway, screaming and wailing like doomed souls locked within the soiled cages of Hell. They skin their knees and elbows climbing over each other, leaving only the three evil Miss Pervy Vanderpervs still seated around the candles on my bed.

Yes, here I am, the legendary naked girl who left the ghost prints of her dead hands on the doorknobs of this very residence hall. Miss Madison Desert Flower Rosa Parks Coyote Trickster Spencer. Here I am, returned to you for just this one night, the dummy dumb-ass spoiled daughter of a movie star. I gaze down at these three with their pointed ballet feet smudging my bed and the knobby hip bones of their anorexic butts digging into my old mattress, and as easy as keystroking Ctrl+Alt+D, I slam and lock the hallway door. I seal them inside my room just as my mother would hold some Somali maid hostage until the bathroom tile truly gleamed.

In the time-honored ageless way the dead have always sent messages to the living, I wail my subsonic attack on their shriveled Miss Sleazy O'Sleaznoid bowels, roiling and boiling the watery contents of their so-abused digestive tracts, bubbling and churning the stewed refuse contained in their intestines, stomachs, colons. I push the mess in violent peristaltic waves, making the three grab at their own midsections, their nether orifices erupting in methane clouds, exploding the tiny candle flames, dousing the room in stinking, suffocating darkness. I force outward the hot slop of their past meals, pushing it against their clenched oral and anal muscles. Trumpeting this scalding putrescence in a slurry against those confining fleshy walls.

Their hands clamped to cover their burning mouths, the girls scream between their fingers, wailing and calling for aid. They clutch their bloating midriffs. In the hallway, beyond the locked door, the assembled students and faculty wrestle with the locked knob.

Only then do I announce myself, that I am arrived. I am Madison Spencer, the nominal ruler of Hell. Making my soprano voice all eerie and wailing-ethereal, I warn that the three Harlot Von Harlotty girls must make all efforts to not find themselves damned . . . for if they do, they will suffer my wrath for all eternity. They will be subject to my whims and endure the endless tortures which I shall decree. Like Archer ranting and railing in his cemetery at night, a human lightning rod, I decree that should these three girls find themselves condemned to Hades, I will force them to stand lips-deep alongside Hitler and Company in the Swamp of Partial-birth Abortions, forever.

The acrid, sulfurous stench of Hell already wafting out, spouting, issuing from their own lithesome, ballet-trained bodies, the three girls weep and beg for forgiveness and release. The locked door reverberates with the pounding fists and shouted entreaties of those students and teachers excluded in the hallway.

"Heed my words," I tell them. From this moment forward,

in order to save themselves, they must utilize the hideous terms *nigger* and *fag* at every opportunity. They must never wash their hands after using the toilet. They must refrain from ever covering their mouths when they cough or sneeze, especially while aboard crowded airplanes during in-flight meal service and filmic presentations of *The English Patient*. Oh, I just go on and on. Damn, but I'm having so much fun. And at the last possible instant before they choke totally to death, mired in their own pungent filth, I throw open the door, allowing every one of their peers full view of what these three Miss Twatty Twatlanders have become.

There they sprawl, moaning in their own slippery degradation for all the world to observe.

And yes, I am petty and vengeful, but I have places to be and flowering trees to plant. I have evil hordes and bloodthirsty armies to command. According to my sensible, durable wristwatch it's twenty minutes to Halloween midnight.

To anyone reading this who isn't already dead, I wish you luck. Honestly, I do. You just keep swallowing your vitamins. Keep jogging around reservoirs and avoiding secondhand cigarette smoke. Cross your fingers . . . maybe death won't happen to you.

And yes, I am thirteen and dead and a girl. I might be a touch of a sadist and a little bit jejune . . . but at least I'm not a victim, not any longer. I hope. I hope, therefore I am. Thank God for hope.

For the rest of you, please don't be afraid. If you go to Heaven, bully for you. But if you don't—well, look me up. The only thing that makes earth feel like Hell, or Hell feel like Hell, is our expectation that it ought to feel like Heaven. Earth is earth. Dead is dead. Another insider fact about the afterlife: If you miss your midnight curfew on All Hallows' Eve you'll be stuck wandering the earth, a ghost trapped among the living, until the next Halloween.

Now, if you'll excuse me, it's late, and I'm in a terrible, terrible hurry to go kick some satanic ass.

To be continued . . .